MYSTERY IN RED

MYSTERY IN RED

SIDNEY WILLIAMS

Introduction by
JOHN BETANCOURT

WILDSIDE PRESS

To
WARD BRINTON
My Pilot in Deep Waters

INTRODUCTION

Sidney Clark Williams (1878-1949) is one of those Golden Age mystery authors about whom little is known. My research reveals that he was born in Wells, Maine and considered himself a Maine writer, even after he moved to Massachusetts then Pennsylvania. He donated some of his papers and books to the Maine State Library, which has recently digitized the correspondence.

Williams spent his career writing and editing for newspapers, serving as the literary editor first at the *Boston Herald* and *Boston Evening Record,* then at the Philadelphia *North American,* and finally the *Philadelphia Inquirer*. He retired from newspaper work in 1939 when his health began to fail. He spent the last 8 years in and out of hospitals due to heart problems, and finallyl died in Norristown State Hosptal at the age of 71.

In between his newspaper work, Williams published 9 well-received books, most of them mysteries. The complete list of titles to look for is:

> *A Reluctant Adam* (1915)
> *The Eastern Window* (1918)
> *An Unconscious Crusader* (1920)
> *The Body in the Blue Room* (1922)
> *In the Tenth Moon* (1923)
> *Mystery in Red* (1925)
> *The Drury Club Case* (1927)
> *The Murder of Miss Betty Sloane* (1935)
> *The Aconite Murders* (1936)

Interestingly, he filed copyright renewals for his last 2 novels after his death. (Talk about a ghost-writer!) More likely, he left his estate to a friend or relative, who didn't know how to renew the copyrights properly.

As for *Mystery in Red*, it received rave reviews in a number of magazines, including *The Saturday Review*, which wrote in the May 9, 1925 issue:

> In totalling the list of attractions which combine to present a first class show of its kind, we may cite conspicuously: One murder, two abductions, two rapid-fire love affairs, intrigue, and mysti-

fication, all materializing with an adroit swiftness which keeps one constantly, if blindly, on the alert for what will happen next.

And not the least agreeable feature of the whole lies in Mr. Williams's style which, for a novel of this sort, is singularly readable and cultivated. If there must be mystery stories (we are one who owns to a secret weakness for them), their quality could be immeasurably bettered were less creditable workers in the field to study Mr. Williams's prose as a guide to the mastery of pure and yet intensely vital diction.

The Bookman (June, 1925) had a shorter writeup, saying simply:

"Bootleggers spoil a holiday, and their punishment provides numerous thrills."

So sit back and enjoy this fine New England tale of bootleggers—and murder!

—John Betancourt
Cabin John, Maryland

CHAPTER 1

DELANCEY OPENS THE DOOR

Said he, "My son, you'll rue the day,
    To me way hay yoh yah!"
Said he, "My son, you'll rue the day,
    And a long time ago.
"When off to sea you go away,
    And a long time ago."
And often since have I thought of his word,
    To me way hay yoh hah.
And often since have I thought of his word,
    And a long time ago.

With a supplementary "Ago-o" the voice died away in a meditative rumble. The only immediate comment was the sardonic "Ah!" of a passing gull. At the impact of an extra-vigorous roller the boat gave slightly to starboard.

Now the voice aft of the cabin resumed its contented droning:

"A monkey's heart and a donkey's liver,
    Blow, boys, blow,
A monkey's heart and a donkey's liver,
    Blow, my bully boys, blow."

The two men smoking forward by the rail exchanged tolerant smiles. A curious pair. In his trim yachting clothes the elder somehow suggested a figure from "Pinafore." Small and chunky, with twinkling blue eyes, and a short gray beard that edged up his cheek bones.

The younger and taller was rising six feet, with the leanness of a grayhound. A Roman nose of the most authoritative mold, and gray eyes with the glint of steel. Something about him a little scornful, but nowise bitter. And the air of a man ever ready to spring to action. He removed the briar that rested comfortably on his outthrust chin to say:

"Ed's happy."

"He usually is with himself, Slim."

The elder man pinched his Havana. "Ed's a romantic cuss," he resumed.

"So are you, Pop."

With his puckered lips, the smoke of the little man's cigar spiralled past the tip of his nose.

"What's one to think when Caswell, the eminent neurologist, is seen shepherding flappers at roadhouses and all-night cabarets?"

"Just how do you pick up this information?"

The tall man laughed.

"Oh, I'm a scientist."

Rotated against the reef of beard, the little man's cigar came to rest in the corner of his mouth. He clamped it there for further observation.

"Delancey, the chemist, is less scientific in such inquiries than Caswell, the physician. Besides, I'm a harmless old feller. And besides—again— I've got an excuse. After tinkering sprained minds all day it's healthy to relax with gals that haven't got any. . . . Now Ed——"

His suspended utterance was due less to delicacy than to overwhelming competition of the voice preceding a face by a far corner of the cabin:

> "Ramble-away, Ramble-awa-ay,
> Here comes the young kid they call Ramble-Away."

The chantey-man regarded his companions quizzically. With his high-rolled ducks, and soft shirt open at the throat, he was a picture of power at ease. A big fellow of thirty or so, with a superb chest, a slope of thigh and leg trim as a clipper ship, and a large, smooth-shaven, deeply sunburned face.

"What's doing?" he asked.

"Nothing," said Caswell. "We're praying for a little more wind."

"If the Lord fails to furnish it, we're going to set you to singing against the sails," added Delancey.

"Go to the deuce. We're out; and that's the great thing. Isn't it?"

He looked about with vast appreciation, and proceeded to answer himself:

"It sure is. Thanks to you, Pop. And God bless Columbus for being born to-day; especially this year, when it comes Friday. . . . Three days without even a square root. How'd you think of this, Pop?"

"Don't know. Maybe Andersen made me. I could see he wanted one more cruise before tying the old *Viva* up for the season. And I thought there might be a lark or two left in the meadows. Then I like Nyatt without the summer litter of off-islanders from Sepoya and Screechhaven."

He waved his cigar to port.

"You see where we come in, Ed," Delancey observed.

"He can't hurt my feelings."

Anthony turned to examine the horizon.

"What time will we get there?"

"By sunset, I guess."

Caswell consulted his watch.

"I thought of asking Andersen to start the auxiliary. He will anyway, if he needs it. Wind's freshening a bit."

He cocked an eye at mackerel clouds proceeding in tidy procession. Then he shaded his eyes, suddenly alert.

"By George, there it is."

"What is?" asked Delancey.

"The island."

Overboard went the cigar.

"I don't see it."

The three lined up at the rail.

"Over there."

Caswell gesticulated.

"See that bit of scarlet?"

"Is it a painted island?" asked Anthony.

"Painted by the hand of God."

Caswell grasped the rail impatiently, as if he would push the boat on. Stooping a little, Delancey got his head in line.

"Right," he said. "What is it?"

"It's bayberry, and sumach, and scrub oak, and heather, and rambling vines. All the divine litter of Nature ripening in the sun."

Anthony stood with feet wide apart, his slate-gray eyes fixed on the still small, but growing, spot of bright color. In anticipation he savored its richness.

"Thanks," he said without turning his head.

"Welcome," replied Caswell.

With a little screwed-up smile he reached for a button set in the rail. Then as quickly turned with a muttered, "I forgot," to call to a man standing at the wheel:

"Shall we be in before sunset, Andersen?"

The *Viva's* skipper turned his straw-colored mustache and faded blue eyes to the still brilliant but fast setting October sun.

"If the wind, she don't fail, Captain," he answered.

The wind did not fail. A fresher following breeze sent the *Viva* flying with effortless speed that makes the boat under canvas one with sky and water; with Nature herself in benevolent mood.

Now and then they passed boats of the scallop fleet, like themselves Nyatt bound, but slower with their burden of bivalves for city markets.

Once a power boat passed them,—a long, black boat with slender lines and powerful engines, tearing towards the island like a flying fish. And just before Grant's Point was sighted the steamer from the mainland overtook the *Viva*. With the usual vague smiles, and waving of hats and handkerchiefs by passengers clustered on the deck, she went ahead.

Now the sun was low. And into its splendor gulls were flying with crimsoned wings. With brighter color, almost magenta it seemed in comparison, the moors stretched their low rampart to the left of the town.

As the island's horseshoe opened to receive them, village houses seemed to advance in welcome. No monumental pile, but a profusion of seasoned brick and old frame houses of mellow aspect. Some with ivy at once affording protection and claiming support. Others with cupola and captain's walk reminiscent of wives that watched no longer, and whalers that went no more to sea. Here and there plumes of autumn foliage showed yellow and scarlet above the serried roofs.

Alert for the narrow and winding channel, Andersen stood with the chart before him. The steamer was already discharging her passengers as they picked their way past the lighthouse on the Point. A half-turn of the wheel to port. They dropped anchor as the old bell brought from Portugal chimed six in the North Tower.

Now Caswell let go the rail, with an impatient shake of cramped fingers, and smiled at Andersen with a lift of his mouth that mounted to a wave of his beard.

"Good," he said. "Have a cigar."

Andersen gravely accepted the token, and tucked it away.

"So," he said. "You will go ashore, Captain?"

Caswell looked at the purpling sky.

"What do you say?" he inquired of Delancey and Anthony.

"Yes." And, "Ditto," they replied.

"All right. I'd like to feel the island under foot to-day. Just that. Dinner on the boat, Andersen."

The skipper touched his cap.

"Yes, Captain."

He turned to a sailor lounging aft with curt command to lower a boat, and went below to complete his instructions.

"Want anything?" Caswell asked his companions.

"Only my cap."

Turning, Anthony plunged down the companionway. Delancey smiled, and tucked away his pipe.

Presently they were sliding through a clear expanse of amethyst water. Over the harbor, smooth as a mill-pond, drifted the pleasant smell of burning autumn leaves. The little boats off the Point sat like birds that settle for the night with drowsy head under a wing.

As they landed at the steamboat wharf the usual reception committee was frankly engaged in examining the *Viva*. Hackmen turned chauffeur with admission of motors to an island really too small for anything but a Ford; scallopers who had tied up early, or not gone out for the day; two or three old deep sea sailors with mahogany color set for life by ocean winds; truant boys, and a smattering of the riff-raff of the town.

A little apart stood a tall man examining Caswell's boat with marine glasses. Possibly able to say, had he experience: "About sixty feet over all. Good lines. Probably good speed. Looks like a Herreschoff," etc.

He turned as they stepped on the wharf, and virtually brushed aside their first questioner, interrogating them about a taxi.

"Are you Griffis?"

The tall man looked at Delancey, who returned his regard with interest. As he delayed his answer the question was repeated:

"Griffis?"

"Suppose I am."

At Delancey's smile Caswell looked nervous.

"What," he said to himself, "is Slim going to do now?"

"Ericsson is expecting you," said the would-be identifier.

"Oh, is he?"

"He's up to the hotel now."

"Thanks. I'll try to look him up in the morning."

As Delancey turned to Caswell and Anthony, standing a few feet aside, the persistent stranger stepped between.

"Better come now."

"I can't leave my friends here."

"Bring 'em along."

"But, my dear fellow, it's about dinner time."

"Well," said the stranger, "there's plenty of grub at the hotel."

"Now what's this all about?"

The man gave no ground.

"They told me to get you. . . . There's a room ready."

Suddenly Delancey laughed.

"Oh, well," he said. "If that's the case, come on."

"My car's here."

Their guide limped on ahead. That he was lame Caswell had noted as he listened to his colloquy with Delancey, sizing him up with a physician's eyes. A big man, he stood above six feet and probably weighed over two hundred pounds. There was a look of strength, limited to the discerning by signs of disease. While his right foot was not deformed to the extent of club malformation, it was misshapen and braced. His face was brick-red. Behind one ear were several yellowish scars, with kindred scars on the back of each hand. They looked like signs of some disorder of the blood.

His clothes meant nothing. They were the sort "tailor made" for men's shops. And his general personality was about equally revealing. He might be a plasterer at fifteen a day, or a corner grocer scraping out four or five thousand a year, with his bottler's license withdrawn. But neither of these would sport the motor to which he led them,—a seven-seater with a hundred-and-forty wheel base, and its wine-colored upholstering of a sort seen commonly in road palaces of motion picture stars.

"Hop in," he said, motioning for Delancey to take the seat beside him. The others followed, with Caswell's "Be back at nine" to one of his crew waiting by the dinghy.

"It seems you spotted me," Delancey remarked as they settled themselves in the car. "But I don't know you."

"Bjerstedt. Come from Dakota. . . . Mostly called 'Buster.'"

Ejecting his words gustily, the big man stooped to the self-starter. The engine roared, and they were suddenly under way.

Up the wharf and past the Yacht Club, its flag still flying but no sign of life about. Across North Milk Street, with its museum where reposed the bones of whales, and hard by harpoons driven by the hands that slew them. Through the Square, on the right flanked by a shuttered, melon-colored caravansary, and sharp left to the gate of a rambling frame structure with "Stimson House" neatly framed over the door.

The ride so soon over, it seemed almost like taking a Pullman to cross the street. Bjerstedt stepped out a bit awkwardly, giving himself the benefit of a half-minute or so in announcing, "Here we are."

Limping a little, he led on to the door, which he opened without hesitation, and stepped through an entry into a room on the right. The office, seemingly, and parlor, too. The open register invited from a marble-topped table, and a bottle of ink beside it.

Delancey stooped to pick up the pen—then hesitated. By Massachusetts law registration under an assumed name is almost as heinous as forging a bank check. However, Bjerstedt spared him pangs of guilt.

"Kate's out somewhere," he announced with a cursory inspection. "I know the room. Come on."

With now and then an impatient clutch at the banister he conducted them up a rather dark flight of stairs, their tread heavily padded in the middle; then up another, after a turn to the right.

The door he opened was almost at the head of the second flight. As he fumbled for the electric button, for it was twilight now,—a sound like that of a chair overturned on a hardwood floor came from the next room on the right.

The room they stood in seemed simple enough with the flooding light. They took inventory without Bjerstedt, who at once departed to find Ericsson. A rather large, square chamber with a neatly made double bed. Straw matting on the floor, and a maple set. By the crockery pitcher on the commode stood a bottle.

"Well?" said Caswell, as Delancey moved to examine it.

"Well, what?"

"How are you going to get out of it?"

"I thought you said you wanted adventure."

"Maybe I did. But——"

"Then don't be ungrateful. I'm giving it to you."

"What will you do when this chap Ericsson comes?"

"Let's not worry about that. Do you suppose this bottle's good?"

Delancey shook it a little, and turned it bottom up for a sign of tampering with the glass.

"Looks all right," he observed. "And 'Lawson's Dundee' is a nice label."

By a convulsion of his whiskers Caswell managed to convey,—"Well, I wash my hands." Then he turned to Anthony with a dry little laugh:

"Isn't Slim the biggest ass, Ed?"

Anthony had surveyed the pair with elation of a lad out with his elders. Now he smiled broadly, and reverted to his favorite medium:

> *"My gal's a high-born ladee.*
> *She's dark, but not too shadee;*
> *Feathered like a peacock, just as gay——"*

"Do you teach mathematics by singing, Ed?" asked Caswell.

"He certainly never teaches singing that way," Delancey volunteered.

"How do you know?" asked Anthony.

"Oh, any boob could tell."

"Ask this one."

Three pairs of eyes focussed on a figure just inside the half-opened door.

"What is the question?" the newcomer inquired, as he closed the door behind him.

"It seems to be,—'Who are you?'"

Delancey carefully put down the bottle.

"My name is Ericsson."

The newcomer affably complied. He had the air of a man ready to oblige in anything.

"Then you're the man——"

"I hope you don't mind."

He interrupted Delancey's magisterial declaration. Then hurried to conciliate:

"I assure you it's all right."

"That's comforting, of course. But we're not here for theatricals."

Mr. Ericsson put forth a protesting hand.

"Of course. I know how you feel. But I assure you I can explain."

"Well," said Delancey, "why should I play Griffis?"

"No reason if you don't want to. But I'll be obliged if you do."

He looked inquiringly at Caswell and Anthony, who had retired to the side-line. Next at Delancey. Finally, at the bottle.

"Suppose," he suggested with a sudden smile, "we lubricate discourse."

"Well, since you're the host——"

Delancey regarded him ironically. At the thrust his rather ruddy cheek showed rising color.

"Take my word, it's good Scotch," he said.

"Oh, it's your bottle——?"

"I had it sent up."

"If that's the case——"

Delancey retired to a chair with a half-apologetic smile.

"Thanks. Allow me."

Ericsson produced a corkscrew. As he worked at the bottle his involuntary guests took stock of his appearance. He was probably thirty-odd, with flaxen hair and blue eyes. Of medium height, thick rather than fat. His voice low and well pitched counteracted the impression of his slightly theatric attire, including the belted coat of Broadway. With his very pleasant expression he seemed somehow ingenuous. Delancey modified his first impression that here was a beguiling fellow.

"Ah," he sighed, when he had removed the cork with authentic "Plop!" and ritualistically up-ended the bottle.

"Now we're set. For once they didn't forget the glasses. . . . Say when. . . . Take it neat? . . . Rather have charged water? . . . Is that right? . . . Here goes. . . . Happy days!"

Sitting with much content, he sipped, and smiled.

"Now," he said, "let me get this off my chest. I did expect Griffis."

"What Griffis?" asked Delancey.

"What one? The moving picture man."

"And what's he supposed to be doing here?"

"Why, making a picture."

Ericsson looked surprised. Delancey put on again the expression of the duelist.

"Don't you think it's pretty cheeky?"

"Not when you know," Ericsson protested.

"I can't go on with the masquerade."

"Not until Monday?"

"What happens then?"

"Griffis will be here."

"What will I look like then?"

"Oh, we can pass it off as a little joke."

For the moment Ericsson looked perturbed. Then his face cleared.

"You know, you do look a lot like him."

"Thanks," said Delancey. "But you could hardly know that in advance of seeing me. So I suppose there must be some other reason for wanting me to pose as Griffis."

"Well, to be perfectly candid, there is."

"Out with it."

"Won't you help yourself? . . . All of you."

Ericsson pointed invitingly to the bottle.

"Thanks. Not just now," said Delancey. Caswell and Anthony declined with murmurs.

"Sorry. I think I will."

Ericsson poured himself a stiff drink, sipped it appreciatively, and plunged in.

"You see, I'm making this picture with Griffis."

"What is it?"

"Oh, an island idyl. Most characteristic stuff in the world here. It will beat 'Cape Cod Folks' by a mile."

"No doubt. . . . Now why must I be Griffis?"

"No real reason. Only some of the boys got uneasy."

"What boys?"

Delancey crooked an inquiring finger.

"I'm afraid I am a roundabout fellow," said Ericsson. "But I'm coming to it. I mean boys that have taken stock in the company."

"Does it happen Mr. Bjerstedt is one of them?"

"Yes. Stumpy has some."

"That explains his pressing warmth in bringing us here. About what, may I ask, are the boys uneasy?"

"Oh, they don't understand about these things. They expect a screen play to happen like a mushroom."

"About how much of it has happened so far?"

"I've got the preliminary work done. Picking the sites, selection of supernumeraries; all that sort of thing."

"Now they want action."

"In a hurry."

"Which they get——?"

"When Griffis comes. . . . I'm no technical director."

"I see. How many are sighing to see him?"

"Oh, a dozen or so."

"So many questions. And I don't quite see it yet."

Now Delancey poured himself a drink, and took it thoughtfully.

"What makes the islanders so impetuous?"

"They're mostly off-islanders."

"What's Bjerstedt doing here?"

"I'm not quite sure. Came to rest, I think."

Delancey put down his glass.

"Much as I would like to oblige you," he said, "I'm afraid I must decline. You see, while it happens I've never been here before, my friend Caswell knows the place well. I don't want to do anything embarrassing to him."

"All right. Of course, it's only a joke."

Ericsson was pure affability.

"I wonder," asked Caswell, who had luxuriated in an armchair, watching the smoke of his cigar spiral to the ceiling, "if you were ever at Harvard, Mr. Ericsson."

"Yes."

"Didn't I see you in a performance of the 'Agamemnon'? Let's see,—about ten years ago?"

"I was the Queen."

"Thought so."

Caswell's cigar rotated to the other corner of his month. And a quiver of satisfaction slightly agitated his beard.

"Know the Carley Simkinses?" he pursued.

"Oh, yes."

Ericsson was aglow with pleasure.

"The salt of the earth. Carrie was no end kind in my undergraduate days. And old Carley is a trump. He tolerated me in spite of the bad bridge I played. . . . They're friends of yours, I suppose."

Again Caswell's cigar travelled to the opposite side.

"I brought up the children. . . . Met you there once." . . . Puff, puff. . . . "Not surprising you don't remember me. It's my job to be inconspicuous. And look at people all the time. Tiresome business. . . . Ah, Slim . . ."

Now the smoke screen drifted towards Delancey.

"Why not give the young man his joke. I don't mind."

"All right then," said Delancey.

"But I'm afraid you don't relish the idea at all," Ericsson protested.

"It's done."

"Well, you're a trump. Of course, you are dining with me."

"But we haven't asked Bjerstedt's permission."

Ericsson laughed.

"Oh, he'll be there. He's one of my best little watchers."

"To be perfectly honest, I'm considerably obliged by your consent to be the temporary Griffis. Bjerstedt, and a few other chaps he brought in, are rather on my nerves. I don't know what sort of men they are used to dealing with. They've acted, these last few days, like race-track gamblers who suspect the bookie means to double-cross them."

"When this picture is under way sufficiently to show the stuff in it, I hope we'll be able to take up the stock these wise men seem to regret buying, and get 'em out. They're not a sort I like to deal with. . . . And that's that."

He picked up his hat.

"See you down-stairs in a few minutes, if that suits you," he said as he breezed out.

At the sound of the closing door Delancey turned to Caswell.

"What's the idea, Pop?" he inquired with slight asperity.

"Which idea?"

Caswell's expression was one of perplexity.

"Shoving me into an impersonation of this moving picture feller."

"I thought that was your idea. Didn't you mean to go through with it?"

"You know I didn't."

"Now that's too bad. I thought you meant what you said about furnishing the old man an adventure."

Rising, Caswell deposited the butt of his cigar in a convenient cuspidor.

"Anyway, it's only for a couple of days. And you'll have the bright companionship of Ericsson and Bjerstedt, while I have only the society of birds. That's supposing, of course, I find a lark, or a black duck to play with."

"What am I going to do?" asked Anthony. "Go into storage, or take the *Viva*, and go sailing?"

"You? By to-morrow noon you'll be sitting with the old salts of the Pacific Club—spitting at the air-tight stove, and roaring chanteys."

Delancey regarded Caswell with mock-admiration.

"You certainly have it fixed all nice and pretty. . . . I guess I'm the goat. And maybe it's my fault. But don't forget I owe you one, Pop. . . . Now let's hunt the bathroom, the secret place of a country hotel. If I had a job of murder on hand, it would be my selection for the spot."

Delancey's misgiving was ill-founded. They came to the bathroom by guessing the first turn to the left. Only Anthony, leading, stumbled over something unseen in the dim light. It was a case left by the baseboard. At the same time was disclosed a gaslight in the wall above.

"May as well save the other fellow's toes," observed Anthony as he brought the light into action. Then he stooped again with:

"Hullo! What's here?"

Painted on the top of the case with bold stroke was a red triangle.

Delancey laughed.

"I knew that case was floating fast off the Shoals, this afternoon. But I didn't think it would get settled in the house ahead of us. Wonder what it is."

Touching it with his foot, Caswell favored his companions with a gnomelike smile.

"Perhaps somebody is running a hooch farm."

At a slight noise behind them they wheeled as one. Seemingly, there was no one there. They hurried with their toilet, and went down-stairs.

"Will you come in here?" Ericsson called from the office as they reached the lower hall. He stood by the table, waving a shaker with a gesture of invitation.

"I timed you pretty well," he went on, filling the glasses on a tray before him.

"My dear boy," said Caswell, with a tug at his whiskers. "Is your company going into liquidation?"

"Only this way."

In high spirits he conducted them across the hall, to a room already occupied by a group of diners. There were four of them, two men and two women. Two facing the door nodded casually as Ericsson brought his party in.

"It looks as if most of the guests belonged to the eat-and-run club," he remarked as he shook out his napkin. "Would you like to have those people over there join us?"

"Of course, if it's the custom of the country," said Caswell.

Ericsson laughed, quite unabashed.

"It's not that. And they won't bore. It just occurred to me it would be nice to have them in on a little surprise."

"Another one!"

Delancey pushed back his chair, as if resolved to leave.

"Oh, you'll like this one," said Ericsson. "Is it a go?"

"We can't resist you."

"Then I'll tell you all I know about them,—and it's precious little, before I bring them over.

"You can pick out the Englishman all right. Name of Guy Beddle. Kate tells me there's an 'Honorable' tacked on his letters. Supposed to be an embassy man. I don't know what he's doing here. May be just staying with his sister. She's the woman on his right. The Countess Sacardi. Married an Italian who's not in evidence. Don't know anything about him. She looks sad. But, say,"—with an eloquent shrug, "she can be an icicle."

He suspended his commentary while a rosy-cheeked waitress served the soup.

"The other chap," he resumed, "is one Horace Flaherty. He was a year ahead of me in college. Never saw him from that time to this. Heard he was a consul, and secretary of legation in some Godforsaken country. Maybe it was Bulgaria. Lately he turned up here. Health, I suppose."

Ericsson paused for a smile of sophistication, and rewarded himself with a generous bite from a roll.

"One remains. The girl who looks so unlike it is Bostonese. Name of Strong. Fearfully rich family, I believe. She was staying with some Edgecombes who have a nobby old house up Quince Street. They went away a few days ago, but she's still here. Flaherty seems to be rushing her hard.

"That's all. Now for it."

He half-rose, but sank back into his chair with a broad smile.

"That would have been funny. . . . The way I came in to-night, like a man up for sentence, there was no introduction at all. Excepting Dr. Caswell, who identified himself, darned if I know who you are. Of course,"—to Delancey, "you're Griffis with them. And much obliged all over again. But between ourselves——?"

"I'm Richard Delancey."

"And——?"

"Edward Anthony."

"Thanks. Now we're set. Will you excuse me a moment?"

With the word he rose and hastened across the room.

"A breezy young man," said Caswell. "It seems he is going to increase our acquaintance considerably. Thanks to you, of course, Slim."

"Do tell us how they make moving pictures, Mr. Griffis," jibed Anthony.

Delancey looked half-angry.

"I suppose this is a splendid joke to you. I've got to do the acting. And I'm all at sea."

"But Ed will do the singing."

Repartee was ended by Ericsson's return, shepherding the party across the way. And trailing the waitress came, to rearrange the table.

"We have company," he announced. "I told you you would like them. And I told them they would like you. It's up to you all to back me up. Now here," with a wave embracing the delegation from the *Viva*,—"are Dr. Caswell, Mr. Griffis,—all unknown to fame, and Mr. Anthony. There," a wave in the opposite direction, "are the Countess Sacardi, Miss Strong, and Messrs. Beddle and Flaherty. Break ranks, please——"

By casual readjustment Delancey found himself seated beside the Countess. Nearly opposite was Anthony, beside Miss Strong, with Flaherty, who looked glum at being dispossessed, at the end of the table next Beddle.

"Now," said Ericsson with much satisfaction, and called to the waitress somewhere outside: "Oh, Stella."

"Coming, Mr. Ericsson."

She appeared with a pail. A pail containing ice and gilt-crested bottles.

Delancey, sitting with Ericsson on his left, read the label: "Roger, 1914." Also he saw above the year a red triangle. It looked as if made with carmine ink and a pen.

Seemingly, no one else noted it. As Ericsson busied himself with the demeanor of one that serves at a shrine Delancey made swift appraisal of those at the board.

Always abstemious, Caswell peered from his whiskered retreat with the slightly amused look of one who marvelled at nothing, and found a reason for all. Anthony, who was little used to liquor, was sitting with a flush accentuating sunburn, one elbow on the table, and half-turned towards Miss Strong, who seemed to be doing most of the talking between them.

A girl of striking appearance. Slender rather than thin; and a little pale, with eyes of the blue of northern waters, and blond hair that recalled wheat sheaves in autumn sunlight. Fine boned, with turquoise adornment of small ears beautifully modelled. Her simple dinner gown of black suggested sophistication rare among girls of twenty. In gesture, in carriage, in various ways she conveyed an impression of strain. Quite steadily she smoked one of the brands of cheap cigarettes young women of fashion became enamored of in the world war.

Flaherty who was evidently an insatiable raconteur, alternated anecdotes of the beau monde in Newport and Belgrade with fleeting spasms of unnatural glumness in which he regarded Anthony, quite unaware of his displeasure, with baleful eyes. He was a tall middle-weight, with a square smooth-shaven face and twinkling black eyes. He had suavity, and verbal dexterity beyond the average.

Beddle, who seemed rather remote and above proceedings, was one of those with the gift of putting the world on the defensive. He was not large or handsome. Certainly not arrogant. But something emanating from this undistinguished appearing, gray-eyed person caused the average to ask themselves,—"I wonder what he thinks." Very quiet, he seemed to turn, whenever he was not engaged in conversation, to something far away.

"Is this your professional deportment, Mr. Griffis?"

A little belated, and doubly startled, Delancey turned to find the Countess regarding him with an expression of amused speculation. At his look of surprise she elaborated:

"I mean, are you playing the Napoleon of the silent drama?"

"I don't feel," he assured her, "in the least like one."

"Well, you don't look like one."

"Like what——?" he suggested.

"Oh, I won't give that away all at once."

"Just a little, then——?"

"I would rather wait until you have had champagne."

"Your reason, please?"

"Men are most natural when they drink."

"Every man?"

"I rather think so. Now Guy," with an appraising glance for her brother, "becomes more congealed. Had it not pleased God to make him an English gentleman, nature might have used him as a cooler in a Paris restaurant."

"You think ill of us."

"By no means. I am not a feminist. Certainly not a—what is the feminine equivalent of misogynist?"

"There isn't any."

"Then certainly I am not it."

"To Harmony!" observed Ericsson from his stance at the head of the table.

From the silence of sipping emerged the voice of Caswell:

"If it's not impertinent, and certainly I am appreciative, how do you do it, Mr. Ericsson?"

"Oh," said Ericsson, with an airy gesture, "Spain is off there."

"And only," observed Flaherty, "a few thousand miles away."

Delancey turned again to the right. What he saw saluted the eye pleasantly.

"May I remark that is a very charming frock," he said.

"'Frock'? What a sophisticated man."

As the Countess smiled a softer brightness entered the hazel of eyes he first had thought rather cold. Banished also the impression of severity in a profile that reminded him of the face in a precious Roman coin. With her olive complexion she looked rather Italian, but habitually belied it by her coolness of manner.

"Since you seem an apt child," she said, "I will tell you that 'frock' is right. And it is blonde lace. Also I sometimes wear with it a pale yellow hat.

It came from Cheruit. But that means nothing to you. . . . Now tell me all about moving pictures."

"I would rather," he asserted, "tell you anything else."

She sighed.

"I can't call this the modesty of the artist. For usually an artist hasn't any. Now I'd suspect you of being a business man—if it were not for that look in your eyes."

"Really? I can't see it, you know. What is it?"

"Inquiring, and undisciplined."

"Now we're getting on."

"Yes, famously. . . . What do you think of the situation in the Ruhr?"

"Check," he conceded.

Little time remained for talk of any sort. Bjerstedt seemed responsible for the sudden break-up of the party. Delancey had a glimpse of him standing in the doorway, and fancied Ericsson had seen him a moment earlier. At any rate he soon offered an excuse to go, with a look at his watch in a spasm of memory.

"I don't want to break this up," he apologized. "And I hate to go. But I'm late with an engagement. Wish I had forgotten altogether. Won't you all just stay?"

"You are highly hospitable. I'm sorry to say I must return to my boat."

Having settled the matter for himself, Caswell turned to Delancey.

"Shall I send the dinghy back for you and Ed?" he inquired.

"Not for me. I'm rather tired. And I guess I'd better go with you."

"Mr. Anthony can't go," the Strong girl announced.

"But I'm afraid I must."

"It can't be done. I need you."

By her positive accent Anthony seemed slightly disconcerted. On Flaherty's brow appeared a thunder-cloud. With a restraining effort of will it quickly vanished. Addressing Anthony, he even forced a smile.

"You may as well give in. With or without a reason, Miss Strong always gets her way."

"There's a reason now," she said. "I want him to play bridge."

"I'm not much good at cards."

"Then I'll take you for a partner, and share the suffering."

Anthony looked at Caswell. His struggle was feebler now.

"Sure you don't need me for anything?"

"Nothing at all. Delancey and I will just turn in. The boat can come for you at any time."

"Better spend the night ashore," Miss Strong offered.

"Why not?" Ericsson interjected. "The room I took for Griffis will be vacant unless some of you use it."

"That's nice. Then we won't have to hurry about anything."

Miss Strong dismissed the matter as settled.

"Shall I see you later?" Flaherty asked with obvious effort at an air of unconcern.

"You might drop in to Rose's house."

The party was breaking up as conversation proceeded. Caswell and Delancey went, with Ericsson bustling ahead, and Flaherty coming after with Beddle and the Countess. Their last look at Anthony showed him putting a wrap about Miss Strong's shoulders, the while she enveloped him with her sudden air of intimacy.

Delancey spoke first, as he opened the gate that admitted them to Lime Street, with its widely spaced lights filtering softly through the maples.

"That's very quick work. I hope Ed remembers it's leap year."

"A good thing if she popped," said Caswell with a smart tap of his stick.

"Just how do you figure that?"

Taking another trip, Caswell's cigar came to rest in the left corner of his mouth. Then observation in a spray.

"All the Strongs are neurotic. They lay it, when they admit it, to some woman that married into the family about a hundred years ago. . . . Too much blame on the old girl. The trouble is mostly inbreeding. Old Boston habit, you know. . . . That, and too much money. Family's richer than mud. Began with leather, and branched out into real estate. Now they just spend, and rot. Two of 'em suicides in the last ten years; and most of 'em queer."

"Well," said Delancey with a sardonic accent. "Then I don't see why you think it would be a good thing for Ed to get involved with them."

"Plain enough. They need simple, honest blood."

"As for Ed——"

"Needs romance."

"It seems to me he moons too much now."

Caswell tossed his cigar into a neighboring yard.

"That's it," he sniffed. "Look at him. Great tackle, star swimmer, champion hammer thrower. Designed by Nature for strenuous living. . . . And what does he do? Teaches mathematics to mutton-headed little boys! And all his spare time he hunts models of sailing ships, or practises torture with chanteys. . . . Bah!"

"On your own statement he's unfit to cope with the Strong tribe," Delancey insisted.

"Nonsense! He needs interest in women. And there's a life job. He'd never understand her. But she right away understood him. That's good biology, my boy."

Lighting another cigar, Caswell gave it position one, and beheaded a spray of aged goldenrod. Then he went on:

"Nice girl, I hear. Just a little skittish. Settle down all right, if she gets the right sort of man."

When Delancey laughed it ended in a sort of falsetto chuckle.

"I see," he observed, "you and the girl have settled it. Am I expected to be best man?"

"Why count me out? Think I'm too old? . . . Just a moment, Slim. If you don't mind, let's take a little stroll in here."

On their way to the shore they had reached a corner a short distance above the wharf. On one side a street of small houses largely occupied by power-boat fishermen; all that remained where once was manned a famous square rigger fleet. Many were Bravas born of dark-skinned adherents old whalers brought from the south seas. To the left was a comparatively open stretch, with little save a fringe of summer houses standing dark and empty. From this side came the perfume that arrested Caswell's attention.

The odor of late meadow grass, cut and stacked, mingled with the salt breath of the sea. Its rote came to them with a low note of mighty and peaceful breathing. And the punctuation of crickets unaware their days were nearly done. For a few minutes they walked in silence, savoring it all.

"What do you want——?"

Less question than a command, the salutation came like a blow.

Stepping from behind a hut by the path, a man barred the way. In their second look they realized he carried a gun. Before they recovered from the surprise of that discovery he barked again:

"Well, what is it?"

"This is a public highway," said Caswell, giving no ground.

"Maybe it is," said the man with the gun. "But it's unhealthy for nosey strangers."

"See here!" Caswell exploded. "What do you mean?"

For answer the man brought his gun to half-cock. A businesslike proceeding with a sawed-off shotgun.

"It's an outrage."

"I think I know what's up, Pop," said Delancey.

He had strained his eyes during Caswell's exchange with the blockader to verify an impression of something happening at the near-by end of the bathing beach.

Right or wrong, he stirred the belligerent one to decisive action.

"Vamoose!" he ordered.

"Oh——!" sputtered Caswell.

"Quick!"

The gun came to the stranger's shoulder. As they did the sensible thing he barked after them:

"Keep moving."

With a long-visored cap pulled down over his nose, they had no distinct impression of his face. It was only evident that he was of medium height, and stocky. And, judging by his voice, one of nature's rough-and-ready ones.

"Isn't that the queerest?" said Caswell, when he thought it discreet to speak. "What do you make of it?"

"Rum runners."

"What makes you think so?"

"What I saw. You know I'm a sort of owl in the dark. And while you had your little say to the gunman I saw proceedings on the beach beyond us. Maybe two or three hundred yards away.

"There's a boat off there—a short distance from shore. And men are wading in from her with something on their shoulders. I saw them going and coming as we stood there."

"Probably some of Ericsson's stockholders. Your stockholders, too. I forgot that in my excitement," said Caswell dryly.

"That's an unpleasant suggestion. More and more, I feel I am foolish to have anything to do with Ericsson."

"Oh, well," said Caswell soothingly. "What's that——?"

From behind came the explosion of an engine brought into action. And the crescendo of triumph as its power was liberated. Then a loud hum, and thundering progress in their direction.

It came with such suddenness that they exchanged no observation. By common impulse they quitted the sidewalk. And largely concealed by a hay cart left outside a stable door, they saw a furiously driven truck go crashing by. It was loaded with something covered by a tarpaulin. And two men crouched on the tail end.

The truck passed the corner they had lately left, and with still accelerating speed vanished in the water-front street that led out to the moors.

"I guess you're right, Slim," Caswell conceded as they regained the road. "Let's get down to the boat before somebody else threatens to pot us."

The short distance to the wharf they covered without misadventure. Only as they reached its head a rocket was discharged from the shore just back of the light on the Point. Scattering fiery particles, it soared, curved, and fell in swift descent, abruptly extinguished against the dark curtain of sky.

Nothing further occurred until they had walked to where two of Caswell's crew waited, with the dinghy tied up to a float at the foot of some steps. Then, as they stepped in, came an answering signal from the direction of the Black Rip Lightship. Fainter, because some miles distant, a blue rocket answered the red.

Not caring to discuss the problem before the sailors, pulling industriously towards the *Viva*, they exchanged only commonplaces on the way across. They climbed the ladder with a sense of relief.

"I snum," said Caswell as they reached the cabin way. "The old island's become a lively place."

Out at sea, some miles to the eastward, a gun barked. From the sound a four- or five-pounder. Its diminishing echoes came racing landward. . . .

Silence.

CHAPTER 2

A BOUT AND ITS SEQUEL

The street seemed empty as Anthony and Miss Strong emerged from the hotel. Not even the honk of a distant horn, or "Clop-clop" of horse's hoofs on asphalt.

They stood a moment, drinking the beauty of the night. Then she spoke, putting an impulsive hand on his arm.

"Oh, this is good."

An exhalation, half-sigh.

"I'm tired."

"Let me get a taxi," he said, instantly solicitous.

"Tired of people, I mean. Besides, there isn't any taxi. And I want to walk."

"With those heels?"

"They're not monumental. And Rose's house isn't far. . . . If you don't mind giving me a little support."

"Of course," he said. "Glad to."

"Then I'll make fast."

She tucked a hand into the crook of his arm. Thus they walked some yards in silence punctuated by her heels clicking on the venerable sidewalk. Anthony emerged from meditation.

"Please excuse my wool-gathering. You must find me stupid."

"Oh, no, I don't. I was just thinking you must find me brassy."

"But I wasn't. I don't," he said earnestly.

"What do you think of me?"

"I don't know yet."

"Are you going to find out?"

"If you let me."

"I don't seem to be offering any opposition."

Suddenly she laughed, a silvery laugh like the voice of some little mountain stream abruptly released.

"What's the joke?"

"You and I."

"I don't quite see,"—half-suspiciously.

"That's what I like."

"Then you do like me?"

"Of course . . . Silly."

Some unfathomed impulse of mirth in her vexed him vaguely as they strolled on to the corner. She felt and met it with a slight pressure on his arm.

"Which way?" he asked, looking up and down the elm-flanked street.

"Rose's," she pointed, "is up there. But I don't want to play bridge now. Let's walk down to the water."

"Won't they curse us out for breaking up a table?"

"Don't tell me you're an infant at bridge. Now I know you are an addict."

"I only thought," he explained a bit stiffly, "that cutting off that way would be inconsiderate."

"Oh, they'll fill in," she said carelessly. "And we're only being a little late. . . . Don't you want to do it?"

"Of course," hastily.

"See all the time we've lost."

He gave up bewildered.

Nothing piercingly personal was said as they walked slowly down the incline to the shore. It was mostly patter in which Anthony recognized himself with secret amusement.

"Not my line at all," he said to himself.

But he was happy.

Once they paused in the shadow of a big tree, and watched figures whirling past the open windows of a dance hall across the street. It seemed a hectic affair, with shouts of sheer exuberance occasionally rising above the saxophone that imparted to frenetic music its dominant rhythm.

Tightening her hold on Anthony's arm, Miss Strong executed a few little steps, like a boat tugging at its mooring.

"Do you ever feel as if you could fly?" she asked.

"No. But I have."

"I wonder if it's nice," she speculated, "to be literal minded."

"I'm afraid you will never find out."

"No. . . . Tell me. Have you ever noted a horse that is nervous, but doesn't know why, getting ready to run away; and it doesn't know where?"

"Perhaps. But I didn't know it."

"I'm like that," she announced.

"Only now and then, I hope."

"I'm going to run away to the foot of this street."

"Look out," he said in alarm. "Those heels."

Instantly after her, he brought the chase to its end, just as she stumbled. He saved her from a fall.

"Well," she panted, "you certainly can run."

"This isn't much compared to the two-twenty."

With an impulsive movement she pushed him away, as if to acquire a fresh perspective.

"Are you Anthony, the dash man?"

"I was," he admitted.

"And a varsity tackle, and champion boxer."

"How do you know?" he asked, much astonished.

"Of course I know. I'm crazy about sports. . . . Track games, baseball, football. Even rowing races, that never start on time, and almost always end with everybody wondering which crew won. . . . You know I saw you play football when I was fourteen years old, with my hair in a long pigtail down my back."

"Venerable man," he admitted, blushing a little in the dark.

She laughed again, with the rippling sound that came so pleasantly to his ears.

"Oh, you're the youngest thing I ever saw."

With perfect amiability they resumed their stroll down the street.

"I'm sorry," she reflected presently, "I never saw you box."

"I can't say that I am. And I don't suppose you ever will."

"You might as well say, 'I don't want you to.' And that makes me want to say, 'I will.'"

"We can find more probable things to quarrel about, if you insist upon it."

"Now that I know who you are, I'll be afraid to quarrel with you at all. . . . Look! Isn't that heavenly?"

Piercing attendant clouds, the harvest moon put a golden band upon the quiet harbor. As they looked a white sail drifted through.

"Let's go now," she suggested. "That's the best. And I never believe in waiting for the rest."

Quite silently they retraced their way up Main Street, until pulsations of jazz abruptly reasserted earth's grosser charms. As they neared the entrance to the dance hall saxophone and banjos burst suddenly into a nerve-clutching crescendo.

Because his companion paused, so did Anthony perforce.

"Let's go up," she suggested.

"But you can't," he said aghast.

"Why not?"

"It's no place for a lady."

"Perhaps you will allow me to be the judge of that."

She spoke haughtily.

"You know what I mean. I'm not trying to dictate to you."

"Then let's go up."

She put a foot on the door-sill.

"You mustn't."

Despite his disclaimer, he was driven to the imperative.

"No one says that to me."

"You force me to."

Now he was frankly angry.

"Good-night, Mr. Anthony."

As she gained the bottom stair he caught her hand.

"You can't go up there."

"I *am* going up there."

Her voice frigid, she was looking straight ahead.

"Oh, no!" he said, and gained the step beside her.

"On the whole," she said, "I prefer to go alone."

"Well, you won't," he assured her with equal rudeness, and took his place ahead.

Somewhat slowly, because the staircase was narrow, and he would not hasten, they climbed to the second floor. And with each step the music of measured delirium grew more insistent.

"Hurry," she said with a little push. "I want to get there before they stop."

Now his face as he turned back was furious. Before he could speak she laughed in pure delight. And his look grew puzzled.

"Of course, you don't intend to dance."

"Maybe not," she answered gayly. "But if I do, I suppose I'll have to dance alone."

He pushed open the hall door, and they went in. A dramatic entrance, since that instant the music stopped, so that they shared the attention of waiting couples with the orchestra. Anthony felt all eyes were on them as he escorted his imperious charge to vacant chairs in a rear corner of the room. There they were better able to pay reciprocal attention.

Through a haze of cigarette smoke supported by vigorous puffing they observed a hall of moderate size, with a fringe of chairs and settees along the sides. Established by the stage, the orchestra wailed and raged away under the draped Stars and Stripes; and a drop curtain proclaiming the power of Polchack's cologne.

A somewhat miscellaneous assemblage. One got an impression that only the Bravas, better fitted than all the others to enjoy blessings of jazz, were barred. There were men off the scallop boats, and obvious sports of the village; finally, a small contingent Anthony could not definitely place.

Some bore the stamp of urban life, with a style of dress familiar at race tracks and pool rooms. But Anthony was not familiar with the type.

With interest he noted Bjerstedt, who must have come for something besides dancing, in earnest conversation with a stout, round-faced man of middle age who presently put him under the observation of a pair of twinkling little black eyes.

"Is he all right?" the round-faced man was asking, with a guiding jerk of his head.

"I suppose so," said Bjerstedt. "He landed with Griffis this afternoon. That looks O. K."

"All right, if you say so. Sam just slipped me the word he's been nosing round the wharf to-night."

"Oh, he's got a girl. That's all."

Bjerstedt grinned, and their talk took another angle.

Anthony saw first the men. But Miss Strong's first inventory was of the women. Most of them quite obviously village girls in, or just out of, their teens. Some seemed to have come out of the kitchen. And some, only a few, wore the inquiring look of birds of passage. One such, a tall, strapping blonde with straw-colored hair, presently approached Bjerstedt. After a brief colloquy they left the hall by a door to the left of the stage.

Once more the jazz band sounded its call. And the floor immediately filled with swaying, shuffling, shimmying couples. Watching dancing of the catch-as-catch can variety, Anthony and Miss Strong did not note the appearance of Flaherty, who saw them first and gradually worked his way through the eddying crowd. A question was the announcement of his presence:

"What are you doing here, Nell?"

"And what are you doing here?"

She raised her eyes, seemingly unannoyed by his proprietary manner.

"That's very different," he said.

"I don't think so," she responded.

"I wouldn't have brought you here."

"For that matter, Mr. Anthony didn't."

"Then——"

"I just came, of course."

"But I don't see——"

"That you are being rude to Mr. Anthony. If you are bound to draw inferences, you might assume I came because I wanted to. If you feel you are entitled to particulars, he came when he didn't."

"Oh——" said Flaherty, turning with an expression of reluctant apology to Anthony, who sat flushed and silent, boiling with suppressed resentment.

What might further have passed between the three was side-tracked by an intrusion.

"Will you gimme a turn?"

The inquirer stood at Miss Strong's elbow.

"Thank you. But I'm not dancing to-night."

"Oh, come on."

"See here," said Flaherty. "Don't annoy this lady."

"Chase yourself," the accoster observed contemptuously, and rested a hand on Miss Strong's shoulder.

Anthony's spring and his blow were the beginning and end of a rhythmic movement. With a certain fierce pleasure he drove his right to the point of the jaw. The man fell like a tree at the decisive stroke of the axe. But falling backward he landed in a chair. As he sprawled there with helplessly extended arms neighboring dancers stopped, curiously interested in the next stage of proceedings.

"What's the row?" asked a man who looked like a longshoreman.

Anthony did not answer. His interest seemed centered in a barked knuckle.

The man he had hit showed signs of revival. By a movement in which he drew in his legs, and brought his hands to his knees, he slowly sat up. Then he touched his chin reflectively, and located Anthony with opaque eyes.

"You hit me," he said heavily.

"I did."

"Think you can fight?"

"I can punch a thug."

"Yeh. Well, you're goin' to get a chance."

"Suit yourself."

"Right now."

"Do you think this is a fit place?"

"I'm takin' no chance on yer runnin' away."

"I guess we'd better go outside."

"Oh, that's all right. We don't mind a little boxing match."

The latest observation came from a black-mustached individual who seemed to be managing the dance.

"Sure," called somebody from the crowd. "Hot stuff."

"Probably," said Anthony in even tones, "you never had your head bumped on a hardwood floor."

"Cold feet," came a new voice.

"We'll fix you up," the black-mustached one assured him. "There's canvas in the closet. Had a bout here last week."

The man Anthony had hit was on his feet again, and came a step closer.

"Will you take your lickin' here?" he inquired.

"If you can give it."

"You'd better get away."

The only attention Anthony paid to Flaherty's advice, given in a half-whisper, was his step away from the hand laid confidentially on his shoulder. Unlike his antagonist, who tried to make the first round of all a battle of eyes, he wore a look of preoccupation.

"Please take Miss Strong home," he said without glancing in her direction.

"I don't want to go," she protested.

"You will go."

"But——" she began, stopping when she saw his eyes.

The honest gray was changed to slatey color. And pallor underlay the sunburn on neck and cheek. He was cold and strange, as he stood there waiting for her to speak. Her defiance evaporated.

"I will go," she said meekly, "if you think I should."

"Thank you. Good-night."

"At least let me wish you good luck."

She extended her hand, and he held it a moment, staring at her slim, nervous fingers.

"That will help," he said quietly.

When she left the hall with Flaherty he seemed oblivious. Men and women made room for them respectfully enough, so that she paused on the threshold for a last look. Anthony still stood where they had left him, regarding preparations for the fight with an air of indifference.

It was evident that no question of propriety had occurred to the escorts of other women. Here and there little groups were chattering with pleased excitement.

Now Ericsson entered, bustling as usual, and came rapidly to where Anthony waited alone.

"See here," he said excitedly. "Do you know who you're up against?"

"No."

From Anthony's manner one might have thought the matter did not interest him.

"It's Sam Lever."

Still no manifestation of excitement.

"Professional," Ericsson added. "Light heavy-weight."

"That's interesting."

Anthony gave further attention to his slightly discolored knuckle.

"I'm afraid it's a plant," observed his comforter.

"No. I hit him."

"Boozy, I suppose."

"I think he had some liquor in him."

"That's his trouble, I hear. He is in bad with the New York boxing authorities. . . . How about your hand?"

Anthony flexed the hurt finger.

"All right, I think. It seems to be nothing but a slight bruise."

"Fine. Now I've given you all the bad news I could, will you let me act for you?"

A trace of Anthony's habitually frank and engaging expression lightened his face an instant.

"Thanks," he said. "I'll be grateful."

"Probably I won't be much good as a second. But I used to chore that way sometimes in college. . . . I see Lever has disappeared. So I suppose we'd better get busy. I'll be back in a jiffy."

As he hurried away Anthony watched the stretching of canvas for the ring. Many hands were making light work. One individual, however, spared time to accost him.

"Say, feller, do you know who you're fightin'?"

"I don't care."

Anthony answered without turning his head.

"You'll find out all right," his would-be informant declared gloatingly, and went his way.

From the other end of the hall Ericsson beckoned. He waited there for Anthony, who picked his way leisurely. A beckoning finger waggled over Ericsson's shoulder drew him on to a small anteroom, where on county convention days small fry candidates made large preparation to address their fellow-citizens. Now another kind of fight impended.

"Our headquarters."

As he spoke Ericsson was closing the door.

"And here are the fixings. I never knew a scratch fight with such a complete outfit. 'Mushy,'—that's the black-mustached impresario, says they bought a lot of stuff for some local tryouts. Anyway, here it is; and all brand-new. . . . First choice for you. Everybody's suspiciously pleasant."

With both hands he extended a collection of trunks to Anthony, who made casual selection.

"Ah, the Black Knight," rattled Ericsson. "According to Scott he was a rather good fighter. Now the gloves."

This time Anthony gave more careful attention. And he asked his only question, as he looked at the stitching of a glove, and bent it back to test its flexibility.

"How does this professional fighter happen here?"

A film of reticence slightly veiled Ericsson's ruddy countenance.

"Got me," he answered. "The island seems more or less littered with strange arrivals nowadays."

Without further comment Anthony made his toilet for the ring. Ericsson's eyes bulged as he stepped from his street clothes.

"I'll be darned," said the voluble one. "You didn't look it."

With open admiration he surveyed the powerful shoulders and clean strength of leg; the deep chest, and easy play of rippling muscle as Anthony went through slight exercises of a loosening order.

"What's your weight?" asked Ericsson with eager interest.

"About a hundred and seventy."

"Well, I don't mind saying that when I volunteered I felt like a philanthropist. Now I feel like a discoverer. That's the way my nerve is. . . . How about yours?"

"All right."

"Say, are you the——?"

An idea that smote Ericsson went unexpressed; the door opened in the middle of his sentence.

"Ready?" inquired the individual whose head was thrust in.

For answer Anthony moved towards the hall, his voluble second after him. As they entered they paused a moment surveying the crowd.

Not the usual assemblage in tier on tier of faces like luminous blotches in a thickening haze. But the aggregate effect of the hundred odd men and women sitting expectant was much the same. At a slight distance their utterance suggested the vocalizing in animal cages before meal-time.

Surveying it all with a feeling of detachment, Anthony felt Ericsson jogging his elbow.

"Better rest a bit," he suggested.

"I'm all right."

"Like to see Lever?"

"Not especially."

"If you change your mind, he's over there."

With a characteristic jerk of his thumb Ericsson was off to confer with the man called "Mushy." Presently that individual did a surprising thing. Producing a large key from his pocket, he walked to the door and carefully locked it.

Now he made his way to the ring, and stood there with his left hand raised in appeal for attention. The hum of conversation sensibly decreased.

"I want to say," he announced, "that this fight is going to be a square fight. Anybody that tries to interfere with it will get hurt."

In his right hand, which had dropped to a hip pocket during proclamation of fair play, he now held a revolver. It was a heavy weapon, its ominous appearance nowise lessened by his affectionate regard. He patted its barrel with his left hand, and returned it to his pocket. Nobody disputed the following conclusion:

"I'm going to run this show."

As the self-appointed referee turned towards him Anthony felt sudden tightening in the crowd's tension. There was fight in the atmosphere, fight on every man's tongue. Responsive to a beckoning hand, he climbed through the ropes.

"Edward Anthony, of Boston," announced the referee.

A ripple of perfunctory applause subsided in serious interest. Those that waited gaily for a slaughtering felt their first misgiving, as he stood at ease. A picture of compact power, with clear color of good health and the satiny skin of a well-groomed athlete.

"Looks like he's got guts," said a hoarse-voiced individual.

The referee turned to the other side of the ring.

"In this corner—Sam Lever, of New York."

Mr. Lever rose and bowed to a demonstration of cordial regard. Evidently he was well known.

"This fight," the referee went on, "will be a fight to a finish." It was news to Anthony, who wondered if Ericsson had been informed. Now he looked at Lever with more searching interest, and a flare of the cold flame of anger. There had been no desire in his heart further to hurt the man he struck. In forcing him to fight Lever had acted according to his code. But if it was proposed to reduce him to bleeding pulp—there would be two with a say in the matter.

Lines of grimness about the mouth that had helped to quell sauciness in Nell Strong were deep again as Ericsson bent over the fastening of his gloves, and his eyes paled with fixed regard unwelcome to those that once provoked it.

"What's your plan?" asked Ericsson sotto voce.

"To lick him."

"Ready," called the referee.

They advanced to shake hands. In the final appraisal Anthony guessed Lever to be about his own age—perhaps younger. He had rather massive shoulders and a short neck. One might have thought Nature intended him for a six-footer, but ran short of material. He seemed light, however, on his feet, with a heavy cording of muscle. As he stared at Anthony a black forelock lent point to his scowl.

"Say you—you piece of cheese," he announced. "I'm going to knock your block off."

Anthony did not answer. But he stepped in a bit closer. The bell sounded, and the fight was on.

Lever came with a rush. His right, and then his left. The right grazed Anthony's chin. The left slid harmlessly over his shoulder. In blocking, as he felt Lever out, his blood ran warmer with the zest of battle.

Taking his turn with the offensive, he penetrated Lever's guard with a right hook that landed on the side of the jaw. An expression of pain rewarded him.

Lever rushed again, but less furiously. As they clinched after a harmless exchange he muttered, "The next round will be your finish." Anthony smiled.

"Break away. Break clean."

The referee came pushing between them. In a quick glance at his foe's feet Anthony saw a shift to the left, and shot a slashing blow to the kidneys.

"Atta boy!" bellowed his hoarse admirer.

Then the gong sent them to their corners.

"Going fine," said Ericsson with enthusiasm. "I see you had it doped all the time."

Anthony saved his breath, while a towel was waved furiously before him. All about the crowd buzzed like a hive of excited bees.

At the sound of the gong Anthony came to his feet with a spring. And Lever was equally prompt, his ugly look intensified.

"You're all in," he muttered in Anthony's ear as they came to a clinch after rapid exchange of infighting.

By this time each had felt the other out, and knew the work ahead of him. And with varying intelligence each realized he had handicapped himself in condition. After two days of sailing, and drink to which he was unaccustomed, Anthony missed the perfect coördination of eye and hand that is the boxer's joy. And Lever, who was by no means in the best of condition after some months of varied indulgence, found the prey he proposed to maul "within an inch of his life" threatening to turn the tables.

The round ended with both wary. And the crowd disappointed.

"Bananas!" yelled a straw-hatted individual lolling comfortably on a settee.

"Yeh! Lean on yerself," another admirer advised as Lever held Anthony cautiously to still a flailing left.

"Wait! He ain't ready," urged another.

Three rounds more, and both men still on their feet. Anthony was studiously encouraging Lever to set the pace. That a man whose means of livelihood was, or had been, fighting with fists could outbox him was no surprise. But he was the quicker, and able at least to offer a stout defence. There would come, he felt, some chance for a decisive blow. Burning within him was a fanatic resolve to win.

In the fifth he saw an opening, as Lever forced him back to his corner, and collected energy for a hurricane assault. For an instant his guard was low, and shifting suddenly Anthony landed on his chin. By an adroit movement Lever avoided its full force, while a glancing blow made his head ring. Momentarily dazed, he half-fell into a clinch.

It was Anthony's second to administer the coup de grace, while the crowd roared encouragement.

What stopped him?

As Lever half-fell with upraised arms Anthony's amazed eyes beheld in the right arm-pit a Red Triangle. Very small it was, with the look of something done by a branding-iron.

A second of amazement cost Anthony the opportunity for which he waited. As the referee came between them Lever regained sufficient poise to block attack for the minute that was left of the round.

Anthony walked wearily to his corner. Astonishment and disappointment combined to let him down. He felt a new weakness in his knees; and his hands seemed tied.

Lever came briskly in the fifth. Now his attack was changed to a stinging short-arm tattoo on the ribs. Anthony felt his body vibrate with blows. His enemy was fighting confidently, but cautiously, taking his own time to finish the work. Anthony fought on doggedly, holding him off with a still formidable left. So the round ended.

"How do you feel?" asked Ericsson, solicitously kneading his calves.

"Low," he said wearily.

Early in the sixth a downward blow on the back of the neck temporarily paralyzed his power of reason. But his feet did not falter as he doggedly pursued the routine of battle. He fought on as one in a mist, with a vague feeling of irritation that Lever was so remote.

Another reprieve distressingly short. Vaguely grateful for cold water poured down his back, he wondered what it had to do with the waterfall roaring in his ears.

"Hang to him," implored Ericsson.

Meantime in the opposite corner Kid Glowerville, of Harlem, sluiced Lever's weary legs, and offered cheery counsel.

"You got him, Sambo. Just one more round."

In languor Mr. Lever reclined against the ropes.

"Say, Kid," he observed. "That's a fighter."

The gong that brought respite brutally brief summoned again to labor. As Anthony's chair was pulled from under him something flared in his brain. He felt its incandescence flood his veins. Galvanized into activity, he eluded Lever's furious right swing for the jaw, and countered heavily on the left eye.

More amazed than intimidated, Lever gave ground before a rain of short-arm blows. The crowd yelped its delight.

As Lever clinched, and held, he was conscious of slackening tension in Anthony's arms. Eyes he looked into lost their feverish lustre. They were glazed. Once in a mining camp he had seen such pupils in the eyes of a man who lay dying, shot in a brawl. In sudden fear he broke loose, and backed away.

Then the amazing thing happened. Swaying uncertainly, Anthony uncoiled like a great spring. One moment he seemed about to fall. The next Lever was prostrate, his smitten jaw pressing the canvas. With a left flush to its point he had gone down swiftly, as one falling from a great height.

As he leaned against the ropes Anthony heard the referee intone the count. He started climbing through at the sound of the fateful ten. The crowd was quiet with an unwelcome victory, now that blood-lust was appeased. He was outside the ring when the referee called:

"Hey, Mister Anthony! Sam wants a word with yer."

By this time Lever was half-sitting up.

"That was a sock!" he said, as Anthony looked down at him, with his elbows on the rope. "My head buzzes like a top."

"It was a lucky one," observed Anthony.

"Mebbe. You're some puncher." Lever touched his chin gingerly.

"But say—I'll get you yet."

He rolled over with a curious smile.

"Good-bye," said Anthony, and turned away.

Too sore and weary to feel elation, he proceeded to his dressing-room. Ericsson waited there jubilant with reflected glory.

"I guess you'll get the whole of the sidewalk in this old burg," he said as Anthony towelled his aching ribs.

"More likely the gang will do me up."

Ericsson snorted, and lighted a cigarette.

"Whither goest?" he asked with the tying of Anthony's cravat.

"To the hotel. And to bed. I'm dead tired."

"I suppose so," Ericsson assented. He seemed a little disappointed.

They went out into the nearly empty hall, and down the stairs to the street, parting with a handshake, and a mutual, "So long." Anthony stood on the sidewalk a moment, as Ericsson set out briskly in the direction of the harbor.

"Congratulations," came a voice in his ear.

He whirled and stared in amaze. At his elbow were Nell Strong, who looked radiant, and Flaherty, a sulky appearing individual.

"I don't understand," he said.

"You were splendid," she explained.

"But you don't mean——"

He paused with a red wave mounting his forehead.

"Of course, stupid. I mean the fight."

"But you weren't there."

"On the fire-escape—every minute. Looking in through the window."

"But you were going home."

He turned accusingly to Flaherty, who exchanged a scowl for his frown. She laughed, delighted.

"What men you are. First he blamed you because I insisted on coming here. Now you blame him because I wouldn't go home. . . . Don't you know I always do as I please?"

"I congratulate you."

Anthony bowed stiffly.

"Good-night."

"I thought you were taking me home."

Astonishment with which she contrived to color her tone was honestly reflected in Anthony's face.

"I understand Mr. Flaherty assumed that responsibility."

"Don't you want to?"

"Is that a fair question?"

In weariness of mind and body, after the ordeal just passed, his temper was getting a little out of hand. Whether Flaherty felt it, or was really disinclined to make a bad third, he promptly effaced himself.

"The fact is," he explained, "I had an engagement. Have one still, if the man has waited for me. So, if you are free, and Miss Strong will excuse me, I'll see."

"Certainly," said Anthony without the slightest elation.

They had walked a block without a word when she stopped under a street light.

"I want to know whether you are really cross with me," she said.

Though he did not wish to unbend, he could not check a smile. She was so like a mock-contrite child.

"What I do see," she announced, "is that you are threatened with a black eye."

"Am I?"

"The left one. I must put some beef on it."

She seemed quite delighted.

"It's of no consequence," he protested. "You mustn't bother."

"I like to. Come along to Rose's. But we won't go in. You wait outside while I slip into the kitchen, and get the cook to give me the beef."

"I don't like to have you do this."

"Yes you do. Now come along."

To enforce her order she took his arm. At the touch he yielded.

The house designated as Rose's was soon reached. A large white house of colonial type, it stood on a hillside commanding the inner harbor. The fused scent of spacious gardens in the rear came to Anthony as he waited on the porch, feeling himself a conspicuous intruder with a quartet of rather festive appearing bridge players just inside. He was not aware of Miss Strong's return until he heard her whisper:

"Come this way."

He followed around a corner, to a secluded spot in a side garden.

"Now stand still," she commanded. "And you'd better close your eyes."

He felt her light touch about his head, binding a handkerchief and something soothingly cool over the damaged eye. Then something so feathery on the tip of his nose. Was it a kiss? . . . He opened the available eye.

"Now we're ready," she said in a businesslike fashion.

"For what?"

She answered over her shoulder, as he followed at her heels.

"Don't be afraid. You're not being abducted."

From the shadows of a closed car standing in the driveway a liveried man materialized at their approach, and touched his cap as he opened the door.

"Home," she said, and Anthony followed in.

In silence framed by encompassing stillness of the night they rode out of the driveway, and half-way down a cobbled highway climbing from the principal square. Then she spoke:

"What are you thinking about?"

"It's a queer evening, Miss Strong."

"Don't you think you might call me 'Nell'?"

"I wouldn't presume so on first meeting."

"Not even after you've fought for me? And I've done up your eye."

"Well——"

Again the ripple of sheer mirth he was learning to anticipate with pleasure.

"All right," he assented.

"That's nice. Now we are friends."

With complete content she settled against his shoulder. And Anthony found himself offering a superfluously protective arm.

"Let's not talk now," she said. "I want to listen."

They were running smoothly along the cliff road, fringed with trees on either side, and flanked on the upper by houses set far back; so they were invisible by night, save here and there some chimney or gable picked out in electric light. Below the sea droned, with a slow beat of mighty meditation.

"Don't you think it's like a soliloquy?" she said presently.

"You mean——?"

"The water. I love it most like this. When it seems to be talking to itself. One feels that it understands—everything."

"I wouldn't expect you to feel that way," he said.

"Why not?" she demanded.

"Oh, it's hard to say. But I would have guessed you cared more for the mountains. That they gave you a feeling of peace through being so big and still."

"They don't. Instead they seem so terribly big and stolid. Like a giant you can never escape; and he never speaks. . . . The sea, even if it is cruel at times, has something for all our moods. And it is never twice the same. . . . I don't like ticketed things."

"I'm afraid," said Anthony with a moment's reflection, "you are going to find me very dull."

"That's funny."

Again her laugh.

"You're not half so literal as you think you are."

What he might have answered remained unsaid. For at that moment the car swung sharply into a gravelled entrance on the left, and stopped with a shock that sent them flying forward. By a convulsive effort Anthony managed to regain his balance and check his companion's impetus; so they were not thrown against the front of the car.

Looking out, he saw a dark mass with which the car had evidently been in collision, just to the right and under a big tree. And he heard the chauffeur in indistinct colloquy with some invisible person.

"Let me find out what it is," he said, and stepped into the driveway.

Then he noted an accent of anger in the chauffeur's voice. In the other's, one of surly apology.

"I thought it was Harrington's," the second voice explained.

"Well, 'tis not," the chauffeur rejoined. "And may I ask, do you deliver goods by the front entrance?"

"If I feel like it," the unknown retorted as Anthony drew near enough to see a burly individual in a turtle-neck sweater. A cap was pulled down over his eyes.

"What are you doing here?" Anthony asked.

"Groceries," said the unknown.

The chauffeur snorted.

With eyes by this time adjusted to dim light Anthony surveyed the truck that had stopped them. It was piled high with cases. . . . Of what?

He moved a bit nearer, and the unknown stepped in his way.

"I guess I'd better be goin'," he said.

"How about my damages?" the chauffeur irately demanded.

"I couldn't help it, could I?"

The man had climbed to the seat of the truck.

"You'll bear me witness, sir," the chauffeur appealed to Anthony. "'Twas no fault of mine."

Loudly snorting, the truck started with a jerk, and narrowly missed hitting the limousine again. Then it went thundering down the road to the town.

"What was it, Bruce?"

Miss Strong had also alighted for personal inspection.

"I don't know, ma'am," he said. "Some of those rum runners, I think."

"Is the car hurt much?"

"It don't seem so, ma'am. I think it will turn over."

"If it doesn't, use another in the garage. I want you to drive Mr. Anthony back to the village. He will take me to the house."

"Are you sufficiently protected?" asked Anthony as they reached the first turn of the double curve by which they reached the house steps.

"What are you thinking of—rum runners?"

She seemed amused at the suggestion.

"Well," he persisted, "some of those fellows I saw at the hall to-night I wouldn't trust far—if at all."

"I'm not in the least afraid. And I'll tell you a secret."

"What is it?"

"I keep a revolver."

"Great Scott! You'll hurt yourself."

"Not I. Maybe somebody else. I'm a very good shot."

"But I'd be glad——"

"Only there is no need. . . . I would like, though, to see you to-morrow. Are you awake as early as nine?"

"Any time at all," he assured her.

"I'll expect you here then. I want to take you to some of my pet spots on the moors. They're best in the morning, when the night has left them all clean. . . . Till then."

Before he completely realized it, with a soft closing of the great door she vanished within. Turning, he walked slowly towards the spot where they left the chauffeur repairing the car. As he reached the second curve he cut across the greensward. It was just then a rustling as of foliage agitated came to his ears. It was repeated when he paused. And as he advanced to investigate he heard a soft thud like that of some one landing in a leap on turf.

Covering some fifty yards, he came to a breast-high stone wall. It was absolutely still then, save for the beat of the sea. After listening for a minute or so he dismissed what he had heard as the passage of some small animal;

a dog or cat, maybe, magnified to overwrought imagination. Retracing his steps, he followed the course of the drive down to the gate.

There was the car and the waiting chauffeur, perched on the wall with a glowing cigarette. He threw it away hastily as he heard the crunch of Anthony's feet on the gravel. Then he hopped down, and stood at attention.

"Is the car all right?"

"Yes, sir. 'Twas only the fender bent, and some paint scraped off. . . . By the mercy of God, sir."

Anthony got in.

"Where to, sir?"

"The Stimson House, thank you."

They had hardly started when strained attention to which events of the evening had keyed Anthony yielded to deepening lethargy of sheer fatigue. He could not even concentrate on Nell, much as he wished to do so.

His mind skipped whimsically, this way and that. And there were blanks when the thread of thought was broken abruptly. So he was only casually conscious of the interruption of smooth driving when Bruce grazed the edge of a gutter by an abrupt turn to avoid collision with a great car that came up behind at high speed, and passed with a single sharp summons of its horn.

That was in the outskirts of the village, where meadows began, and the little houses, some of them partly supported by piles that had rather the look of hind-legs in the water. Muttering angrily as he continued to drive with care, Bruce brought his somnolent passenger to the hotel gate. Anthony still lounged inside, not quite conscious of arrival. And he was by no means alert when, having tipped the chauffeur like a nabob, he went up the flagged walk to the white door.

He opened and entered. There was no one about. For the island air, soft and heavy, is a drug to strangers; and native philosophy is nourished with much sleep.

With a look into the empty office, where a gas jet flickered and the open book reminded him that he was an unregistered intruder, he forced his feet up the stairs. There he stopped again, clearing in his mind the location of the room offered by Ericsson.

Apparently, he remembered correctly. For he made the turn, recalled the step down, and concentrated to the best of his ability on doors along one side of the hall. It was a considerable exertion, since by rule or inadvertence the light had been turned off.

Now for the first time it occurred to him that he had no key. To get one he would have to locate and rouse somebody. He did not know who, or where the keeper of keys might be found.

Better test a chance that the door remained unlocked. He thought it had been when he left with Caswell and Delancey. He recalled it as the third to the left. He felt his way along and counted.

As the knob turned under his hand the door opened easily. He closed it behind him. Then he fumbled for the light, but did not find it. After a futile minute or so he gave up.

With the window-shade raised there was a little reflected light of the moon. Sufficient to make out the white spread of the bed, and pallid crockery of the wash-stand. A small rocking-chair he found by hitting an ankle against a corner.

A little disgusted because he lacked necessities of the toilet, he poured a generous measure of water into the wash-bowl located by touch more than the eye, and splashed it over his face. Then he felt for a towel, and picked his way to bed.

His last conscious act was to straighten Nell's bandage over his eye. It was dripping a little on his nose. . . . He sighed, he yawned, and slept.

Seemingly, no one saw Anthony enter the hotel. And no one saw a tall man with a slight limp come from somewhere in the rear of the house about fifteen minutes later. Not venturing on the piazza until he came opposite the door, he took the few steps to it with extreme care, and entered. It appeared the door was never locked.

Slowly, but without hesitation, he ascended to the second floor, and followed Anthony's course of a short time before. In his turn he counted doors, until he came to the one in mind. Then he stooped to the keyhole to listen.

Apparently satisfied by what he heard, or did not hear, he tried the door, which opened easily. Leaving it slightly ajar, he stepped in.

CHAPTER 3

BJERSTEDT'S BOMB

In the pearly mist that presaged daybreak little boats went briskly out to sea. Confident of their way, they pushed past the far end of the breakwater, with a "Put-put!" of engines like exchanged greetings of early birds.

The scallop fleet. With its passing the harbor drowsed. Then it stirred again under its pink coverlet, as the sun peeped over the hill, and oars creaked here and there in dories. Ruffling the water, a little breeze cleared lanes in the fog, so that cottages on the Point showed their dripping faces.

It was then a long black boat crept from its hiding place on the north side of the last fish-house in the row. Keeping close in, but far enough from land to make observation uncertain, it reached the ship channel. Then it pointed with increasing speed for open water. Its engines were almost noiseless. And but one figure, that of a man half-crouched at the wheel, was visible.

Not many minutes later the sun resumed its rule of day. But the black mystery was invisible from shore when the harbor cleared of mist with celerity like that attending the raising of a curtain. Then the steamer for "America," as the islanders styled it in the simple pride of isolation, cast off with hoarse blasts of her whistle to hasten scampering laggards.

On board the *Viva* two barefoot sailors were sluicing the deck.

"Do you think," said one, "'twould be taking too big a chance?"

"It's bloody big money," the second indirectly answered.

"There's the law-breakin'," the first pursued.

"Them Red fellers have a pull."

"All the same, 'tis a crime we'd be doing."

The taller sailor cleared the rail with superb expectoration.

"How'd you make that out?" he inquired. "Everybody's doin' it."

Whatever the question, debate was squelched by the appearance of Andersen, a figure of calm capability in uniform of blue.

"Has Captain Caswell been on deck?" he inquired.

"Had his bucket a short time ago, sir," the sailor called Johnson answered.

"Have you seen Mr. Delancey?"

"Took a plunge. But he didn't swim much." Johnson permitted himself a faint smile. "He went below to get warmed up."

Levity in sailors was unseemly to Andersen.

"It's cold water for swimming," he said, and added crisply: "Get on with your work. Breakfast may be wanted here."

As he went below to prod the cook the pair on deck resumed their swabbing. When Johnson began it Murray chimed in; so they droned away in unison, with measured strokes:

> *"Blow, bullies, blow;*
> *Blow, bullies, blow.*
> *Sugar an' rum an' pearls below———"*

Next the brasswork, to which they gave the final wipe, and went forward. Immediately, as if by signal of "Deck clear," Caswell appeared, wearing his cap at a highly unnautical angle. From a waistcoat pocket he fished the first cigar, then put it back again.

To his nose came something from the shore. With his funny grimace he sniffed ecstatically. The faint breath of the moors, still wet with dew and warming gradually in the waxing sunlight. That with an overtone of burning leaves, fired by some conscientious laborer raking his dooryard before the day's work.

He was in the full tide of enjoyment when Delancey, cool as the morning in white flannels, arrived on deck.

"Cocktail before breakfast, Slim," said Caswell without turning his head.

"Where? And what, Pop?"

Delancey looked about with interest.

"Over there."

Caswell's gesture began with the North Tower, standing white in the morning light, and returned from a tour of beach and billowy moorland.

"Oh! Then you're not being dissipated."

Delancey inhaled in his turn. As they stood a moment in silence Caswell again produced, and a second time returned to his pocket, the beloved cigar. With deliberate sweetness the Portuguese chime in the tower struck seven.

While the echo lingered Caswell pressed a button.

"Breakfast here," he said, when Andersen came gravely up the ladder. Before it was served he had made his third inspection of the cigar, and looked doubtful.

"Why the burning haste?" asked Delancey, smoking comfortably with an elbow on the rail.

"It's a morning for the lark."

"So you're up with that."

A contortion of Caswell's whiskers.

"That's a rotten joke," he said reproachfully. "Just to punish you I'll smoke one of those marvellous cigarettes. I know you hate to see me."

"Well, you smoke cigarettes like an old woman," Delancey said kindly, passing his case.

Caswell turned it in his hand, admiring its exquisite tracery of hammered gold, and the springing vine from which a woman's head emerged in aquiline beauty.

"Pretty thing," he observed. "Every time I see it I want to steal it. Where did you get it?"

"A present. It's Moorish stuff, I suppose."

Caswell carefully inserted a cigarette in his mouth, then threw it away with relief. Breakfast was served.

"What about the lark?" Delancey asked presently.

"It may sing."

"Replacing Ed, I suppose."

Caswell's nose wrinkled with disgust.

"You needn't bother," he said maliciously. "In fact, you won't have time. Is it to-day you start making the island movie?"

"Oh, Ericsson won't carry the joke that far."

"Remember his determined customers," said Caswell delighted.

Delancey put down his napkin.

"I don't think I will go ashore," he said. "You're a pleasant companion."

"Don't get cantankerous, Slim. After all, you're only palmed off on Bjerstedt. And the real Griffis is due on to-day's boat. . . . So that's that. Come on."

"If my host commands, I suppose I must obey," conceded Delancey. "I'll call on the birdies."

Presently they were being rowed towards the Point. As the oars cut the water they sat back in luxurious enjoyment. It was so bright and still, with gracious heat. Little sounds of village life made their way over the quiet water.

Past the Point, they skirted the curving shore, with its inlets where tall grass waved in the tide, and the meadows spread their carpet leading to reddening slopes. Then a celestial warbling came to their ears.

"Stop!" Caswell barked to the rowers.

As their oars trailed in the water the song went on. Somewhere far above its spiral was prolonged, until with a last long trill its melody vanished in silence.

"Put in there."

Caswell pointed to the piling of a little wharf just visible above the reeds and grasses of an inlet some fifty yards beyond.

"What for?" asked Delancey, viewing the immediate landscape with disfavor.

"It may roost," said Caswell with half-subdued excitement.

"What of it?"

Caswell looked at him with bare tolerance.

"I haven't seen one on a bush or hedge for years."

"Well, I can picture it for you, if you haven't sufficient imagination."

Pulling gingerly, the sailors brought the dinghy in to the wharf.

"Take Mr. Delancey on to the steamboat landing," Caswell directed as, eager to be ashore, he scrambled over the side.

"Why the banishment?"

Delancey was leisurely preparing to disembark.

"I don't want to bore you, or insult the lark."

"I'll assume the latter risk, if you'll take the former."

With a long step Delancey gained the wharf. Caswell was already under way, pegging up the narrow footpath that wound through the meadow with a course conforming to conditions of soil. Hastening to overtake him, Delancey slipped in a moist spot, and nearly measured his length. He regained his balance with a half-smothered imprecation.

"What's the matter?" asked Caswell without turning.

"Nothing but muddied white buckskin and flannel trousers."

"Shouldn't have worn them." Caswell kept going. "This isn't Bar Harbor."

Further sharpshooting was prevented by the lark. Again its song, like the far trill of angels, gushed from the sky. They stood and listened.

So far as they observed, heaven's feathered messenger did not come to earth. After considerable tramping, in which Delancey somewhat glumly followed his eager guide, they set out for town.

"The scene of our hold-up," Caswell presently observed.

Sure enough, they had reached the corner patrolled by the man with a sawed-off shotgun. A bit beyond was the yard in which they had found shelter behind a cart.

"I wonder what Ed's up to," said Delancey.

Caswell was hunting the inevitable cigar, which he clipped and lit.

"Somewhere singing, I suppose," he suggested after the first puff.

"Warbling about 'sugar, and pearls, and rum below,' to Nelly Strong."

"What makes you think he is with her?"

Caswell's cigar travelled to the left corner of his mouth.

"Because I know women."

"That impression," Delancey observed, "is supposed to be a mark of inexperience."

"Not in my case."

Now the cigar swung to the right, and smoke poured from Caswell's mouth gustily.

"It's been my job to study them," he continued, "for about thirty years. Why shouldn't I understand them? As a sex, of course. One woman is different. When you take a personal interest, your eye is put out."

"Then you think Ed——"

"Is a goner. Good thing."

"It's a pity he doesn't know you have it all settled for him."

"It would be a good thing for you, too," said Caswell, quite unruffled.

"Just why?"

"You're too self-centred."

Delancey decapitated a stalk of goldenrod with a vicious swing of his stick.

"I think," he said, "there's no immediate danger of my reformation."

The much-travelled cigar stood out at a rakish angle.

"Maybe," remarked the busy smoker. "It looks like quite a lively cruise to me."

"Huh!"

With that observation Delancey turned to look at a motor brought to a stop beside them with furious grinding of brakes. In it sat Bjerstedt.

"I've been looking for you."

His manner was accusing.

"That's very kind of you," Delancey responded with suavity thrown away. "Since you're on the lookout, I wonder if you have seen our friend, Anthony."

"No."

"Then Ericsson, maybe?"

Bjerstedt turned in his seat to face Delancey squarely.

"No," he said slowly. "I haven't seen Mr. Ericsson, either."

"Such a pity."

Delancey looked at him genially, and lighted a cigarette, completing his observation with the first puff.

"Everybody's out, it seems. Or in."

As he reached back to open the door of his car Bjerstedt's face was topped by a frown.

"Get in," he said curtly.

"We're only going up to the hotel," observed Caswell, who had seemed oblivious of the colloquy between Bjerstedt and Delancey, as he peered at something in the foliage of a neighboring tree.

Bjerstedt's hand remained on the open door. He waited patiently.

"So am I," he said. "No use walking when you can ride."

Clamping his cigar afresh, Caswell stepped in. And Delancey followed. Hardly settled, and then out. The ride seemed ridiculously short.

"Thank you," said Delancey as they alighted at the gate to the hotel yard.

"Hold on. I'm coming."

Slowly, and with the mental effect of cursing his ailing foot, Bjerstedt got out of the motor. Then he turned to Delancey with a bald observation:

"I want to see you."

Caswell took the cue.

"I'll look up Ed," he remarked.

"Not now," said Delancey. "I'll be with you in a few minutes. . . . What can I do for you, Mr. Bjerstedt?"

The big man hesitated, looking doubtfully from one to the other.

"We'd better talk it over up-stairs."

Having sought and found a fresh cigar, Caswell made his quest of a match excuse for stepping aside.

"I guess you don't need me," he offered.

"I want you. I don't know what it is Bjerstedt has in mind. But there's no mystery I'm aware of."

"I'll tell you all right."

Bjerstedt met Delancey's accent of irritation with a rougher note that suggested anger. For what?

"Come on," he said, and went clumping ahead.

They followed up the first flight, and then one more. Their guide went heavily down the hall that ran to the rear of the house, with a window at the far end, until he came to the last door but one on the right. Fitting a key, he pushed open the door for them to go in.

Before Delancey and Caswell could take stock of the place they heard the turn of the key behind them. That was disturbing; and the rest more so.

What presumably was meant for a good-sized chamber had been turned into a sort of office. There was a flat-topped desk planted in the middle of the floor, with a swivel chair behind it. The rest of the furniture was a hat-rack, half a dozen of what are known in the vernacular as "kitchen chairs," a filing cabinet, and a telephone.

All this was not instantly evident, for the light was poor, with the morning sun partly shut out by a drawn curtain, behind which bars stood out in shadow lines.

The air was heavy with tobacco smoke. Counting Bjerstedt, there were six men in the room besides Delancey and Caswell.

Two of them stood up as Bjerstedt brought in his charges, and vacated their chairs for a seat on a case in a corner. Painted on the end next the door was a Red Triangle.

Had they known them, Delancey and Caswell would have identified "Mushy," the black-mustached manager of fistic proceedings the night before; Sam Lever, Anthony's defeated foe, and his second, that hatchet-faced individual, the "Harlem Kid." The others present were a small, snub-nosed man with the look of a comedian; a paunchy fellow, with a toupee, and a sanctimonious expression; last, a man who might have passed as a bank teller. In fact, he had been one.

Proceedings, conversational and otherwise, ceased with the entrance of Caswell and Delancey. They stood there under a barrage of eyes. Whatever the party's interest might be, evidently Bjerstedt was expected to enlighten them. But there was no haste with it.

"Have a seat," suggested "Mushy."

He indicated the vacated chairs.

"No, thanks," Delancey replied. "We only stepped in for a moment."

Caswell busied himself with a fresh light.

Bjerstedt barked a question:

"Are you going to come through?"

While no name was appended, he looked at Delancey, who answered in bewilderment:

"I don't know what you mean."

"You're Ericsson's partner."

"I am not."

As Delancey made his crisp denial the room was circuited with a flare of anger.

Leaning forward, to emphasize his remark by tapping the table with a forefinger, Bjerstedt resumed:

"Now see here, Griffis——"

"I'm not Griffis," Delancey cut in.

"Last night you was. And I guess that's good to-day," said Bjerstedt grimly.

"That was only a joke to oblige Ericsson."

Again that forward movement in every chair. Delancey put up a hand, feeling his forehead moist with sudden perspiration.

"That's rich," sneered the "Harlem Kid," ignoring Bjerstedt's shifted frown. "Great little jokers, you and Ericsson."

Delancey's temper began tugging at its leash. He took a step forward.

"I don't know what you are driving at," he said sharply. "So far as Griffis is concerned, I don't know him. I never even saw him. . . . It was foolish, I admit, to let anybody confuse me with him. But it was only a joke, as Ericsson will tell you. Send for him."

"Where?" inquired Bjerstedt.

"I don't know. Wherever he is staying."

"He skipped the island last night."

Delancey stared his astonishment at "Mushy's" slashing statement.

"And took my boat," Lever added.

"And seventy-five thousand dollars of our money. Damn him!" was the venomous contribution of the man with a toupee.

"His company is a blasted fake," observed the "Kid."

"If you're swindled, I'm sorry. But I had nothing to do with it."

"You've got to show us," said Bjerstedt.

As Delancey stood up to the fire, he mentally cursed both Ericsson and his forebears. "Fire away," he invited. "What do you want to know?"

"If you ain't Griffis, who are you?"

Bjerstedt took up the cross-examination.

"My name is Delancey. I'm a Boston chemist."

"What are you doing here?"

"I just came for a sail with my friend, Caswell."

"What's he?"

Caswell emerged from a seeming day-dream, framed in smoke, to answer for himself.

"I'm a bird man."

"A what?"

Bjerstedt cupped his ear.

"I am looking for a lark," Caswell continued placidly.

"If you think this is a joke——" the "Harlem Kid" burst forth. Without turning Bjerstedt thrust back a hand that nearly entered his open mouth, as he leaned forward to speed up the observation. Once more he subsided in a rumble.

Bjerstedt pondered a minute that seemed much longer.

"And what," he asked at length, "is the other man with you? This Anthony."

"A school teacher," Delancey answered promptly.

"A what?" ejaculated Lever.

Reflectively he caressed a spot on the left side of his jaw.

Bjerstedt turned to "Mushy," as if seeking guidance. That worthy tugged at his mustache, considering judgment. From a general air of expectancy Caswell and Delancey gathered he was the immediate arbiter of their fortunes.

"All right," he said at length, "if you're telling the truth. If you lie,"—with a reflective movement he pressed his bulging hip pocket, "it'll be the worse for you. I guess that's all."

Six bodies relaxed to slouchy ease.

"Then we'll go along," Delancey suggested.

"Let 'em out, Max," Mushy ordered.

But as they started he held up a hand to stop them.

"Not thinking of leaving the island to-day?" he suggested.

"We might," said Caswell, who had not thought of doing so.

"I wouldn't."

"Why not?"

Delancey took up the burden.

"It's a bad day to try."

While Mushy did not raise his voice, his meaning was obvious.

"Are we to take that as a threat?"

"Not exactly."

With a fresh cigar in his hand, Caswell felt for a match.

"What's the obstacle?" he coolly inquired.

"It's easy to get around it, if you want to."

"Just how?"

"Tell us where Ericsson is."

"We've already told you," said Delancey hotly, "that we don't know anything about him. We never saw him before last night."

"Of course, if you stick to that——"

Mushy's manner was indulgent.

"I'm in favor of keeping them here," interjected the "Kid."

"Oh, are you?"

"I am. Ericsson made his getaway. D'you want them to give us the slip, too?"

"I'll handle this."

Mushy's voice was suddenly of edged steel, that softened again as he turned to Delancey and Caswell.

"Better stick around," he said blandly. "Let 'em out, Max."

The paunchy fellow with a toupee produced a key.

As they left the room they heard the "Kid's" furious outburst.

"I say it's foolish to let them go. If they give us the slip, that money's gone, too. . . . Like the dough Max got us to dump in Higgledy-Piggledy. . . . Fine business to be in. We never keep anything. Now——"

The door closed softly. And the key rasped.

"Well," observed Caswell, when they had put a few yards behind them,—"that was a lively little interview."

"I'm sorry," Delancey said earnestly, "I got you into the mess."

"But you didn't. I gave you the last push with Ericsson."

"That scoundrel!"

"No. Hardly that."

"What else can you make of him?"

They were quickening their pace to round the corner.

"Not vicious," said Caswell. "Only weak. Pleasant fellow, without any backbone. Might rob his mother; but he'd dislike to do it. Simply no conscience where money is concerned."

"He has certainly got us in Dutch."

Caswell shifted his cigar.

"Oh, that will straighten out. Those highbinders back there can't take away money we haven't got. And they'll find out we're straight. I have friends here, you know."

Delancey rested a hand on Caswell's shoulder.

"I suspect," he said, "you are trying to cheer me, Pop. Thanks for the effort. . . . Now let's find Ed. Maybe he's had some adventure."

Caswell cogitated.

"Let's see: Which was the room?"

After trying two doors without even a response from the wrong person they went down to inspect the register. No success there. The office was empty; and, so far as Anthony was concerned, the register a blank.

As they stood in the doorway, proposing inquiry, a large man came lumbering down the stairs. He had whiskers, and a medicine case in his hand. Also the air of one exasperated with life. With some sulphurous, indistinguishable observation he charged past them, like a buffalo on the way to a water-hole.

"He looks like a sweet consoler of the sick," observed Pop with his crinkly smile.

Now they went on through a sitting-room, with the stove set up for winter, and opened the door to the room in which they had dined the night before. Empty also.

But as they turned to go, the apple-cheeked waitress so eagerly responsive to Ericsson appeared from the region of the kitchen.

"Mr. Anthony?"

She seemed puzzled by Delancey's question.

"Oh, you mean the gentleman with you last night. . . . No, sir. I haven't seen him since."

"Didn't he have breakfast here?"

"No, sir,"—very positively.

"Are you sure?"

"I waited on everybody this morning."

"Could we speak with the proprietor of the hotel?"

Caswell took a hand in the inquiry.

"With Miss Stevens? Yes, sir. She's in the kitchen."

"Then——?"

"Just a minute, sir. I'll call her. . . . Oh, thank you, sir."

With a somewhat startled look at the bank note Caswell pressed into her hand, she fled through the swinging door.

Presently Miss Stevens came in, still rubbing hands just dried. A stout and affable woman of forty or so, with a candid expression.

She could throw no light on Anthony's whereabouts. Obviously he was not in the hotel. For nobody had seen him. And his name was not on the register.

To her this fact was evidently a clincher. To be sure, the office was sometimes left without any one to tend it. But no gentleman would think of going up for the night without registering. It was against the law.

Parting from her without largess, they retired to the hotel porch. As they stood there undecided Bjerstedt came from the house. He was walking slowly, with roving glances right and left.

When near the gate he located them around the corner, and stopped. It was evident he meditated speaking, but decided against it. But he stared hard as he stood there, swaying a little with the uncertain balance of his club foot.

Once his decision, whatever it was, solidified, he went clumping out of the yard, and turned left towards Main Street and the Square. In that short stretch he turned twice to look over his shoulder, as if to assure himself they were still on the porch.

"What do you think?" said Delancey after the second demonstration of pressing interest.

Caswell's cigar brought up in the right-hand terminal.

"I'd rather see him outdoors than in the house."

A silent moment in which the cigarette's pale spiral stood out against the darker smoke column of the cigar. Then Delancey rose abruptly.

"Where do you suppose Ed is?" he asked.

"Probably gallivanting with Nell Strong."

Caswell's small and neatly shod feet still rested on the porch rail.

"Then you're not worried?"

"Why?"

"Oh, I don't know. Nyatt may be your pet island. To me it seems a queer place."

"A little piratical just now," Caswell admitted.

"A 'little' is conservative. What do you suggest?"

Inspecting his Corona, Caswell saw one side going faster than the other, and turned it to equalize the burning. That attended to, he gave deliberate reply:

"It seems a fair morning for gulls."

"For what?"

Delancey distrusted his ears.

"There's an inlet," Caswell pursued, "a few miles out on the South Shore. And bright mornings like this they're apt to caucus out there. I've seen hundreds."

"And I've seen thousands," Delancey said satirically, "at sea. What's the difference?"

Caswell thrust his hands a little deeper in his pockets, and feet still on the rail, pushed himself back in his chair.

"Did you ever," he asked, "see their bills?"

"What of them?"

"Ah!"

Now the cigar took an extreme station to promote freedom of speech.

"You unenlightened landlubber. Many of them are beautiful. Now take the herring gull. Its bill looks somewhat like a sunset sky. There's an orange spot on the lower mandible to represent the sun. You never noted it?"

"Never," admitted Delancey unenthusiastically.

Caswell's feet came down.

"There's a lot in beaks. If you get a chance some time, see how the stork clatters its mandibles together like a pair of castanets."

Delancey threw away his cigarette.

"At the present time," he observed, "I'd rather see Ed."

"Well, there's a chance for another inquiry," Caswell suggested.

"Where?"

For answer Caswell pointed up the street. Delancey turned to see what was indicated.

Coming leisurely, Beddle and his sister approached on the sidewalk next the hotel. Beddle raised his stick in casual salutation, and Delancey led in walking out to the gate to meet them.

"What adventures this morning?" inquired the Countess.

"Well, if you've an hour——" Delancey began.

"Which she hasn't," interjected Caswell.

"That depends," she said. "This sounds interesting."

Delancey was taking an observation. If she had looked thirty-five the night before, this morning she seemed no more than thirty. Only he was not so precise in his impression.

And her slight accent of world-weariness had vanished with the dark. A sub-tone of Nature's red in her olive cheek. In her eyes a look half-quizzical. A woman would have noted she wore a frock of dark blue, with a gilet of white silk embroidered on the edges in black. A straight frock that emphasized her slender fineness of line.

A small hat moulded close to the head crowned the chic effect. When he had vaguely possessed himself of all this Delancey became acutely conscious of his mud-stained knee and shoe. But the Countess seemed oblivious. With Caswell she carried on conversation that left Delancey and her brother, who never bothered to speak unnecessarily, on the side-line.

"Don't let your cigar spoil," she said, when Caswell in homage to beauty put Lady Nicotine behind him.

"Are you sure you don't mind?"

He brought it to view again.

"Not the least bit. Unless," with a smile, "you let it go out."

He puffed with alacrity, then freed his mouth for a question:

"You haven't seen our friend Anthony this morning?"

"Not yet. But I've been nowhere. Just from our house to here. If I do meet him, is there a message?"

"Better still, take him along," with a gesture to Delancey, "if you're going nowhere in particular."

"And why not you, too, if you are going nowhere in particular? We aren't."

"I am. I am going out to the South side to scrape acquaintance with some gulls. But he doesn't want to go."

"I never said so," Delancey protested.

"Just the same I know. Right now you're down on the lark because you got mud on your toe. I'd rather take no risk with the gull."

She turned to Delancey.

"It's no use to struggle. You are condemned to our society."

"'Condemned' isn't the word. 'Blessed' would be much better. But I can't let Caswell attach me to you, just because he doesn't want me on a bird hunt."

"Please don't feel embarrassed," she urged. "We really want you."

Then Beddle made his first, and characteristically succinct, contribution to the conversation:

"Glad to have you along."

"Done," said Caswell. "And I must be trotting. Morning's the time for gull confabs. . . . Meet you at the hotel at twelve o'clock, Slim. That is, if you happen to want to be there. Otherwise just telephone, and I'll have the boat sent in for you any time. . . . Good-bye, everybody."

With his parting observation he was under way. The Countess looked after him with amusement.

"Isn't he rapid?" she remarked.

"Where birds are concerned," said Delancey, "he develops the executive fervor of a factory superintendent."

After watching him a moment longer they turned in the direction of the Cliff road, with silent Beddle strolling beside them.

Walking energetically, Caswell turned the corner by the church tower, and proceeded with unslackened speed down the street to the right, with another square just visible in the distance. When he reached it he spent no time inspecting the Soldiers' and Sailors' monument in its centre.

But he did go hurriedly into a small corner shop with "Cigars, Confectionery, and Soft Drinks" blazoned over the door. A mental reminder of his need came when he had turned into the road to the moors. So he went in by the side door to investigate the storekeeper's supply of famous five- and ten-cent cigars.

"I sell a lot of these," that worthy suggested, and held out invitingly a box of gaudy-banded "Prince Hokum."

Holding one to his nose, Caswell flinched a bit. But he put a half-dozen in his pocket, and went his way.

Meantime a man who wore a T-shirt, and had more the look than the walk of a sailor, reached the Square some fifty yards behind Caswell, and quickened his gait as the small figure was lost to view.

When he also made the turn by the tobacconist's he stopped in astonishment. Since there was no one in sight on the Moor road, he looked to right and left without success. Then a thought sent him up the shop steps.

Caswell was completing a purchase as he entered. With an elbow on the show-case he lounged while the transaction was completed. A glance was exchanged, seemingly with equal indifference, as Caswell left the shop. But the man with the T-shirt kept an eye on the window while the storekeeper reached for a requested package of cigarettes. No one had passed it when he pocketed his change and started for the door.

A look was enough as he stood outside. In plain sight Caswell again headed for the moors. Without conspicuous haste, since his stride was longer, the man with the T-shirt went after him.

While they kept to a sidewalk with wide and yet wider gaps between little houses of laborers and fishermen, the distance separating them remained about the same. Caswell's turn into the Commons, once public grazing ground for any householder's sheep and cattle, was his pursuer's signal to fall back.

Seemingly, Caswell did not know he was followed. Even a look behind him might not have made the fact evident. Various errands are explicable in a public highway. But out in the open it is difficult to hold a trail without alarming the quarry.

The man with the T-shirt leaned against a side of the gate opening into the Commons, and puffed a cigarette until Caswell was a considerable distance ahead. Then he followed, keeping a sharp watch for signs of suspicion.

Not crystal clear, as bright days are in the mountains, but a radiant hour. The old windmill sunned itself on a slight elevation that caught in boisterous weather the full sweep of ocean winds. Only little puffs now, warmed by sunlight in which the sea seemed to sleep. Its distant breathing came faintly, regularly to the ear.

Caswell struck out briskly, sometimes keeping to a narrow footpath; and when it vanished, as it had a trick of doing, taking to the middle of the sandy, rutted road worn by generations of beach carts and buggies.

The course of the road was serpentine, and seemingly erratic. For no engineer had contributed; and there were pitfalls to be avoided. Here a marsh, and there a hill that citizens working out taxes had no ambition to tunnel through. And fresh-water ponds dingy in contrast to the blue-green of sparkling sea offered for inspection their autumn harvest of red-brown reeds.

Ahead the gentle elevation of Paul's Hills, with their approaches of more luxuriant vegetation. A carpet of sumac, and bay-berry, and scrub-oak, with moss and various grasses. There were flashes of scarlet, purple patches and sweeps of deep brown. And what in spring had been a fresh green was now nearer a sage color. All this at a distance took on the reddish hue that so delighted Caswell at sea.

In the midst of it all, and happy alone, he was humming to himself some childhood ditty. Not once had he looked behind, with so much to allure in the distant prospect.

No pause until a faint sound, coming nearer, brought him to attention. Had he possessed forefeet, he would have lifted one like a pointer. He turned to the north, pulling his hat over his forehead to take an observation.

The sound waxed and clarified in the blend of many voices, brazen voices of honking geese. They came on, some hundreds in varying formation. From a long line abreast they swung into a V-shape. Great birds, each with its long neck stretched towards the south, driving with superb pinions to the winter home. The babel of their voices swelled in climax, and dwindled to peace.

With increased energy, since he now had intensified vision of herring gulls gossiping on the shore, Caswell struck out again. And the man with the T-shirt rose from his shelter behind a dwarf pine to take up the trail once more. Now he lessened somewhat the distance between them.

A solitary vireo, with slate-blue head and curious white eye-rings, popped out of a bush briefly to claim Caswell's attention. But an inlet clear enough to the mind's eye was a stronger magnet as he cut down intervening space.

He saw the cut in the bluff, where the sandy wheel-tracks swung in a rough circle reminiscent of many picnics. And waves advancing playfully upon a strip of white sand.

Some minutes later he stood on the beach, looking about in disappointment. Tracks aplenty, but not a gull. Since no wind had arisen to blur impressions, he saw the visiting cards of a considerable flock clear in the sand. Traces of gulls, and maybe of other shore birds. Probably, he thought, a few crows.

With a field-glass drawn from a coat pocket he went up and down the beach, studying the tracks earnestly. Thus engaged, he was wholly ignorant of the fact that he was himself under observation from an old horse-shed on the bluff. There the man with the T-shirt peered through an opening in loose boards. His left elbow rested on a beam, while he tightened half-consciously his grip on something in the right hand held at his side.

Once he sighted as Caswell brought his glass to bear on a boat a mile or so at sea. But he changed his mind, and resumed his attitude of watchful waiting.

From the upper air came another sound that speedily identified itself. The waxing drone of a great dragon-fly. It swept overhead and out to sea. Then it returned, dropping lower, and swung in circles above the beach.

Caswell saw the aviator at the wheel, and thought he meant to land. But he pointed upward when only a few hundred feet from the beach, and flew towards the town.

Now fate, which had seemed malignantly disposed towards the yachtsmen, at last did Caswell a good turn.

His casual interest in the aviator had been more earnestly returned. As the airplane picked up pace in departure from the shore something white was released from the cockpit, and came fluttering down.

A folded sheet of paper. It came to rest in the gravel, almost at the corner of the horse-shed in which the man with the T-shirt kept watch. He saw it and hesitated, one eye still on Caswell, as he went peering up and down the beach.

Presently he stepped out to snatch it from the ground, and hastened back to his post. Then he opened it in earnest inspection. While the light was poor it sufficed for reading the few lines scrawled.

Still the man seemed doubtful, distrusting eye or wits. He looked from the paper to Caswell, and back again. Now he took a step in the direction of the beach, but paused again to consider. Resolved at last, he stuffed the paper in a pocket, and with crouching posture covered the few yards between the horse-shed and the rampart of vegetation topping the bluff. Still keeping low, he headed with what speed he could command in rough going towards the north side of the island, some five miles away.

Meantime the pilgrim of the beach continued his research with increased interest, and quite unconscious of peril. If he had missed the gulls, a Cape May warbler came to reward his interest. He stalked it carefully, noting with joy the tiger-like markings on its face, its spotted sides, and the yellow rump. Presently some whim in its tiny head turned it from flitting about, almost within arm's length, to swift flight.

Caswell watched it vanish, and straightened up with a little shrug of weariness. His eyes roved inland, as he sensed rather than saw heather-clad expanses that released their fragrance in the mellow midday heat.

Through the cut a slight elevation, rounded and domelike, came into the middle foreground. And as if posed there, on its summit he beheld a figure.

"Darned if it isn't Ed," he said to himself in amazement.

He waved once without response. Then he took out his binoculars. But it was too late. As he lifted them to his eyes the man commenced descent of the far side of the hill. All Caswell got was a rear view of his disappearing head. But one with the habits of a naturalist is not easily stumped.

"I'll find out," he soliloquized, and scrambled up the bluff.

To the top of the obscuring hill was perhaps a quarter-mile. As Caswell puffed up the last yard he completed a quick climb. But fruitless.

His amazed eyes had no sign of Anthony. No trace of any one at all. Incredulous, he swept the open expanse before him with careful gaze. There was no sign of human life.

He brought his glasses to bear, so that details of vegetation, and whorls of sand, came distinctly to view. And it was still the same. Directly below the hill was coated with little shrubs and brownish grass. Beyond the unbroken sweep of winds that, some scientist said, would carry the island away in five hundred years had left its sandy soil nearly naked.

No human being stood between hill and sea. The only possibility of concealment was behind a clump of dwarf pines freakishly placed near the base of the hill. He went down to look behind them. Nothing there.

Half-accusing himself of an optical delusion, he at last turned towards the town. Still not quite satisfied, he was moved to look about him again. Sweeping the ground with his binoculars, he completed the circle. The only fruit of his effort was conjecture. He thought he had seen Anthony. Who was it? And where was he?

Pondering the question, he set out again. And presently his figure seemed no more than a moving spot on the moor.

CHAPTER 4

THE TRIANGLE IN THE CLOUDS

"First," said the Countess, "forget them."

"Forget what?"

"The spots."

"Oh!"

Slightly disconcerted, Delancey surveyed his soiled knee and toe.

"I'm afraid," he confessed, "I am what New Englanders call 'nasty neat.'"

"It's a fault," she observed, "I wish more men had. Of course, there are some, Guy for instance, who absolutely cannot help it. Drop him in a mudhole, and he would emerge without a spot on his collar."

Apparently, Beddle, who had been swinging along ahead of them in the narrow footpath, did not hear this jibe at his immaculateness. It was then, at the fork of roads respectively leading to shore and hilly fields, that he paused with a question:

"Which way are you going? It has just occurred to me I promised to see Fotler this morning. Something about my boat."

"We'll go on to Scammon's Pond," said the Countess promptly. "That is, if Mr. Griffis leaves it to me."

"I am happy to do so."

He bowed.

"Then that is settled. I can promise you some nice reeds, with a funny name. The villagers call them 'Cat-o'-nine tails.' . . . Back for lunch, Guy?"

"I think so. But don't wait for me."

Casually saluting, Beddle went towards the shore with a leisurely stride. For a moment he evidently absorbed his sister's thoughts.

"I wonder," she said, "what is the matter."

Mutely Delancey asked his question.

"I was only talking to myself," she explained, meeting his eyes. "But Guy has something bothersome on his mind these days. I feel it."

"I'm sorry," said Delancey.

"Of course you are. Because you are a nice person. . . . Now tell me who you are."

"Well——" he began. Then she interrupted.

"You might begin by telling me who you aren't."

"I don't understand."

"Then let me help you. You are not Griffis."

"How do you know?"

He was astonished.

"I knew last night. By the way you acted when I invited you to tell me about making pictures."

"I must say you are clever."

"Not very. But you may say, if you wish, I am not stupid."

"You are right," he conceded.

"Why do you pretend to be Griffis?" she asked.

"I'm not pretending any more."

"What was the object?"

"None," he answered, helping her over a stile.

"Then I don't see——"

"Oh, it's simple enough," he assured her, "and stupid. When I landed with my friends, last night, a fellow calling himself Bjerstedt practically took possession of me on the wharf, and told me I was Griffis. In one of the spasms of freakish humor that sometimes break out in me, I let it go."

"Rather foolish, wasn't it?"

"Very. And it's led to some unfortunate results."

"What?" she asked, with lively interest.

"That's quite a long story. Before I go into it tell me why, if you thought I was an imposter, you didn't turn me down this morning."

"Simple enough," she said. "After the varied, not altogether charming experience of a field nurse and ambulance driver I think I know a gentleman almost anywhere."

Delancey blushed.

"You are kind."

"Not in the least," she assured him. "I look to you for help."

"Command me," he said warmly.

"I've been bored."

"Oh!"

He was chagrined.

"Now let us see," she went on coolly. "You are not Griffis. That is settled. But who are you?"

"My name is Delancey, and I am a Boston chemist," he answered. "And who are you?"

"My friends call me 'Greta.'"

"Yes?" he said encouragingly.

She went on with a slight grimace.

"I belong to an old, and what was once known in England as a noble family. My father missed a peerage by one life, and married an Italian woman. I have kept up the tradition by taking an Italian husband."

"I see."

His tone was unenthusiastic.

"Not quite," she went on. "He is very handsome, and equally charming. But——"

She waited a moment to enjoy the struggle in his face between polite interest and regret.

"I had to divorce him."

"You did?"

Somehow he felt relieved.

"Yes. He was quite worthless."

As they climbed a hill he was silent for a minute or so, wrapped in thought. Presently she laughed.

"What is it?" he inquired.

"Don't you think we are being very intimate in a first meeting?"

"I'd rather think of it," he said promptly, "as the first of many."

"But probably it isn't. That is my excuse for being unladylike."

"What is 'unladylike'?"

"Men have always decided that. Why ask me?"

"This reminds me," he observed, "of 'Puss-in-the-Corner.'"

As she puzzled over the expression they passed the last gate and came to the crest of the hill.

"My favorite spot," she said.

While his eyes roved the expanse she went on, with a certain vehemence.

"It's lovely, of course. But more than that, it blots the consciousness of boundaries. I've never liked islands. Perhaps because I lived in Malta as a child. And it wasn't a happy childhood."

Some recollection she greeted with a shrug of impatience. He did not break the current of her thought. And after a silent minute she went on:

"Ever since to me islands are like prisons, which I can imagine too vividly without experiencing them. A sense of constraint in definite bonds. Of course, we are all eternally in prison, but blessed in not knowing it. . . . Don't you feel it so?"

He sent a wisp of withered dandelion flying as he answered:

"To be honest—no."

"You were never married?"

"No—again."

"Why?"

"To give only one reason, I never really wanted to be."

"Oh," she said, and seemed to ponder his answer.

In this personal colloquy neither had looked at the other. Now she turned with an impulsive movement he was learning to recognize as characteristic. An occasional lifting of the veil.

"I trust," she said, "you don't think me impertinent."

"On the contrary, I thank you for wanting to know."

She colored a little at that, and invited with a gesture his attention to lands below.

Over light brown of autumn stubble the eye travelled to stagnant, opalescent pools, from which russet reeds raised their serried fingers. And a rampart of green-gray hills high enough to cut off what was beyond, so one more easily imagined the galleons of light autumn clouds sailing on to eternity.

"Wouldn't you like to rest here?" she suggested.

"Immensely."

Without further ado they settled in a corner of the old stone wall that wandered up and down the hillside, comfortably braced against a granite slab.

Now they raised their eyes in instinctive salutation to the sun. And a great bumble-bee like minded circled them once, in his droning way to hive and home.

"Now tell me about it," she invited.

"About what?" he parried.

"What happened through playing Mr. Griffis."

"For one thing, I'm threatened."

"By whom?"

The intensity of her tone was disproportionate to his lightness of expression.

"By persons unknown, and Bjerstedt."

"Are you armed?"

"Certainly not."

Quizzically he met her look of anxious interest.

"Aren't there arms on the boat?" she asked.

"I'm sure I don't know. What if there are?"

"Before I explain, tell me your story."

"I fear," he said, "it won't justify your solicitude."

She urged him on by her tense attitude.

"As I said before, this fellow Bjerstedt started the silly thing. He met us at the wharf, last night, and called me 'Griffis' with such authority I half-expected him to add, 'You are my prisoner.' But all he had to say was that Ericsson expected me at the hotel."

"Oh," she said, "is he in this trouble?"

"He was, but isn't now. That's how I come in."

"Is he gone?" she asked quickly.

"Why do you jump to that conclusion?"

"I don't quite know. But it wouldn't astonish me."

"It happens you are right. Now I wish I'd been allowed the benefit of your intuition when I landed. But I wasn't. So this happened.

"Caswell had made moan about lack of adventure, and something prompted me to accept identity thrust upon me—just as a joke. I expected to shake it off at the hotel. Then Ericsson appeared—to play the persuasive stranger."

"He has a way," she commented.

"He said Griffis was due on his boat yesterday. Apparently ours was the only yacht that came in."

She nodded.

"So Bjerstedt's mistake was natural enough. But what came out later I don't like at all. . . . Do you know anything about a moving picture company?"

"Yes," she said. "I believe Guy was bored into taking a few shares in it."

"There's the trouble. Ericsson explained himself as Griffis' partner in some 'Way Down East' production. And some men who put money in through him grew suspicious because work had not started. So, with Griffis on the way, it would be a great favor if I allowed them to think of me as the magnate—just for a night."

"Why did you trust a stranger so?"

"I don't know. Lunacy, I suppose; and the fact he knows friends of mine in Boston. That popped out accidentally."

"I see," she said, and added: "I like generous indiscretion better than cold caution."

"Thanks. But I can't feel laurel is deserved. . . . Not to talk interminably, Caswell and I came ashore this morning. And Bjerstedt met us again, with another pressing invitation to visit the hotel. There was no reason to refuse, since we meant to go there for Anthony. . . . Are you sure this isn't boring you?"

"Go on," she said.

"Instead of a friend we found a nest of scorpions. Bjerstedt led us up to a room, and locked us in with a delegation that tagged me as Ericsson's partner and invited me to 'come through.' You may gather that means to pay his debts."

"Did you know any of them?" she asked.

"Never saw them before. I don't even know their names. But they claimed investments in Ericsson's mythical company. And since he took French leave last night, they expect me to square him. Or rather, they did."

"What did you tell them?"

She seemed impatient for the full story.

"That I wasn't Griffis. That Ericsson was a stranger to me. And I wouldn't pay his bills. There were a few other remarks, not important. Now I'm out on bail. That's all."

"Don't jest. How did you get away?"

"We walked out when they unlocked the door. That was after a fellow acting as moderator of the meeting gave us a pressing invitation to stay here for the present."

"Was that just before you met us?" she pressed.

"Only a few minutes. Queer occurrence, wasn't it?"

"I think," she said earnestly, "you are in grave danger."

"But how? Nyatt isn't the frontier, or the bush."

"That is true. It seems a quiet and simple place. But strange things happen on this island. Guy was shot at a few nights ago."

"Are you sure?"

"How can I doubt it? He was coming in from the gate, and the bullet meant for his head lodged in the side of the house."

"Perhaps it was a stray shot," he suggested.

"I don't think so. And he doesn't think so, though he pretends to laugh at my fear."

"Has he any enemy you know of?"

In the problem of Beddle, Delancey forgot his own predicament.

"None I know of," she said thoughtfully, and sat looking meditatively over the marshes. Presently she added, as if speaking to herself:

"I wish I knew what he is looking for."

"If it is not intrusive——" he said hesitantly.

"Not in the least. I opened the way."

"Well," he said, "when I met you I wondered how you happened to come here."

"I can only answer for myself. I came because Guy suggested it. We were in Washington, and he said some one there told him the bird shooting in Nyatt was fine."

"It is supposed to be," Delancey assured her.

"But he never goes shooting. When we arrived we learned it was too early. Still we stayed. We have been here now for nearly three weeks."

"And you don't like it?"

"I might, if my mind were easy. There is something Guy keeps from me. I know he is in danger."

"Why not ask him what it is?"

She drew her shoulders away from the supporting rock with a shrug of impatience.

"If you knew him better, you would never ask that question. He is the best of brothers, but the most taciturn. Fortunately, he never married. The sort of woman he'd care for he would drive mad."

"How?" asked Delancey.

"Just by his stillness. He thinks women are spared anxiety by never being told things. Our reasons for coming to this country were to help me forget Guido, and find our brother, who came over after the war and disappeared in the West. I am equally interested, you'll concede. But Guy almost never mentions Stephen to me."

"Perhaps," he ventured to suggest, "things have gotten a bit out of focus with you through being overwrought."

"Do I seem flighty?" she demanded.

"Not in the least," he confessed.

"Then let's leave femininity out of the question."

"That is difficult."

She tossed away a twig she had toyed with, and ignored his offered hand in rising. Her air was disdainful.

"You seem averse to compliments," he said.

"I thought we were in serious conversation."

"We were. . . . And I struck a false note."

As she stood there, high-spirited and handsome, with the light of vexation in her eyes and mounting color in her cheek, he capitulated. And with his surrender her irritation evaporated. Of a sudden she laughed.

"Did you say 'overwrought'? Here I am proving it. But I am in earnest about this thing."

She paused, as if questioning herself. Then she put a hand lightly on his arm, as he leaned against the gate.

"Promise me something," she said.

"Done," he answered.

As if to emphasize her unuttered thought a sound came through the still autumn air. A sound like the cracking of a distant window-pane.

She flinched, and breathed with a sharp intake.

"Promise me," she urged, "you won't go about this island again without a revolver."

"But I haven't one," he said. "I don't think Caswell has, either. And I don't believe I can buy one on the island."

"That doesn't matter. I have one for you. Will you take it?"

"And rob you?"

"Don't quibble. I have two. And I know how to use them."

As if punctuating her declaration the sound of the second shot from the same direction as the first, but nearer.

Instinctively they turned to locate the spot from which it came. No smoke was visible, and no form appeared. They could only speculate.

"What do you think that was?" she said.

"Probably some gunner shooting out of season."

"But what is there to shoot down there?"

In her gesture she swept the brownish hillside, marked only by patches of juniper bushes and boulders, and moist fields in which an occasional willow took root beyond.

"I don't know," he confessed. "But then most gunners don't know, either."

"Will you promise," she pressed, "to take the revolver, and keep it with you?"

He regarded her mock-seriously.

"I promise."

"Thank you."

In a way he could not fathom she seemed much relieved. At once her attitude became one of friendly ease.

"Do you think," she asked, "we have stayed here long enough?"

"That, of course, is as you wish."

"But don't you know it is past lunch time?"

"I didn't until you told me."

"But this is being too polite."

She was frankly amused.

"I wonder," she speculated, "if you could live until dinner on chocolate, and a little spirits."

"I could, but I haven't got them."

"I have."

She pointed to her hand-bag reposing on the ground.

"This is delightful."

"Wait."

She raised an admonishing finger.

"Afterward can you walk another mile?"

"Any distance."

"Then sit down. . . . But first———"

He suspended the process of relaxation, and stood waiting as she opened the bag. From it she took a small flask, and handed it to him.

"See if you can find any non-poisonous water."

With recollection of a small spring shaded by overhanging rock he climbed the wall, and went back to it. When he returned she was resting again in the corner by the gate. With one hand she extended a duplicate of the flask he held, as with the other she indicated a place beside her. Next she produced from a little leather case a jewelled drinking cup in the shape of a thimble.

"So we're lawbreakers, too," he observed, as from the second flask rose to his nostrils the aroma of fine brandy.

"No," she corrected him. "You see, we're in the Embassy, and have a right to possess it."

"Oh!" he said.

"But I shouldn't have mentioned it," she added contritely. "It's not supposed to be known."

"I have forgotten already," he assured her.

"Then let us drink a little toast to friendship. That is, if you do not think it unmanly to drink toasts with women."

"What is taboo to women now?" he inquired, handing her the first portion.

"A good deal decreed by nature. But I don't think anybody ever appreciated brandy more than I did before starting a day trick in a base hospital after all-night service. Sometimes it was necessary."

"I'm not a prig," he said, as she handed him the thimble.

"I'm sure you aren't. I should apologize for dragging in one of those earth-shaking subjects. Only I am a little shy with strangers since the local doctor found occasion to tell me, the other night, he thought women had no right to smoke."

"What's he like?" Delancey asked.

She reflected.

"Rather like heavy columns, supporting a large trunk, with superimposed whiskers."

"To the life. I knew I had seen him."

"And have you seen Natty, the town crier? Grand as a beef-eater, with his bell, and his list of lost articles. And maybe there's a meat-auction."

Upon ignorance confessed she launched into racy portrayal of Nyatt worthies. Delancey marvelled at such vivacity in one who seemed at first coolly self-contained.

"It's the Italian in me," she explained, sensing astonishment.

Such feeling is infectious. They went on gaily, until suddenly she became conscious of the westering sun, and prepared to rise.

"It's time to visit Nancy."

"Nancy who?" he said blankly.

"That's a secret you'll learn at the end of the walk."

"At least you might say whether she is blonde or brunette."

"Neither."

"I give up. . . . Have you noted that curious cloud, just to the right of the sun, like a heron with extended wings?"

"If you mean a comparison with Nancy," she responded,—"no."

They were descending the hillside, as she set the course and a lively pace. And conversation became spasmodic, with little said until at the foot of the hill and a corner of a bordering field he opened bars to let her through. As he followed they turned right. Both paused in astonishment.

Beside a clump of willows previously concealing it, and standing in a grassy roadway that zigzagged in the direction of Simms Point, stood a Ford. A Ford runabout apparently abandoned. Its engine, however, was still turning with a faint whir.

It was loaded with something, and Delancey came near for a better view. Two cases with marking that drew from him a low whistle.

"I'm getting curious," he said, "about a Red Triangle."

"I wouldn't be," she suggested nervously.

"Why not? This is the third time I have seen it since we landed yesterday; and I'd like to know what it means."

"What do you think?"

There was an undercurrent of eagerness in her voice now.

"In this case," he said promptly, "it looks very much like bottled goods. And it did in the others, also."

She was silent a moment before asking:

"Isn't that a hint to let it alone?"

"But why?" he persisted. "I'm not a prohibition agent."

"These people do not investigate. They strike first."

"Well, if you're an authority——" he began half-jocularly; but stopped at the look of unmistakable distress in her face.

"Forgive me," he said. "I didn't mean to tease."

She summoned a smile.

"I know I'm unreasonable. If you don't already, you'll come to think me a silly female."

"Absurd," he assured her. "Let's get on."

Though both saw it, neither spoke of a brown cap in the grass by the roadway, perhaps fifty yards from the machine.

Soberly, and at a rapid gait they pushed on to the Point. As they drew near Delancey was again conscious of the beat of the sea. Thrust like a forefinger into the Sound, the Point was approached from the distant village along the crescent of a pleasant shelving shore. On the other side unhindered waves advanced in direct attack. Planted at its base a long, low building.

"A queer place to live," said Delancey to himself.

To the Countess he remarked:

"That looks familiar."

"Then you guess?" she said.

"What?"

"Who Nancy is, of course."

"I don't see how."

He was frankly puzzled.

"I'll tell you now. It's a machine."

"Oh!" he said, still unenlightened.

"Don't look so puzzled. I mean a biplane."

"How could I guess," he asked, "that 'Nancy' was a plane?"

"Women, you know, have to name everything."

"I see. Who did you christen it for?"

"It's my own."

She courtesied.

"Yours!" he said, incredulous.

"My own," she repeated. "And I have a pilot's license."

"You begin to seem to me," he said, "a mysterious person."

"But not evil, I hope," she responded.

"By no means."

"If it's at all important to you, you have to thank Nancy for meeting me. Without her I would not have stayed."

"Then you fly here?"

"With the Atlantic beneath me."

She spoke with a straightening of her figure and a deep breath. And stood for a moment facing the water with extended arms. A figure of victory. After a minute or so her arms fell, and she turned towards the hangar, separated from the beach by a short stretch of grass.

"I supposed," said Delancey, "the Simms Point Station had been abandoned."

"It was kept, I am told, as an experiment station for hydroplanes," she explained.

As they entered the hangar several mechanics lounged near the great doors. Evidently they were used to seeing the Countess, for they gave her an informally respectful salutation, without speaking or getting up. A sergeant with a ramrod back was the only visible person in uniform. Delancey's presence was accepted without explanation.

He followed past berthed hydroplanes to a more compact and spirited machine. She touched it affectionately, and he caressed its polished side with a one-word observation:

"Farman?"

"Oh," she said, "you know about airplanes."

"Escadrille Americaine," he confessed.

"What was yours?"

"A Bleriot—after I got to know a little about flying."

"I suppose Nancy seems clumsy to you after that?"

Her tone was defensive.

"By no means. I think she's a fine family machine."

He was examining the compass, the altimetre, the revolution-counter. By force of habit he even moved to inspect the contents of the petrol tank. She watched him silently until he paused with a little nod of approbation, and stepped back.

"How much flying," she asked, "have you done since the war?"

"Not any."

"Isn't that rather strange?"

"Not in the least. I was shot down three times. And I'm still here."

"Does that mean——"

She hesitated, considering the word she was about to use—"That you have lost your nerve?"

"It means," he explained without resentment, "that I am prudent, but not cowardly."

"Will you go up with me?"

He looked from her to the plane, and back again.

"It's a double control machine," he said at length.

"Yes."

"Will you turn it over to me, if I ask for the stick?"

"Yes," she said again.

"It's a bargain."

She smiled now.

"And I have the better of it. For if anything happens to me, you may not get your chance."

"I'm not worrying," he said with a shrug. "I only mean to be sensible. My concern just now is getting some flying togs."

"I think the sergeant will oblige us," she suggested.

And the sergeant did. At mention of Delancey's name he unbent in a fashion that caused the Countess to regard her drafted observer with fresh interest.

They put on helmet, goggles, and leather waistcoat, and stood waiting for mechanics to push out the machine. When it was turned facing the wind, a westerly breeze newly risen, they climbed into their seats, and fastened the safety belt.

"By the way," said the Countess casually, "if you want to speak, and can manage to make me hear, you may call me 'Greta.'"

"Thanks."

"It saves breath," she added.

As she nodded to the mechanic Delancey caught, "Coupe, plein gaz" on the tip of his tongue. It seemed monstrously odd to sit silent and passive.

At her nod the mechanic started the propeller.

"Switch off," he sang out.

"Switch off," she echoed, and complied with his request.

"Suck in," the mechanic shouted.

She moved the lever. Now the mechanic put forth his full strength in revolving the propeller. As it turned life-giving petrol was sucked into the cylinders.

"Contact," he shouted.

The Countess switched on, and the propeller turned faster. Then the vital moment of the starting engine.

For a minute or so assisting forces held the machine back, and Delancey felt his own heart's responsive beat to the deep throbbing of the motor. Presumably the heart of the Countess did also. But a pilot has no leisure for self-analysis.

She waved her hand in signal for release, and they taxied across the aerodrome with increasing speed. She opened the throttle wide, and the plane pointed up. A slight movement of the elevator, and they were climbing in earnest. With a couple of circuits over land and sea they were some hundreds of feet up.

Once or twice Delancey caught a furtive glance by which Greta sought to assure herself of his serenity. She put the plane through a dive and a steep bank. And somewhat to her chagrin he seemed more interested in the landscape. He was seeing the panorama of Nyatt, all its dramatized geography for the first time.

Flying at moderate speed, and within a thousand feet of the earth, details of contour were distinct, and houses clear in miniature. There was the village, with its pool of pitch roofs emerging from the tapestry of embracing trees, and the inner harbor flowing like a robe of silver-gray from the shore. Toy boats rocked on its breast, or bustled about as energetic midgets.

Away in the northeast the moors, subdued by distance to a dominant violet tone; and leading out of town pale courses of highways, with here and there dispersed houses wearing the look of travellers that had paused to rest. The hills seemed like emphatic thumb marks of a great hand. And all about the living green of the sea.

As a wing dropped slightly in an air pocket Delancey's attention came back to the machine. Greta caught his flash of anxious interest, and smiled.

"Allez! en route!" he called with cupped hands.

They pointed up again, climbing steadily to a strata of cloud so white and fluffy it seemed like snow. A little higher, and their shadows were cast on the brilliant white below. Shadows fantastically fringed with rainbow hues.

They passed into the fibrous tresses of thin, fast flying clouds. Against wind bearing these heralds of a great storm the plane made slow headway, and its pockets complicated the problem of equilibrium. Still handling the machine with composure, Greta half-turned to Delancey with a significant nod. He leaned forward to take the second set of controls.

He throttled the motor, and the plane dipped abruptly downward. Tilting to a steep bank, and with controls set, it descended in a close spiral. With dizzy smoothness the plane fled downward.

In momentary check Delancey threw the controls over, so that the spiral was reversed. Down they went again until suddenly conscious of a warmer temperature. Their goggles steamed as they passed through the cloud bottom, so that Delancey, jogging along on even keel, was unconscious of other invaders of the sky until the roaring of an engine different voiced than the Farman sounded under its right wing.

He instinctively put the nose up and switched on power. The strange machine shot ahead and above them with few yards to spare, and left Delancey staring wide-eyed. He had glimpsed the Red Triangle on the under-side of one of its wings.

It was no optical illusion, for the unknown aviator returned. Flying at greater speed he swept over them with so slight a margin that Delancey dropped sharply, and cursed the intruder.

This time he saw it was a monoplane, apparently of Italian make. Of its pilot he glimpsed a hawk-like nose. That was about all.

But the man in the monoplane was evidently bent on further knowledge of them. He followed like an inquisitive terrier. Once he turned his nose down suddenly and swooped behind them. Then Delancey instinctively acted as experience had taught him to do when such manœuvers with machines bearing the black cross were followed by the pop-popping of a machine gun. He did a vertically banked about turn, and went slap for the other plane.

Their position as they dived in turn was ideal for return fire. But there was no gun on the Nancy. And Greta was an observer who did not quite understand proceedings. Delancey smiled grimly to himself, remembering other planes with black against their silver wings, turning over and over as they fell in flames.

Their tormentor was evidently alarmed by the demonstration, for speeding up, he drove straight out to sea. In their descent they had come over the water, perhaps two miles from shore, and handling the plane Delancey was not too busy to see a two-masted schooner swinging at anchor.

Apparently a mother ship, for several launches were near by, either going or coming. At the time of their close contact with the annoying plane one boat rather larger than the others had just put out.

Pointing for the aerodrome, a few miles distant, Delancey put the machine into the wind. They came down in a swooping spiral, and landed gently.

It was near sunset as they stepped from their seats. Palely beautiful, the crescent of the young moon stood out against the darkening curtain of the sky; and above it, in perfect alignment, the first evening star.

As they looked a point of greenish white light, dazzling in its brilliancy, appeared suddenly above the schooner waiting offshore. It sailed and burst with showering particles.

"A rocket," said Delancey. "I suppose it's a signal that we have landed."

"You'll take the revolver, as you promised?" Greta questioned.

"I wish I'd had it," he assured her, "twenty minutes ago."

"Thank you——?"

"Dick," he supplied.

In harmony they struck out across the meadows. Towards first lights of the distant town, yellow twinkles in the dusk.

And as they walked a faint humming from the north came to their ears. Powerful overhead, it faded in the distance.

Delancey voiced Greta's thought:

"I wonder where the pirate berths his machine."

CHAPTER 5

"A HOLE IN THE HILLSIDE"

Anthony awoke from the sleep of exhaustion. He struggled upward from its stupor, yawning widely in the morning sunshine. As his eyes registered unfamiliar details of the room he had a moment of doubt.

Then it all came back to him. And he sprang from bed to look at his watch. Eight-forty. But twenty minutes to meet his engagement with Nell Strong.

It is better, he reasoned, to apologize in advance than afterward. He looked for the telephone, and looked in vain. Evidently the instrument he had seen screwed to the office wall was deemed sufficient for guests of the hotel.

Stumped in his first enterprise, he rubbed his chin, and so came to fresh anxiety. No razor. In sheer desperation he poured water remaining in the pitcher into the bowl, and towelled himself vigorously.

His hasty toilet completed by slashing attack on somewhat insubordinate hair, he ran down the stairs. No time for breakfast, and a shave would have to be dispensed with. Had he better telephone? He paused in momentary indecision, one foot inside the office door. Again a negative decision was forced upon him.

"Gosh!" he said ruefully. "I remember the place, but I've forgotten the owner's name."

In his quick turn he nearly ran down Stella, come on some errand from the kitchen.

"Good-morning," she said, with a discreet smile for stalwart simplicity and good looks.

"Good-morning," Anthony reciprocated with a step towards the street.

"Two gentlemen," she pursued, "was here to see you."

"Why didn't you tell me?"

"I didn't know you was here."

"I suppose not. You see, I came in too late to register."

Evidently Stella did not see. And Anthony admitted to himself that his explanation savored of burglary. A little flustered, he turned back to inquire:

"Do you know them?"

"Same two gentlemen that was with you last night," said Stella fluently.

"When were they here?"

"Just a few minutes ago."

"Leave any message?"

"Not that I know of."

"Well, if they come in again, tell them I'll be back by noon."

Starting to leave, he added in afterthought:

"My name is Anthony."

"Yes, Mr. Anthony. . . . You goin' to have some breakfast?"

"Thanks. I haven't time."

He had his hand on the door. But Stella was not defeated yet.

"Was you disturbed last night?"

"No," he said with a tinge of impatience. "What was there to disturb one?"

"There was a man chloroformed in the house."

She released the news importantly.

"Was there? Who was it?"

"Mr. Higgins. He's a ladies' notions drummer from New Thetford."

"Robbed?" asked Anthony.

"Nobody knows," Stella answered indirectly, "who done it, or what he was after."

"Queer times," he observed, again edging towards the door. "Is he very sick?"

"Pretty sick, I guess. Dr. Pugh says he won't be out for two or three days."

"I see. Thanks for the news."

With the screen door open, he furnished easy entrance to a wandering autumn fly.

"Is there any word you want to leave?"

"Only what I told you. If those two men come again, tell 'em I'll be back at noon."

He fled to the gate, in the nick of time to hail a passing taxi. It was one of those multitudinous products of Detroit that in Nyatt seemed to have inherited leisurely habits of livery nags superseded. One almost expected them to do the impossible, leaning heavily in the traces.

"Where to?" the man at the wheel inquired with mild interest, when he had refreshed himself with a chew of tobacco.

"Out that way, over the bridge,—you know," was the best Anthony could do, with a wave of his hand.

They went rolling westward. Anthony consulted his watch anxiously. Still five minutes leeway. Probably he would be passably prompt; but he was abashed as he reflectively rubbed his stubbly chin.

When the bridge was passed Jehu paused in silent inquiry. Again Anthony resorted to a gesture, leaning forth to refresh his memory.

"You know that place up the hill," he suggested. "The second right beyond the turn. Red roof, and a flock of dormer windows."

The driver started again, with a nod of assent.

"Confound him," thought Anthony. "Why doesn't he tell me whose place it is?"

Until they arrived he somewhat feared memory had betrayed him; but the second turn in the drive reassured. He could almost place the spot where he had turned off the night before, to investigate what was stirring in the screen of trees.

The next minute he saw Nell standing at the top of the steps, a figure in cool white, with the sun bringing out the brightness of her hair.

"You get a prize for promptness," she called as he paid his fare.

"I haven't passed inspection yet," he warned her. "What's more, I fear I won't."

"Why not? Let's review you."

He stood at attention before her.

"The eye is not bad," she said judiciously. "Only a little puffed, and plummy looking. I'm pleased with it."

"And the rest," he observed, when she withheld further comment, "is silence."

"Well, of course I can see you haven't shaved."

"There was neither time, nor a razor."

"That means, I suppose, you have had no breakfast."

"I don't mind that," he hastened to say.

"Politely untruthful, but I'm not going to let you suffer for it; or myself, because you are uncomfortable. How much time do you give to shaving?"

"Oh, ten or fifteen minutes."

A bit disconcerted by the turn of conversation, he reddened under his tan as she went on:

"That's good work. My father dawdles with his razor for half an hour, and my brother is worse. Neither has as much work as you to do."

"I suppose it looks pretty bad."

He covered his chin with a protecting hand, feeling the spikes of beard like autumn wheat.

"Don't look sad. I like it."

What Anthony was about to say was left unuttered. Suddenly she laughed. And he could not be resentful.

"Come with me," she commanded.

He followed, obedient but wondering, into the hall and up a flight of stairs, then on past doors, until she came to a second-story room on the side next the water.

"There."

As she opened the door he looked over her shoulder and saw she had conducted him to a bathroom, with a dressing-room beyond. From its appointments a room used by a man.

"Jim invites you," she said, "to use his rooms. That is, he would if he were here. I think you will find all you need. Meantime, I'll be useful."

"Thanks. I'll get on all right."

"You needn't look alarmed. I'm not offering to be your valet."

"Of course, I never imagined——"

He paused, hesitating to put the thought in words.

"But I would, if you needed me."

"What are we driving at?" he blurted.

"Nothing," she said airily. "I'm only testing your patience. If I keep on, your beard will be like Rip Van Winkle's. And you'll be hungry and cross enough to eat me up. So tell me what you usually have for breakfast."

"Grapefruit, coffee, two eggs fried, bacon and coffee," he promptly answered.

"The bacon?"

"Crisp."

"And you didn't mention the toast. I take that for granted. Now I'll let you alone, and negotiate with Bennett. He will feel morally wronged in my request to serve another breakfast; but it will be ready when you are."

"You know, you're being exceedingly good to me," he said warmly.

"It's for my own good. Uncomfortable men never pretend to be anything else. . . . Would you like breakfast on the porch?"

"It would be fine."

"Then look for me there. Now I am going. I may as well. You haven't paid me a single compliment."

"But you know——" he protested.

"Yes, I know. After all, why should you? Good-bye."

She vanished, and left him staring. Slightly dazed, he went about the business of shaving, speeding up as he realized he had a time limit and reputation to sustain. Still he could not stifle speculation concerning this remarkable girl. A stranger last night, she had seen him fight. And now she was ordering his breakfast in a strange house, while he shaved in the bathroom of a man he had never set eyes on. It was a rum situation.

As he lathered his chin he absent-mindedly broke into singing:

"A-rovin', a-rovin', oh, rovin's been my ruin,

I'll go no more a-rovin' with you, fair maid——"

Then he stopped guiltily, fearing his voice carried below stairs. If it had, he must have seemed discourteous. But once more, as he administered a final dash of bay rum, his voice escaped him:

> *"Blow, bullies, blow.*
> *Sugar and rum, and pearls down below——"*

He throttled the end at the head of the stairs, and started down, schedule perfect. Seated comfortably in the sun, Nell pressed a button as he appeared, with her other hand pointing to a box of cigarettes.

"What's the pirate's ditty?" she inquired.

"That's a bad habit I have," he confessed as he established himself. "I ought not to do it in a strange house. Delancey says I should never do it anywhere."

"And who is he?"

"Don't you remember? You met him last night."

"Did I?"

Between her brows appeared a little wrinkle of perplexity.

"I thought your friends' names were Griffis and Caswell."

"But 'Griffis' isn't Griffis. He's Delancey."

"I can't understand that. Here is something definite."

Bennett, a butler worthy of a bishop's apron, had appeared with a tray and a look of hauteur. At Nell's smile and "Thank you" he unbent slightly, like a stiff-necked bird, and retired.

"It seems all right."

She inspected the tray, and reseated herself.

"Now I expect you to show appreciation."

"Of the most practical sort."

He attacked breakfast with gusto, for the zest of pleasure deferred was increased by heavy exertion of the night before.

"Now about 'Griffis' Delancey," he said when the first cup of coffee was dispatched.

"Yes," she invited.

"That's a joke."

"A 'joke'?"

"I know it seems curious," he apologized. "But really it's a simple matter. In a way, that clump-footed fellow, Bjerstedt, is responsible. I don't suppose you know him."

"Sight is sufficient," she observed.

"That suits me, too. He met us at the wharf, last night, and took possession of Delancey in the name of Ericsson, dubbing him 'Griffis.' And Delancey let him do it. God knows why. . . . I beg your pardon."

"You needn't," she said amiably. "That is what I think about it. It's all incredible. Go on with the fairy story."

He buttered another roll.

"It sounds fishy, but it's true. Bjerstedt toted us up to the hotel, where Ericsson took hold. Bjerstedt had mistaken the man expected to arrive on his boat; the great picture man was delayed. 'Sure to come to-day,' Ericsson said, and he wanted Delancey to play Griffis,—just for a night."

"Why?" she inquired, as he paused to light a cigarette.

"I don't quite get it. Some idea about investors in an island movie getting hot under the collar."

"It seems," she said judicially, "a silly thing to do."

"We can't quarrel about that."

"Is he restored to his right name to-day?"

"Hope so, but I don't know. I haven't seen Caswell and Delancey since we left the hotel last evening."

"I suppose I am horribly selfish; but," she added with a little grimace, "I'm not sorry."

"Neither am I."

"Still, wouldn't you like to telephone a message to the hotel?"

"I left one for them when I came away. That I would be back for lunch. That's safe, isn't it?"

"I think so."

She meditated a moment, and asked:

"Don't you think they would lunch with us here?"

"You might ask them."

"If you'd like it, I will. There'll be time enough when we get back. . . . Are you afraid to drive with a woman?"

"Where?"

"Oh, over the moors, and little hills, and through meadows."

"Is this," he asked, "a sea-going carry-all?"

"By no means. It's a runabout."

"Since it's you——"

"You will."

His look of fortitude amused her.

"I know you prefer Bruce; and he is better at Boylston and Tremont, or Forty-second and Fifth Avenue. But I'm superior in cross-country driving. Anyway he can't handle a wheel to-day. . . . See for yourself——"

As she invited his attention to her chauffeur, just then crossing the driveway, she called:

"Bruce, a moment, please."

The man halted.

"Will you bring my runabout to the steps?"

Bowing, he turned back in the direction of the garage.

"What's the matter with the arm in the sling?" asked Anthony. "He was all right when he brought me back last night."

"You shouldn't feel so exclusive. We have mysteries, too. But with your shaving and breakfast I forgot I had a story to tell."

"Nothing to prevent now," he suggested.

"Then we'll have to sit down again."

As she perched on the piazza rail he leaned against a post beside her.

"Now," he said.

"To make a long story short, or anyway to make it shorter,—after Bruce took you to the hotel, last night, he took the car to the garage. It's quite a distance from the house, with trees just behind it, and on one side, too; just across a little valley that runs down to the shore. Do you see?"

"Yes, I see the valley. Did Bruce fall down hill and sprain his arm?"

"If you don't want to hear the story——"

She dropped from her perch.

"But of course I do. Go ahead."

He laid a detaining hand on her arm. She made no move to evade it as she went on:

"There's nothing vicious about the valley. Something else hurt Bruce. Curiosity in the beginning. . . . He was on his way from the garage to servants' quarters in the rear of the house when he thought he saw something under a tree. There was just a little moonlight, you know."

"I know," he assented. "It was all I had to go to bed by."

"So he moved closer to look again. Then he saw it was a motor truck. It seemed deserted, but he hesitated to go near it."

"Wise Bruce."

"He watched for a few minutes, standing just around a corner of the garage; and he heard voices of men coming up from the shore."

"So he went down to meet them."

"Bruce has got common sense," she flashed. "He hid, well out of sight, while they panted up to level ground and put down what they carried. One suggested they leave it there until they brought the rest of the 'stuff' up from the boat."

"I don't suppose," said Anthony, "by any chance this 'stuff' was in cases."

"You're a smart young man."

"Bootleggers."

"Can one steal from them?" she asked.

Anthony laughed.

"I'm not a lawyer. But I've been told that with loose liquor finding is keeping. That is, if the police don't nab you. Have you been taking some?"

"Don't be silly."

She smiled in turn, and struck off at a tangent.

"The men rested long enough to smoke a cigarette, and Bruce says their talk was interesting."

"About the Bok Peace Plan, I suppose."

"About ways to tell good liquor from bad."

"What all the world is seeking. What did he learn?"

"I may not get it straight, but they said a lot of the whiskey that people think so fine nowadays is really nothing but a combination of things."

"'Combination' of what? I thought this was to be a revelation."

"I can't remember," she confessed, "but I think they said that next to having a chemist analyze it the best way to test a drink is to half-fill a glass with it, and the rest of the way with boiling water. If you sniff the steam, you get the ingredients."

"That is interesting, and maybe true. Did Bruce strain his arm lifting a big one?"

"I misjudged you at first."

She looked at him appraisingly.

"How?" with lively interest.

"I thought you were tongue-tied."

"As a matter of fact, I'm not garrulous," he submitted.

"Then you'll let me go on with my story?"

"I'm trying to get you to."

"Where was I? You interrupt me so, I lose my place. . . . Now I remember. When the men went back to the shore Bruce thought he would take a look at the things they left piled up. So he did. And he found a lot of——"

"Cases," Anthony supplied.

"That is right. It is easy to guess after all I've told you. Now tell me what was in them."

"Oh, did he get that far?"

"I'm afraid," she said, "Bruce is not an entirely moral man."

"Then he did strain his arm lifting cases. It must have been quite a haul."

"There are two cases in the rear hall. One is supposed to be whiskey; the other, Benedictine. Bruce says the men left them last night in running away."

"What frightened them?" he asked.

"I don't know. According to Bruce, he was standing by the cases, and wondering what was in them, when a man apparently left as a guard crept up to attack him from behind."

"Was he left unconscious?"

"Not at first. He thinks he must have moved just as a blow was aimed at his head. Then he grappled with the man, and they fought for several minutes.

"He says it was a fairly even struggle until a second man appeared from somewhere. The pair were too much for him; so he got out his revolver."

"Do your servants," asked astonished Anthony, "go armed?"

"Not as a rule. I got a revolver for Bruce to carry because he drives me about the moors, and sometimes quite late."

"This sounds," he observed, "like a story of the frontier."

"It sounds ridiculous, but it happens to be true."

"After what I saw last night," he assented, "I dare say you are wise. What did he do with this revolver?"

"He fired once, and thinks he hit one of the men. Before he could pull the trigger again his hand was twisted; and he dropped the revolver. Then a handkerchief saturated with chloroform was held over his mouth. That is all he remembers."

Anthony whistled a bar or two preliminary to his question:

"Are you sure this is all straight?"

She looked at him with a trace of displeasure.

"I don't understand you."

"You're out here," he said, "alone with servants. If things like this can happen, it's a serious situation."

"I'm not afraid. Those men won't come again."

"But don't you think this thing should be reported to the authorities?"

"Somebody else thought so," she said easily. "The housekeeper has already notified the sheriff. The same man, she tells me, that brings out groceries. He proposes to 'go to the bottom' of the matter. That is, I suppose, after all his orders are delivered."

Now Bruce, driving with one hand, appeared with the runabout. "I shall not need you this morning," Nell said as he stopped the car at the steps.

"Thank you, Miss."

While the chauffeur's face was decorous, as he turned away, Anthony felt he was disappointed rather than relieved in being excused from duty. But he dismissed the thought as visionary.

"What evidence," he inquired, "have they for the officer?"

"Not much, Mr. Sherlock Holmes."

She smiled at his earnestness.

"An unmarked handkerchief that has held chloroform. I can tell that. And some blood on autumn leaves. That isn't a visiting card either. And the shot I heard has gone away. . . . That's all."

"You forget the cases."

"Do you want to see those? Then let's have it over with. A bright morning is wearing away. Come."

With waggling forefinger in token of command, she preceded him. As they went through the high, cool hall a great dog with the head of a wolf materialized from the shadows. Anthony stopped as if struck when the animal stood suddenly beside him.

The dog neither snarled nor made any movement towards him. Simply it seemed to appraise him with glowing, greenish eyes.

Nell hardly paused. "Yes, Custer," she said pleasantly. Like a collapsible figure the dog sank to the floor. Anthony hurried on.

"What is Custer's disposition?" he asked, as they passed through swinging doors that gave him an agreeable sense of backing.

"Pleasant to friends."

"The name of 'Custer,'" he pursued. "Isn't it a queer one for a husky?"

"It's just one of Jim's notions. He got Custer somewhere way up north. And he killed some Indians. . . . Mrs. Johnson!"

She called to a stout woman who had emerged from a room ahead on the left when her name was called. She turned inquiringly.

"Where are the cases Bruce found?" Nell asked.

"In the pantry, Miss Strong."

Assuming nothing further was required of her, the housekeeper went on. When they crossed the kitchen the treasure was revealed.

"Um-m," said Anthony to himself as he bent over the cases.

"Um-m—what?" asked Nell.

"That red triangle."

He pointed to a brand in the upper left-hand corner of each case.

"This mark," he explained, "was on a case we saw in the water, crossing the Shoals yesterday. That's not so strange. But it was also tattooed under the left arm of the man I fought last night. Here it turns up again. It means something."

"Perishable goods," she suggested.

"I hope," he said soberly, "it is something we can laugh about."

"Then let's."

With considerable agility, though not much voice, she went through a few of the vocal acrobatics called "Pearl of Brazil."

"That's as much like forced laughter as anything I can think of," she said after her descent from a final trill. "Now let's go out. I need sunshine."

As she somewhat impetuously opened a door an obstacle was encountered. Bruce, apparently in the act of picking up a wrench.

"I'm so sorry," said Nell, with instant sympathy for the injured arm. "Did I hurt you, Bruce?"

"No, Miss," he said gravely.

Evidently feeling no explanation was necessary, the chauffeur turned away. Anthony saw, but said nothing about it,—that he had been stooping directly under the pantry window, which was open but screened.

As they emerged the air was very soft and warm. Then as they turned a corner of the house the breath of the ocean was suddenly stronger. It stimulated but did not sting. They crossed the short stretch of greensward to the runabout, and stepped in.

"Wouldn't you like just to enjoy nature?" Nell asked. "For a little while?"

He answered with a nod. And they went rolling down the driveway, into the Cliff road that stretched more whitely in contrast with deepening blue of the sea. From the browning verdure of banks above armies of crickets intoned their hymn to the sun.

They ran through the tip of the village, over the old mill bridge and past little houses that squatted by the bank of the estuary for purposes of sociability. Next they entered hills clad with the scarlet of October.

Nell had seemed half-dreaming, but she gripped the wheel with decisiveness to swing into barely perceptible cart tracks that went rambling towards the shore. Now she turned to Anthony with a smile.

"This blessed place," she said. "It heals everything."

"May I come in?" he asked.

"If you don't crowd."

Subduing the car to cross-country travel she was forced to keep her eyes on stretches ahead. Presently she asked:

"Did you ever know bayberry so purple?"

"Never," he agreed. "I was thinking just then how like furry little beasts all these scrub trees are."

"Like kittens," she supplemented.

"And yonder the robber's house."

"There's the robber himself."

Anthony followed a gesture of her disengaged hand to a figure rising in the middle distance. An aviator clearing a fringe of trees that screened all but the roof and chimneys of a square, black old house. It rose from a patch of green, strikingly planted in the midst of moorland.

Not with rapid wing-beat, as a bird flies in dashes upward, but in a long arc, the man in the machine rose into the gathering haze of upper air. The throb of his engine diminished to a faint hum. Then silence. And cessation of sound was followed soon by failure of sight. Speeding seaward, a speck vanished in the blue.

"I wonder," said Anthony practically, "how he got his take-off over there."

"I wonder more," Nell observed, "who it is."

"My question," Anthony pointed out, "might be answered."

"Let's see."

She had already turned to the right, picking her way in sandy ruts that showed signs of days when some sanguine farmer, probably more beauty loving than the rest, strove for sustenance where Nature willed to be left alone.

Rickety rail fences still marked the boundaries of closed domain. Beyond were willows rooted in spongy soil; large trees that in their drooping seemed somehow mournful for human failure. And three-quarters encircling the house a hedge that so far surpassed any reasonable expectation it disclosed from the land side no more than the eaves to view.

Not even the sun beating hotly on a blackened roof could quite free the place from a brooding air. It seemed to hint at strange happenings in the locked past.

They left the car a short distance from the hedge.

"I could shiver now," said Nell, and did so.

With momentary hesitation, and feeling unseen guards stood either side of the gateway in the hedge, they passed the rampart of green, and were lost to a speculative observer.

Unwittingly, Nell and Anthony had met the man with the T-shirt. His self-effacement in the encounter was a proceeding of considerable skill. First, he had tacked to avoid them as they appeared in the distance, with apparent aimlessness roaming the moors.

Thus interest was born in him; and possibly suspicion. When their turning threatened to cut him off he dropped to the ground. There he lay, screened and half-suffocated by a spreading juniper as they reached the lower end of the lane and turned in towards the house.

So cautious he maintained a crouching posture, he watched them reach an opening in the hedge, hesitate, and vanish. Then followed several minutes of unwinking watchfulness on his part. Still they did not reappear.

Now the man in the T-shirt turned his back on the house in quest of something possibly half a mile away, and on a hill. Whatever it was he found it, and proceeded to signal. With a pocket mirror he semaphored a message, his arms swinging in circles that sent points of light dancing from the black house towards the shore.

Came answering flashes from the hill. With that he desisted, and seemed to dismiss Nell and Anthony from his mind. Assured a folded scrap of white paper was still in a trousers pocket, he set off at a lope towards the invisible town.

Meantime the innocent intruders, all unconscious of malign interest in their movements, inspected the inclosure. Up the clapboarded side of the house, in which square windows were set high, climbed screening ivy that found entrance by crevices and broken window panes.

"We might get in, too," said Anthony.

Nell withdrew a step at the suggestion.

"Would you feel comfortable," she asked, "when nobody has entered for so long?"

"I'm not sure of that."

As he spoke he pointed to a match-box lying on the ground. One of a common sort, made of pasteboard, and bearing the words, "Made in Sweden." It certainly was not weather-beaten.

Other signs of people lately on the premises were not wanting. As they stood on the slab of slate that served as a doorstep a light streak in the casing showed where some one had taken out a sliver by trying to jimmy the door. A rusty hasp had no present bearing on its fastening.

Peering with shaded eyes, Anthony made out that the door was bolted on the inner side.

"I don't want to be mean," said Nell. "But I'm rather glad of it."

"There must be another way of getting in," he persisted.

"Please don't try."

"All right."

With a smile he desisted. But with lively curiosity he took stock of the room commanded by one of the panelled windows flanking the door. The other side of the hall was cut off by a hanging of rusty brown stuff.

The room on the right was somewhat in shadow, with one window shuttered; but through dusty panes of the other streamed enough light to channel the stained, uneven floor. It was bare, with the dark opening of a capacious fireplace on the far side. Two of the severely plain kitchen chairs popular among New Englanders of past generations lingered near a deal table.

These natural relics of a discouraged tenant's departure. . . . But what was it Anthony saw reposing in the centre of the table?

A heavy revolver. A shining, nickel-plated, efficient instrument of destruction. Sensing his alert interest, Nell raised herself on tiptoe to peep over his shoulder. At a glance she fell back in dismay.

"I feel nervous," she said. "Let's get away!"

Already she was headed for the opening in the hedge by which they had entered.

"But we haven't seen what we came for," argued Anthony.

"Don't you think we have seen enough?"

The intensity of her expression, as she turned, silenced his half-quizzical objection.

"Of course," he said, "I don't want to make you uncomfortable."

As they passed the portal of the hedge a wandering bumblebee boomed a cheerful salute. Nell sighed in relief as her eyes swept great expanses where sun and air made free.

"I suppose I am foolish," she confessed, "but I couldn't draw a free breath in there."

"I think the hedge did it," he speculated. "Somehow it did seem what an old aunt of mine would have called 'Pokerish.'"

Without marked haste, yet with a certain alacrity, they proceeded to put the black house a comfortable distance behind them. When they came to the car there was a moment of uncertainty. Nell solved the unspoken question in each mind.

"Let's leave it here," she said, "and see what's beyond the hill over there. It isn't far."

"That's a good idea. I'd like to stretch a bit. And the car's safe enough. Nobody here to run off with it."

With casual chatter, the while keeping watch for snares of bramble and hollow, they picked their way towards the hill from which the man with the T-shirt had been answered. Perhaps two-thirds of the distance had been covered when Anthony paused inquiringly. To his ears came first a faint, familiar sound. A sound in the distance like the steady buzzing of a great dragon fly. He craned his neck until he located it, so that eyes following suit picked up an advancing object in the sky.

It swooped and clipped, and swung in great circles. Yet with all its appearance of vagrant impulse it drew nearer, coming in from the Sound. When almost over the beach, as they knew it must be, though there the hill cut off their view, it dropped so low Anthony felt sure a landing was proposed. But it rose again.

Its nose pointed sharply upward, the airplane climbed a thousand feet or so before passing over the spot where Nell and Anthony stood. Then it straightened out for some point easterly at high speed.

"Probably," observed Anthony, "that is the fellow we saw starting out from the black house. He acted just then as if he were watching something. Sorry I must leave to-morrow. This place begins to seem quite mysterious."

"Must you go?" asked Nell.

Was there an undercurrent of something more than casual? Anthony vaguely sensed it, but doubted his perception.

"I suppose so," he said in offhand fashion. "I'm a poor schoolmaster, and there's work to do."

"Couldn't anything keep you here?"

Now the undercurrent of earnestness was nearer the surface; but Anthony was a modest man.

"I wouldn't say that," he answered, "but I can't think of anything. Is this a guessing contest?"

From Nell's lips issued the rill of laughter he liked to hear.

"Nothing so stupid," she said. "I'm much more interested in what's over the hill. . . . You know we'll have to hurry to reach home in time to lunch with your friends."

"I'm not dawdling," he said, and went on ahead.

Despite her counsel, Nell seemed in no haste. She appeared to prefer browsing about the base of the hill. One near might have guessed by her expression that something remote from the efflorescence of autumn was first in mind. When Anthony several times called to direct her attention to some discovery he found her a trifle deaf.

"In a minute," she answered his last request. "There's something here I want to see."

As he came to the top of the hill he straightened with the expansive impulse of one coming suddenly on the great moods of Nature. He was conscious of nothing but sky and water, and the far rim of the horizon.

A cry came as a rapier thrust. At the sound he wheeled, feverishly searching the hillside.

The cry was not repeated. And Nell had vanished. . . .

He ran recklessly down. A hundred yards or so covered with a desperate feeling he would never get there. So great was his speed he could not check himself on reaching the spot that must hold the answer to his question; but an unseen hand stopped him.

A stick thrust from behind the clump of pines tripped him neatly; and while still dazed from the shock two men pounced upon him. As one pinioned his arms the other bound about his mouth a handkerchief saturated with something sickish sweet.

Borne inward, and struggling with failing strength, he was briefly conscious of an opening in the yawning hillside, and of something white. Came complete paralysis, and engulfing darkness.

Perhaps three minutes later a rabbit in quest of lunch paused at this spot to munch a berry. Luxuriating in the sunshine, it cocked an eye at the sky.

Untroubled nature.

CHAPTER 6

WHEN THE WHITE YAWL CAME

Caswell sat in a strategic position. From the Stimson House piazza he commanded Main Street from square to square, so it was difficult for any one to pass through the village without coming under his observation.

Thus far his watch profited him not at all. It was late sunset now, with trees rustling a soft farewell to day. In the fading light Caswell squinted a little, forcing fatigued eyes to sustained vigilance.

He had occupied his post for several hours, with nothing to do but watch and smoke. The piazza floor about him was quite carpeted with ashes and burned matches. Still he vigorously puffed, with an occasional grimace at one of the cigars recommended by the tobacconist at the edge of the town.

The lamplighter came up the street, leaving behind him a trail of orange points.

"It's curious," said Caswell to himself, a trifle querulously, and bent his head to look again.

That moment Delancey turned the corner of Main and Wells Streets, and came striding towards the hotel. The short distance to go was half covered when Caswell first saw him. Then he seemed unexcited. Far from rushing to greet the lost one, he settled back in his chair.

Opening the gate, Delancey advanced briskly up the walk. He had a foot on the steps when some movement of Caswell drew his attention.

"Hullo," he said. "Where's Ed?"

"I'd like to know," said Caswell.

"Haven't you seen him?"

"Not since yesterday."

"I'm sorry."

Delancey spoke with lively contrition.

"I wouldn't have stayed away all the afternoon, if I hadn't supposed Ed was with you. Probably he had the same idea about me."

"That's all right. Only I'm worried."

With one of his shrugs like the movement of a bird shaking its feathers Caswell rose, and stepped to the rail to consult his watch.

"Hasn't he left any word for us?" asked Delancey.

"Not since morning. It seems he slept here last night. We just missed him. Nobody knew he was in the house, because he walked in without registering."

"That's odd," commented Delancey.

Caswell produced another cigar.

"Oh, he had quite a night," he observed, "according to all I hear. Took Nell Strong to a dance hall down in the Square, and had a regular ring fight with some pug from Brooklyn."

"What luck?"

"Knocked out his man. Quite the conquering hero."

Delancey whistled.

"So that's our backward friend. I'll be darned. What makes you worry about him?"

"Several things."

"For example——?"

"Well, according to that flighty waitress we saw last night, he left word for us that he would be back for lunch."

"Still I don't see any mystery," said Delancey. "Maybe he has been beauing Miss Strong."

"He was with her. They were seen together."

"I thought," observed Delancey, "you wanted him to be in love."

"So I do," snapped Caswell. "It's a good thing. But Nell Strong is lost, too."

"Just where do you get all this news?"

"From Flaherty. He was here a few minutes ago."

"I don't fancy him," said Delancey.

"Nor I. That's beside the point."

"Anyway, what's his intimate interest in the lost children? If they are lost?"

"Well," observed Caswell, with an astute cocking of his head, "I don't suppose he's heated about Ed. But I guess he thought he had a steady job as squire to Nell Strong. To give the devil his due, he's apparently sent by the people Nell was staying with. They got back this noon, and have spent most of the time since in efforts to locate her."

"Nyatt's a small place," observed Delancey.

"That's just it. They've tried everywhere, and can't find her."

"Nonsense. There must be some clue."

"The only one isn't comforting. They've discovered her car, abandoned about five miles out of town."

"Don't be so fragmentary," said Delancey with a tinge of impatience. "How does anybody know it's Nell Strong's car?"

"Flaherty is positive it's her runabout. Says he has ridden in it a dozen times,—knows the make and upholstering."

Delancey sat for a minute or so, drumming on the rail absent-mindedly.

"Where does the trail stop?" he asked at length.

"Servants at the house say she left with a man,—evidently Ed by the description, about ten this morning."

"They don't suspect him of abduction, I trust."

Caswell flipped his cigar ash away with an impatient gesture.

"Of course not. . . . Let's be serious. Can you offer a suggestion?"

"Interview the chauffeur."

"That's no good. They left him behind. He sprained an arm in some shindig, last night."

"Then my suggestion is no good. What's your idea?"

Caswell looked about him before answering. Then he leaned forward.

"Taken with what I've told you, there's a thing that bothers me. I wanted to get your general reaction before mentioning it; just now, at least, I won't tell anybody else."

"What is it?" said Delancey, falling into a confidential pose.

"Out on the South Shore, where I was scouting for gulls, I thought I saw Ed."

"It seems to me you ought to be fairly familiar with his appearance."

"I saw him so plainly I was dumbfounded by his disappearance."

"That's assuming he was there," Delancey pointed out. "What made you think it was he?"

"I was walking on the beach, and happened to look up; and there he was, at the top of a hill less than half a mile away."

"And then——?"

"I waved without getting an answer. Then I got out my field-glass to make sure. I had a fair view of his back, just as he started down the other side of the hill. If it wasn't Ed, it was his double."

"And who is that?"

"There wasn't anybody."

"Oh!" Delancey sat back with relaxed interest. "An optical delusion."

"But I don't believe it was," said Caswell stubbornly. "There's nothing wrong with my eyes."

"You just said there wasn't anybody," Delancey reminded him.

"Afterward, I mean. When the man disappeared I hurried up the hill after him. In five minutes I was on the spot where he stood; and he'd vanished. Not a sign of him. . . . I poked about the side of the hill, thinking he might have sat down somewhere to smoke; and had my trouble for my pains. . . . I can't understand it."

"I guess, Pop, for once you were wool-gathering," said Delancey.

"I'm not convinced," returned Caswell firmly.

"Which doesn't help us any. Since Flaherty seemingly is the person who knows things that are so, what does he suggest should be done?"

"He's rounding up a searching party now."

Delancey came down from his perch on the rail.

"Then let's get some supper before they come. With nothing but chocolate for lunch, I'm half-starved."

Caswell threw away his cigar in token of assent, and they went in. Early as it was, they had the dining-room to themselves, and Stella's undivided attention. It was evident she did not think they appreciated the latter fact. When she had brought the dishes she was bent on talk.

"Mr. Higgins is better," she said presently.

"Is he?" remarked Delancey indifferently.

"Yes. Dr. Pugh, he thinks he'll be out again to-morrow."

From Stella's air, as she straightened her apron and leaned against the table, it was plain nothing would squelch her but a direct snub. Delancey capitulated.

"Do I know Mr. Higgins?" he asked.

"Prob'ly not."

Stella proceeded rejoicefully:

"He's a lady's notions drummer from New Thetford. One of our regular customers."

"What happened to him?" inquired Caswell.

"Why, you know, he was chloroformed last night."

"Was he?" contributed Delancey.

"Right in this house."

"That's interesting. . . . Do you mind passing me the biscuit?"

She obeyed without cramping her conversation.

"Nobody knows who done it; or what he was after."

"No clue at all?"

"Not that they're sure of. There was a little sticker on the floor outside his door. Dr. Pugh told them to save it."

"There's a name on it, I suppose," suggested Caswell.

"No," said Stella a bit scornfully. "Nothing but a red mark."

"A triangle?" asked Delancey.

At Stella's blank look he proceeded to illustrate on the table-cloth.

"Yes," she said. "That's it."

This moment the arrival of two women took Stella away to the farthest corner of the room.

"This Red Triangle," said Caswell, after a brief silence, "is beginning to make me nervous."

"It began on me," Delancey admitted, "some time ago. One gets to feel he might wake some morning,—or not wake, with it plastered on himself."

"If we only knew what was behind it, we'd have a better idea of its intentions, if any, regarding us."

"I was a fearful ass to let myself be passed off as Griffis," said Delancey.

"That was mostly my fault," Caswell insisted.

"No. You were only a contributory influence. It was my lunacy."

"Well, it's just a little flurry," said Caswell sympathetically. "No great harm done. We'll collect Ed, and get away to-morrow, I guess. I don't see how they can stop us. After all, this is the twentieth century; and we aren't on the Spanish Main."

"Are you sure Ed will relish being rescued?" asked Delancey. "Suppose he's only been larking about with the girl. It would seem rather ridiculous to send a posse after him."

"Maybe," said Caswell, "but everybody here is bent on it; and they know the situation better than we do."

"Here they come," observed Delancey, facing the door.

Flaherty looked in, and they heard voices behind him in the hall.

"Are you about ready?" he called.

Caswell and Delancey rose from the table, and walked to meet him.

"Dr. Pugh," he said, stepping away from a burly figure at his elbow. It was the man they had seen rushing from the hotel with a medicine case in his hand that morning.

"How do you do?" he said.

The voice issuing from his beard was lighter than one would have expected from his impressive bulk; a voice rather cold and metallic.

It was evidently assumed the doctor knew their identity. Delancey wondered whether he was supposed to be himself or Griffis.

Apparently Flaherty thought that with other members of the searching party no introduction was necessary. There were ten of them by Delancey's count. From the general look of the crowd under a street light he sized them up as scallop men, mechanics, perhaps a village storekeeper or two,—representative men of the town. Their talk was low-keyed, as befitted the occasion. As they waited by the gate several tested pocket flashlights.

"We'll be havin' the moon, if we're out late," one observed.

"We'll need it all right," another remarked. "Looks like a blind hunt to me."

"Where's Beddle?" asked Flaherty, as they proceeded to motors parked across the street.

"Not home," answered Bjerstedt. "I didn't leave any message. His sister hadn't seen him since noon."

Standing by the cars, the men waited a moment, uncertain what to do; then proceeded to divide into little groups.

"Better get in with me," said Bjerstedt to Caswell and Delancey. Of necessity, since nobody else offered a seat, they stepped in after him.

Bjerstedt took the lead. As the little procession rolled through the Square, the clock in the North Tower struck seven. It was already dark, with a general twinkle of supper lights behind small-paned windows.

They drove past the Soldiers' and Sailors' monument, out the Moor road, and on past the old windmill, now posed with a certain solemnity against the evening sky.

Bjerstedt, at least, had no doubt about which way to go. Not rapidly, but never hesitating, he set the pace and course.

"Drives like a man on the way to a picnic-ground," said Caswell to Delancey sotto voce.

To Bjerstedt he observed,—"You seem to know your way pretty well."

"Been here before," said Bjerstedt without turning; evidently, for in the expanse of moorland that yielded no detail to unacquainted eyes he pushed on with intuitive dexterity.

Profane ejaculations came to their ears from the rear. Despite the advantage of a pilot car, their associates were finding rough going.

After a while they paused at the foot of the lane where Nell and Anthony had stopped—some eight hours earlier. So much concealed by its surrounding hedge that the emerging roof seemed a part of it, the old black house on the hill was a gloomy spot against the sky.

"We'd better get out here," said Bjerstedt, hoisting his deformed foot over the side of the car.

They stood in silence while the other cars came up, and discharged their groups.

"This is the place," explained Flaherty, the field-marshal of the expedition, "where Miss Strong's car was found. . . . We'd better start the search here, and divide. I'll beat up the hill. You come with me, Bjerstedt.

"Will you,"—turning to Caswell and Delancey, "see what you can turn up in the direction of the bogs? Perhaps you'd better take charge there, Norcross. You know that territory, I understand, better than any one else here."

"I been a foreman there, come twenty years," said a thick-set man who stepped forward from the crowd.

Casting another glance around, Flaherty picked out the doctor.

"Perhaps you'd better come with me, too," he said.

Others suiting themselves, the two parties separated and moved in opposite directions. Caswell lingered a minute or so to look after Flaherty's party, melting into the background of the distant seeming hill.

"Do you know," he said to Delancey, "I believe that's the place where I saw Ed this noon. It's rather strange. . . ."

"Where you thought you saw him," Delancey corrected.

"Uh," Caswell mumbled disdainfully. "We'd better hurry, or we'll be lost, too."

The squad led by the bog foreman was visible only as moving spots that spread fanwise as they advanced. Coming up with quickened pace, Caswell and Delancey fell in together at an end of the line.

Little was said as they advanced slowly over uneven ground. Despite eyes fixed on its surface, some searcher occasionally tripped over a root, or caught a foot in a tenacious vine.

Now and then the spurt of a flashlight betokened helpfulness, and a slight ripple of excitement came and went with the extinguished light. Once a dark form in perceptible movement drew the party post haste to a clump of alders. Three lights flashed as one, and a vagrant cow turned her head, chewing her cud dreamily.

The ground grew spongy, with the scent of mould. After a little of footing in which insecurity impaired concentration, the party halted at its leader's request.

From some neighboring pond a frog boomed,—"Hear ye! Hear ye!"

"This ground is dangerous," the foreman said. "You've got swamps on both sides. There's quicksands. Folks that didn't know how to handle themselves could get bogged easy enough. If the pair we're after are in there, they'll probably stay till mornin'."

With a slight rest from this oratorical effort he proceeded to finish it.

"I'm takin' you a path to Cummock's Pond. There's just a chance we might stumble on 'em. Don't lose sight of me. I'll go ahead."

They fell into single file. A ghostly procession, brushed by tall grasses and wisps of mist. Evident hopelessness of effort to pierce the screen of elusive green on either side led each man to look only at the one ahead.

In this fashion a quarter-mile or so, until they came to the oozy bank of the pond. It stood stagnant, its unrevealing water darkly purple by faint brightness that presaged the rising moon. As the party stood silent at its edge a puff of wind set tall reeds nodding; it seemed they caucused against human intrusion.

"I guess it's no use," said the foreman. "Maybe I was foolish to come. But they may be in here; only we can't see them. If they be, nothing can be done till morning. . . . We'd better be getting back. Mr. Flaherty and the others, they'll have finished their beat. Best let me go ahead again."

As they had filed in, they filed out, each footstep carefully stamped in the slimy trail. Last of all Caswell, whose first cigar since the party took the trail burned a beacon to luminous insects of the night.

"Now let's swing to the left, and make a half-circle on the way back to the lane," the foreman advised on their return to solid ground.

"Pretty hopeless," said Delancey to Caswell, as they brought up the rear. "The town's population would be none too many to cover these moors by night. Why do you suppose Flaherty brought so few?"

"All he could get, probably," Caswell responded. "Big things here are supposed to be announced by the town crier. They'll get him out, if Flaherty's had no better luck."

It appeared Flaherty hadn't. They found his party resting in the cars.

"Any luck?" he asked as they came up.

"Not a trace," said Norcross.

There followed a silent moment, in which each man felt his fellows groping for some helpful suggestion; but none came.

"Well," said Flaherty finally, "I guess we've done all that can be done to-night. Luckily, the weather isn't severe. If they're only lost, they won't suffer much from exposure."

"But if they are hurt——?" interjected Delancey.

"That's possible. Still we can't help it. Hunting these moors at night is a blind gamble. But at least we had to try it. To-morrow we'll go over them with a fine-tooth comb, if necessary."

Flaherty spoke with a slight accent of irritation, as if he felt himself suspected of heartlessness.

Without further conversation the men once more grouped themselves for the return to town. Again Caswell and Delancey rode with Bjerstedt.

Their car went first, and faster than on the trip outward bound. Occasionally they were overtaken by puffs of wind, blowing briskly for a few moments; then followed a dead calm. More weatherwise than Delancey, Caswell took note of the sky, in which outposts of advancing clouds were scudding across the moon. As they rode the air grew perceptibly cooler.

When they entered the village most inhabitants of a community in which early rising was not so much a virtue as necessity had gone to rest. At the hotel they disbanded. While the Nyatt men went their respective ways, Flaherty and Bjerstedt lingered.

"Shall I turn out Natty?" inquired Dr. Pugh, as he sat at the wheel of his car.

"If you will," said Flaherty. "There must be people still awake; and the sooner we have everybody on the lookout, the better."

"About what time will you organize your searching party in the morning?" asked Caswell.

"We'll say eight, and probably get under way by nine."

"We will be here by that time."

"Oh, you're going out to your boat?"

Flaherty spoke as if the idea had just occurred to him.

"If we can get some one to row us out; and I guess that's possible. I'm going to see now."

"Righto. Good-night."

In the exchange of parting salutations Bjerstedt took no part. As they entered the hotel Caswell and Delancey noted he stood at the end of the piazza, staring into the dark.

There was no trouble in engagement of a boatman.

"William will take you out, if he's here," said a shock-headed young man whose ardent enjoyment of some snappy story was interrupted by their entrance. "I'll go see."

"I'm hungry again," Delancey announced after a few minutes of waiting.

"Can you last till you get to the boat?"

Caswell's inflection was satirical.

"I want it now. . . . There was a dish of fruit on the sideboard at dinner."

"None for me, thanks."

"That's where the house wins."

Delancey sauntered down the hall to the dining-room door. It was unlocked, and he entered. With some blinds drawn there yet entered enough moonlight to make his way about. He found the fruit and possessed himself of two fair specimens of the banana. About to go he stood suddenly alert.

From the darkness outside a voice came to his ears. Flaherty's, in unmistakable reproval:

"I'm afraid we're in a mess. With the whole town poking around, we'll be lucky if something doesn't crop out."

Then Bjerstedt's voice in sulky retort.

"Handle it yourself next time. I did the best I could."

That was all. The conversation ended, or they passed out of hearing. Moving with careful lightness, Delancey returned to the office.

"What do you make of it?" he asked when he had repeated the colloquy overheard.

"We both jump to the same suspicion," said Caswell, after a moment's meditation. "And we may do them injustice. If we see anything fishy in their behavior to-morrow, I think we'd best turn to the town officers. Assuming, of course, Ed and Nell Strong are still missing."

"I guess that is the best we can do," Delancey conceded.

Presently appeared William, a long-armed, taciturn boy with soon demonstrated prowess as an oarsman. As he pushed off from the wharf they heard the distant, "Cling-cling, cling-cling, cling-cling!" of Natty's bell preceding his,—"Attention, people!"—and proclamation of the news that a couple were lost on the moors.

Against a wind coming in long gusts, and a rising swell in the harbor, they made their way to the *Viva*. She was swinging at her anchor with no person visible in the rays of light at bow and stern; but as they came up the ladder, Andersen's face appeared at the rail.

"Breakfast at eight, Andersen," said Caswell as he reached the deck.

"Very well, Captain."

The skipper saluted and went below. Almost immediately Caswell and Delancey followed. Preoccupied, they did not note the white yawl anchored near by, an arrival since morning; nor were they conscious of the man slouching in a deck chair who watched the *Viva* from the yawl, pulling at his pipe as the hours passed and the sea rose.

It was past midnight when a long, black motor-boat driven more by rising sea and gale than engines running easily, picked its way along the ship channel, and came briefly to rest on the lee side of the yawl. A few words passed between the lookout on the white boat and a man in oilskins who appeared at the side of the black launch. They spoke with cupped hands, the better to control their voices in the strident wind. A listener near by might have distinguished the word,—"Ashore." Perhaps more.

Backing away, the black boat came around the stern of the yawl and passed the *Viva* on her port side. Precisely then a comber lifted and threw her over, so that she hung for a moment, black and shining under one of the *Viva's* deck lights. Then she plunged with tumbling water into darkness and foam.

Solemnly the clock in the North Tower struck one.

CHAPTER 7

CONCERNING A 38 COLT

The southwester howled under a brilliant sky. A sky deeply blue. From its depths rushed wind that rent the scurrying clouds to tatters. The bosom of the Sound was agitated to violent crescendo.

Over the long line of the breakwater white horses came leaping. With lessened force, but still powerfully, racing waves assaulted the disintegrating shore. Their rhythm, as they curved and fell, punctuated the far-off roar of surf on the South Shore.

Sea-weed, fragments of planking, barrel hoops,—the miscellaneous trophies of predatory waters, were whirled shoreward, played with, and sometimes dragged back to make the wild journey again.

Of the fishing fleet neither sloop nor motor-boat had ventured forth. Their crews smoked on the sheltered side of sheds along the water-front, or stood with feet well braced, speculating on the duration and destructiveness of the gale.

As Caswell and Delancey came on deck in their oilskins, ready for the trip ashore, the morning steamer for New Thetford, which had waited an hour beyond its schedule before casting off, turned tail off the lighthouse and headed back to her wharf.

Though much tossed, the *Viva* was riding easily, her anchorage seemingly secure. Having superintended the lowering of her larger and stronger boat, Andersen called to one of the crew:

"You first, Johnson."

The tall sailor who had cryptically remarked,—"Them Red fellers have a pull" tightened his belt as he stepped to the rail. While the men with the ropes manœuvered energetically he dropped into the boat and picked up the bow oars.

"You, Carlson," Andersen said.

With comparative ease the sailor who had remarked, "'Tis a crime we'd be doin',"—took the stern seat and oars.

Now the captain himself put a foot on the ladder.

"Are you going, Andersen?" asked Caswell in surprise.

"I think it is best, sir."

Nothing further said, he took his seat in the boat with the tiller. Caswell and Delancey followed gingerly, with a squeamish feeling that the boat might not return from one of its sudden drops as seas rushed by.

They pushed off in good order and headed for the shore. With the sweep of wind behind them it was more a question of steering than of pulling at the oars. Above them flocks of screaming gulls were cruising with wings for sails.

Through his inseparable field-glass Caswell took an observation of the nearer shore. With concern he noted how waves lashed at pilings of the wharves. He turned to the right, and the curving shore on which he had landed with Delancey the day before. Though the gale had flattened its waving grasses, the waves scalloping its shelving sands looked less ominous.

Unable to make Andersen hear, as the wind just then blew a tremendous blast, Caswell drew attention by a questioning gesture to the inlet with a little wharf at which he had tied up. The captain nodded, and changed their course.

Now the men at the oars pulled harder; and for a few minutes they shipped water, despite Andersen's adroit handling in the quartering sweep of sea. Then, the Point offering its protection, the water grew comparatively smooth.

Riding easily in long swells, they drove straight to the inlet Caswell indicated with a confirming hand, and came smartly about at the wharf. With more difficulty than Delancey experienced Caswell scrambled up, and turned to Andersen, sitting calm at the tiller.

"Do you want to come ashore?" he asked.

"In this weather, sir, I think we'd best be aboard ship."

"Very well," said Caswell. "You are left in full charge. Mr. Delancey and I expect to be at the Stimson House, not later than one. If it is possible, please have a boat ashore."

Andersen saluted.

"Very well, sir." To his men, "Cast off."

The elder man leading, Caswell and Delancey turned inland, picking their way up the winding path. That morning no lark sang. Excepting rejoiceful sea birds the upper air was swept clear.

As they went up from the shore the wind fused in overtone with the lessened voice of the water. They were at the edge of a brightly carpeted slope when Caswell, leading, stopped with an exclamation:

"Slim!"

"What is it?" asked Delancey, pressing forward to see the thing riveting Caswell's attention, but cut off from his own view by a screen of tall grass.

"Beddle," said Caswell as Delancey stood beside him.

Beddle it was, with something more than his customary iciness of demeanor.

He lay on his back, the right leg slightly doubled under him. His left hand, resting on the ground, clutched a revolver. That and a blood stain over his heart comprised the suggestion of violence.

To a casual passer-by it might have seemed he slept. There was about him an air of complete composure. In the wind-swept night no dew had fallen. His linen was still crisp. Eyes half-open fronted them with the expression of one probably bored, but nowise horrified.

Delancey stooped to touch the body.

"I wouldn't do that," said Caswell sharply.

"Are you sure he is dead?"

"Not a doubt in the world."

As Delancey stepped back Caswell continued:

"In cases of suspicious death it is forbidden to touch the body before the medical examiner arrives; and certainly we don't want further complications here."

"We can't leave him like that," Delancey objected.

"We certainly must. It's our duty to find an officer in the village."

They went on, skirting the marshy region of the Point in their stubborn struggle with the gale. The only person encountered was a bearded ancient who seemed too decrepit for such weather; but he was running before the wind.

"Quite a tem-pest," he cackled with cupped hands as he blew past.

Expectation was surpassed in finding the police. It was Delancey's discovery. He chanced to spy a visored cap and a glint of brass buttons on a man comfortably established in a ship chandler's window. He regarded them indifferently as they entered. A fattish fellow, with dull brown eyes in a leathery face.

"There's a man's body near the lighthouse on the Point," said Delancey abruptly.

"So?" said the policeman calmly.

"Yes. Let me tell you——"

"Guess you'd better go with me."

"Sorry we can't. We've got to get over to the other end of the island."

"Guess you'd better stay here."

The officer neither raised his voice nor changed his lounging attitude. But he unquestionably meant to command.

Now Caswell intervened, seeing storm signals in Delancey's heightened color and a pugnacious set of his head.

"All right," he said. "It's a bother; but I suppose it's our duty. Is there a telephone here?"

"Help yourself."

The proprietor came to the fore with a gesture of invitation towards an instrument resting on a shelf. The hotel was reached, and Flaherty located with little difficulty.

"I'm sorry," he said, after Caswell's preliminary expression of regret that they would be unable to join the party searching for Anthony and Nell.

"What's that! . . . Beddle dead?"

A moment's silence, in which Flaherty seemed to be absorbing this shocking news. Then he began rapid questioning:

"Where is he? . . . How did it happen?"

Caswell gave him the meagre information he had, and he responded with lively sympathy:

"I see. It's awkward. As a matter of law, I suppose the yokels are right. They're bound to take your statement. . . . By the way,—Pugh can make it easy for you. He's the medical examiner."

"Do you think we can get at him soon?" asked Caswell.

"He's right here. I'll have him over to you in a jiffy. . . . Has anybody told Beddle's sister?"

"No. There hasn't been time to do that."

At his end of the wire Caswell could feel Flaherty's painful decision.

"I'll do it," he said presently. "Somebody has to. And you're tied up with the police. . . . I'd better be getting at it. There's a big party waiting to start the search. I hope we won't need you fellows. But if we don't find your friend and Nell Strong this morning, we'll be glad of your help this afternoon. . . . So long."

"Well?" said Delancey, who had heard nothing but Caswell's end of the conversation.

"It's all settled. We wait here. Dr. Pugh will be down in a little while to make the examination."

Unexpectedly soon, considering the leisurely habits of Nyatt, Dr. Pugh appeared, with the village hearse drawn by black horses in his wake. The stout policeman at their elbow, Caswell and Delancey stepped into the doctor's car; and the little procession set out.

A short ride, and a rather silent one, with little to tell and the wind overpowering an ordinary conversational tone. They finished afoot, Caswell showing the way. Presently they came to Beddle's remains.

While Dr. Pugh, accompanied by Caswell, stepped forward the others held back, checked by the layman's feeling of strangeness in the presence of death.

Stooping, the examiner touched Beddle's cheek and took between his fingers the wrist of the right hand rested on the breast; probably raised in a gesture of surprise that was the last conscious movement. Now the doctor tentatively tested the left hand's grip on the revolver. Beddle's fingers would not at first yield.

"How long?" asked Caswell, as the examiner rose from his stooping posture with a little grunt.

"Can't say exactly. Over ten hours dead, I think."

Without comment, and only once taking a note, Dr. Pugh moved slowly about Beddle's body, vigilantly regarding it from every angle. Then he called to the undertaker and his assistants:

"Lift it."

With impersonal gravity his order was obeyed. The examiner's eyes followed the body on its way to the hearse, and swept the spot on which it had lain.

"Now," he said, "let us carefully examine the ground in this vicinity."

The search was unavailing. They scoured the clear ground, and to the last blade pressed down neighboring meadow grass. Nothing conceivably connected with the death was uncovered.

Meantime the examiner held the revolver taken from Beddle's hand. Now it received close attention.

"A short 38 Colt," he said, and wrote a line in his memorandum book.

He broke the weapon, and held it up to the sun.

"One cartridge fired."

Another line in the note-book. Then he wrapped the revolver carefully in a big silk handkerchief, and put it in an overcoat pocket.

"We're through here."

As he spoke the doctor turned towards the spot where they had left the car. The others followed with the sort of conversation that plugs a gap. Only when they were driving into the village did Delancey utter anything bearing upon the grave matter with which they were engaged.

"I suppose," he said, "we are through now."

"No. Not exactly," Dr. Pugh replied, and meditated a moment. "The judge will want your statement. It's about time for the close of his morning session. We might get in touch with him, and have it over with."

"We'd be greatly obliged. You know, we came for a week-end. It seems like several years."

There came a gleam of teeth in the doctor's characteristically guarded smile.

"It must have been pretty uncomfortable for you. . . . I'll drop you at the judge's office. Fitzmaurice's his name. And I'll be over as soon as I make a preliminary examination of the body. . . . Go right up, and tell him what's on hand. I won't be long."

Completing this advice, Dr. Pugh stopped by one of Main Street's massive elms, and pointed to the door at the foot of a flight of stairs.

"Up there," he said. "See you soon."

Delancey and Caswell paused to read a gilt sign:

"NYATT DISTRICT COURT"

And under it:

"Edward Fitzmaurice. Attorney and Counsellor at Law"

They climbed the stairs to a green baize door, knocked, and in response to a voice calling, "Come," went in.

A stout, smooth-faced, youngish man of rather pleasant expression looked up from his desk on the right, and paused in his writing.

"What can I do for you?" he said.

"Are you Judge Fitzmaurice?" asked Caswell.

"So they say."

"Dr. Pugh sent us in to see you."

"What about?"

"The death of Guy Beddle."

"Beddle dead!"

The pen dropped from the judge's hand. He stared in shocked amazement.

"How did it happen?"

"Shot," said Caswell.

"When? It's strange I have heard nothing of it."

The judge was leaning forward now, elbows on his desk, regarding them keenly over his clasped hands.

"We found him less than two hours ago," Delancey explained.

"Oh, *you* found him."

The judge rubbed his chin.

"And I suppose you notified the medical examiner?"

Delancey nodded.

"Quite unusual common sense. . . . I suppose the examiner sent you here to make your statement."

"That's right," said Caswell.

"But why the haste?"

The judge was sitting back in his swivel chair, with a more judicial air than he had previously worn.

"To have it over with. We only came for the week-end."

"I see. May I ask your name?"

"Caswell."

"Oh, yes. They're hunting now for a friend of yours lost on the moor. . . . And your name is Griffis."

He turned to Delancey, who hesitated a moment before making the explanation clearly inevitable.

"No," he said, "that is not my name."

The air of unconcern he aimed at was not quite achieved; and so, perhaps, was added a slight elevation as the judge's brows rose.

"That is strange," he observed. "It happens Beddle spoke of you to me—only last night. You had met him,—hadn't you?"

"Yes," said Delancey.

"I would have sworn he said your name was Griffis."

"That was the name under which he met me."

Delancey was exhibiting the stiffness of one irritated by innocently aroused suspicion.

"A joke, I suppose?"

The judge's accent was a bit satirical.

"Just that. A foolish joke. I'd like to explain it."

"There's no need—now."

The court's spacing of "*Now*" was somehow ominous.

"I prefer to. That is,—if you've time to listen."

Delancey spoke with warmth and heightened color.

"Very well, if you wish."

The judge leaned back again. He seemed fond of a semi-recumbent position. Somewhat assertively Delancey plunged into his tale:

"When we landed yesterday a fellow named Bjerstedt—a stranger to me—met us on the wharf and insisted my name was 'Griffis.' Like a fool, I let him think so. We'd been talking on the boat about lack of adventure. So I said to myself,—'Here's a little lark.'"

What the judge thought was not evident from his expression. Delancey resumed:

"He seemed to have me booked to meet somebody at the Stimson House. We—three of us, I mean, went along expecting nothing more than a laugh over Bjerstedt's mistake. But Ericsson, who sent him, appealed to me to play Griffis; just for a night. I found it was the moving picture man who was expected."

"Ericsson said so," remarked the judge.

"Perhaps I am telling you something you already know."

Delancey paused, uncertain.

"I know now that Ericsson's company was bogus; but I thought Griffis was real."

"Probably he is. I don't know."

To the dismay of Caswell, a helpless spectator of proceedings, Delancey's manner had become distinctly defiant.

"What made you do it?"

"Because I was an ass; with slight extenuation in the fact I found Ericsson knew friends of mine in Boston. He said the joke, as I supposed it to be, would save him embarrassment."

"And then——" began the judge.

"I'm told he ran away."

"You seem well informed, Mr.——?"

"Delancey."

At this stage of proceedings a ferret-faced man entered without knocking. A spare type, with small, restless eyes, and a nose made for sniffing. His look inventoried Caswell and Delancey on its way to the judge.

"Do you want to see me, Sheriff?" asked the court.

"Just a minute, Judge."

The sheriff's manner, looking at Caswell and Delancey as he spoke, implied—"Just a minute alone."

Rising, the judge turned to folding doors behind him.

"Step in this way," he said, and over his shoulder as they disappeared: "I won't be long."

At the closing of the door the two without exchanged unrestrained glances.

"Well," said Delancey with a bitter laugh, "at least they don't suspect we will try to run away."

"That's less a compliment than you think," observed Caswell. "It would be madness to put out of this harbor on a small boat to-day. And we're thirty miles from the mainland. As to the jail, I remember one of the favorite tales with summer boarders is that of a prisoner who sued the town because a sheep got in while he was asleep one night, and bit him in the face."

"Thanks, Pop, for trying to see some humor in the thing. It's mighty good of you."

"Oh, we'll straighten this thing out," said Caswell, with a more jaunty elevation of his cigar. "The great question is, What's happened to Ed?"

"There again," Delancey said with vehemence, "my masquerade comes in. Somehow I fear he has bumped against the bunch convinced I came down here to help Ericsson get away with their money."

"Nell Strong is missing, too," Caswell suggested.

"That's true, and I don't suppose these rum runners, or whatever kind of pirates they are, would have any object in harming her. Maybe I'm wrong, and they're just lost. . . . What day is this?"

"The calendar says, 'Sunday.'"

"Two days since we landed. I feel as if we had been here about two exciting years. Wish the doctor would hustle, so we can have it over with."

They had but a few minutes to wait. In the same moment Dr. Pugh bustled in, and Judge Fitzmaurice emerged from his private office. They exchanged "Good-morning." To Caswell and Delancey the doctor nodded.

"What's this I hear about Beddle?" asked the judge.

"Dead," said the doctor, as he took from his overcoat pocket a capacious bandanna containing articles deposited on the desk. From one corner protruded the barrel of a revolver.

"What do you know about it?" queried the judge.

"Not much. He was shot through the heart. Some time yesterday, I judge. And found down near the Point, just off Peakes' Landing, by our friends," with a jerk of his head towards Caswell and Delancey,—"this morning. Since they're only here for a little trip, I thought we could oblige them by taking their statement now."

"I see."

The judge did not glance at the off-islanders, but the sheriff's little eyes were busy travelling from one to the other.

"Which one," asked Judge Fitzmaurice, "reported the crime?"

"I think the officer said he was informed by Mr. Griffis," Dr. Pugh answered.

"Mr. Delancey," the judge corrected him.

"Oh," said the doctor, plainly astonished.

"Then we may as well begin with him."

The judge settled himself in his office chair, and picked up a pen.

"What is your first name, Mr. Delancey?"

"Richard."

"You knew Mr. Beddle?"

"I met him twice."

"That was——?"

"Night before last, and yesterday noon."

"The first time?"

"At the Stimson House, with a party of friends, the night we landed."

"And the second time?"

"Yesterday noon. In front of the hotel. He was walking by with his sister as Dr. Caswell and I came from the hotel. We stopped for some conversation."

"And then you parted?"

"Not at once."

"Tell me about it."

"As Dr. Caswell wished to take some notes on birds, a thing not very interesting to me, the Countess Sacardi suggested I join herself and brother for a walk. I did so."

"I see. And at what time did you part from them?"

"Beddle left us soon after, and walked off in the direction of the spot where his body was found. The Countess and I went another way."

"You never saw Beddle again?"

"Not alive."

"Only when you found the body?"

"Yes. This morning."

"Now let's see, Mr. Delancey. When Beddle turned off towards the shore, the last time you saw him alive, which way did you and the Countess go?"

"At first, I think towards Scammon's Pond. If there is such a pond."

"Yes, there is."

"I had never heard of it. It was the Countess's suggestion."

"I see. And how long were you there?"

"I can't say. We rested a while on a hill above the pond."

"And then?"

"We went to Simms Point. If, again, I am right about an unfamiliar name."

"There is a point so called," the judge assented. . . . "How long did you remain with the Countess, Mr. Delancey?"

"Until about sunset."

"Where did you separate?"

"At her gate."

"And then——?"

"I joined my friend, Dr. Caswell, at the Stimson House."

"How long were you with him?"

"We went out to his yacht together, and spent the night aboard."

"So you were with him until you made the discovery this morning. Is that right?"

"Perfectly correct."

The judge had been putting questions rapidly. Now he meditated a moment.

"I wonder," he said presently, "how you happened to go ashore this morning at the place where Beddle's body was found. It is a private landing, off on the north side of the harbor, and almost never used by strangers. Why did you put in there?"

"Because, I suppose, it was an easier landing in rough water; but that was not a matter in my control."

"I remember. You were Dr. Caswell's guest."

Turning a little in his chair, Judge Fitzmaurice brought his examination to bear in another quarter.

"Will you tell me, Dr. Caswell, why you put in to this private wharf, instead of tying up to one of the public landings?"

"As Mr. Delancey suggests, because it was quieter water there."

"How did you know about it?"

"I had put in there twice before."

"When?"

"Once about two years ago, and the second time yesterday."

"You mean the day Beddle was killed."

"Evidently, since Delancey and I saw him about noon, yesterday."

"What time was it when you landed?"

"Nine, or thereabouts."

"See any evidence of crime then?"

"Not a scintilla."

"What were you looking for?"

"Larks."

"You mean——?"

"Birds. Ornithology is my hobby."

"Ah, yes. Now tell me,—were there any larks there yesterday morning?"

"I saw none. But I heard one sing."

"Mr. Delancey, I take it, was with you then."

"Yes."

"And remained with you until he went walking with the Beddles, while you started off on another bird hunt alone?"

"That is right."

"We're getting on. . . . Tell me, please, where you spent the afternoon."

"I went out past the old windmill, and over the Commons, until I came to the Sound. I can't say just where. But there's an inlet near Paul's Hills, with an old horse-shed on the bluff behind; and traces, I'd say, of a picnic ground."

"I think I know the place you mean," said the judge. "What did you do there?"

"I was looking for gulls."

"And you found some?"

"Plenty of tracks, but nary a gull."

"Then you went back to town?"

"Not right away. A Cape May warbler came along, and I put in a while looking at bird tracks on the beach. It's quite fascinating."

"I dare say. Did you see any person over there?"

Caswell hesitated, then answered:

"No."

"How did you return to town?"

"I walked back."

"Reached here about what time?"

"I can't say exactly. In the late afternoon."

"Then what did you do?"

"I waited at the Stimson House until Delancey came along."

"When was that?"

"I can't say to a minute. It was just after sunset."

"You agree with his testimony regarding your movements together afterward?"

"Wholly."

The judge settled back in his chair.

"Well," he said, "that seems to account for all your time in which the state is interested."

For a moment he chewed a finger-tip meditatively. Then he leaned forward to turn over articles deposited by the medical examiner in his bandanna. Meantime he addressed that worthy:

"I suppose, Doctor, the Countess has been notified of her brother's death?"

"Flaherty started out to tell her, just as I left to observe the body," the medical examiner answered.

"We should have her testimony to corroborate the evidence of Dr. Caswell and Mr. Delancey regarding meetings, and their movements of yesterday. Would it be cruel to call her now?"

Dr. Pugh pulled his beard.

"As I size her up," he said presently, "she is a level-headed woman. I don't believe she would go to pieces. Being asked a few questions might help her to rally from the shock of Beddle's death in this way."

"Then we'll try," the judge decided. "Suppose, Sheriff, you go to her house. It's McCardle's, just around the corner. Ask her, if she's there, to come here for a few minutes. Just say it's an important matter."

"Sure, Judge."

With alacrity the sheriff was on the way. The judge leaned back, and yawned with hands clasped behind his head.

"Have you a cigarette, Mr. Delancey?" he asked.

Delancey's hand went to his upper left-hand waistcoat pocket, and remained there a moment.

"I'm sorry," he said with a look of chagrin. "I have lost my case."

"Is this it?"

From the bandanna before him the judge lifted a case of hammered gold. Delancey's eyes took in its shape and size, and the woman's head emerging from a decorative vine.

"It looks like it," he said with an expression of surprise.

"I thought it might be. The initials engraved on it are 'R. D.'"

With his equable air the judge turned to the medical examiner, still retaining the case in his hand.

"Where did you find this, Doctor?" he inquired.

"In one of Beddle's pockets, when I examined the body."

"How do you explain this, Mr. Delancey?"

The judge regarded him lazily.

"I can't explain it."

There followed a tense moment; a moment of shocked astonishment for Delancey, of keen anxiety for Caswell.

"I can't explain it," Delancey repeated. "But I've an idea of what may-be happened."

"Let's have it," said the judge encouragingly.

"I lost the case somewhere yesterday. In the afternoon I knew it was gone. My reaching for it just now was one of those instinctive things. Happenings to-day for the time being drove the loss from my mind."

"That's likely enough," said the court. "And where do you think you lost the case?"

"Just where it was found."

"It was found in Beddle's pocket. Are you suggesting he stole it?"

"Certainly not," said Delancey. "What I mean is this: I remember when we landed, yesterday morning, I slipped going up the bank, and nearly fell. In fact, I came so near it I got mud on one knee. I think the case must have been jarred from my pocket then. I had it in my hand before leaving the boat, and I didn't have it when I wanted a cigarette in the afternoon."

"Quite reasonable," the judge observed. "And how do you think the case came into Beddle's possession?"

"I can only guess he came along, and picked it up."

"And then some one came along, and killed him. So there he was with the case in his pocket."

Again the judge leaned back, with hands behind his head. Resting a foot on a half-open drawer of his desk, he seemed a trifle bored with proceedings.

"Have you a revolver, Mr. Delancey?" he asked with eyes fixed on the ceiling.

Delancey briefly withheld his answer:

"I don't own one."

"I meant to inquire if you have one in your possession."

"Yes," said Delancey.

"Did you have it yesterday?"

"Part of the day."

"From what time on?"

"I received it about sunset."

"Who gave it to you?"

"Nobody gave it to me. It was lent."

"By whom?"

"The Countess Sacardi," said Delancey reluctantly.

"For what reason?"

"She thought my life was in danger."

The judge's feet came down from the desk.

"Very interesting," he said. "And how was your life in danger?"

Delancey pondered, more humiliated than apprehensive.

"I don't think I can fully explain that," he answered at length. "Only I had told her about the threatening behavior of men who seemed to think I helped Ericsson cheat them. She attached more importance to it than I did."

"So she insisted upon arming you."

"That's it."

"Have you had occasion to use the revolver?"

"No. I haven't fired it."

"Where is it?"

Delancey's right hand went from the arm of his chair to his coat on that side.

"It's in my pocket, where I put it yesterday," he said. "I'm wearing the coat I had on then."

"May I see it?"

The judge extended his hand, as Delancey stepped forward, holding the weapon. He received it gingerly; an involuntary withdrawal of his head as he looked, with a slight squint, into its black tube of death.

"Aren't you something of an expert with small arms?" he inquired of the medical examiner.

"I've qualified in target practice with the revolver," assented the doctor.

"Then suppose you look at this?"

The judge held out the revolver. Receiving it without comment, the doctor turned it slowly in his hand, and held it under his nose with a deep inhalation. Then he broke it, holding its cylinder up to the sun.

"Well?" said the judge when examination was completed.

"A short 38 Colt, in excellent condition."

"Isn't it a good deal like this one here?"

The judge reached for the pistol in the bandanna.

"As much alike as two revolvers can be."

Now Dr. Pugh held one in each hand.

"And pattern," he observed, "isn't the only parallel."

"What else?"

"One cartridge of this revolver has been discharged."

He held up the one surrendered by Delancey.

"And one has been fired from the revolver I found in Beddle's hand."

Deep silence reigned in the office. With varying interpretation each of the four men present took the implication. The judge's sleepy eyes were studying the pressed steel pattern of his office ceiling.

"What calibre was the bullet that killed Beddle?" he asked at length.

"From superficial examination I would say this calibre—a 38."

"There was only one wound?"

"I feel justified in saying so," said the doctor. "Although, being in haste to get here, I have not completed my examination."

The judge tapped his teeth with his pencil.

"Might the shot through the heart," he said at length, "have been self-inflicted?"

An answer on the doctor's lips was delayed by the opening of the outer office door.

Greta Sacardi entered, followed by the sheriff and an unknown man. She was pale but composed; quietly dignified in her suit of black. If she was astonished by the number and identity of those present, she did not show it. With a slight bow that comprehended all, she turned to Judge Fitzmaurice her inquiring eyes.

"I appreciate your coming here," he said,—"just now. It happens there is something important I need to ask you. If you will be seated?"

"Certainly."

The judge turned back to the doctor:

"And your answer to my last question—is?"

"Positively—No. There is no powder stain on either clothing or body."

"I think that's all for you."

With Greta the judge indulged in a little preamble.

"I hope you understand," he said, "that in such matters as your brother's death officers must do things distasteful to them as individuals. With extreme reluctance I shall ask you a few questions."

"You need not apologize," she said. "I understand."

"That helps. Now may I ask you first if you have any theory about your brother's death?"

"I've no suspicion against any person."

"He had never been threatened?"

"Not to my knowledge."

"When did you last see him alive?"

"We parted at a street corner just outside the village, yesterday morning."

"Any other person present at that time?"

"Mr. Delancey."

"Indeed. I see you have been favored with his right name."

"He explained to me the jest that led to his appearance here as 'Mr. Griffis.'"

She spoke calmly, without looking at Delancey.

"Then excepting yourself," the judge pursued, "he is the last person known to have seen your brother alive."

"The last person I know of."

"Now just to get at all aspects of the matter, will you tell me about your own movements the rest of the day?"

"When my brother turned off towards the lighthouse—to attend to some matter about a boat, he said,—I walked in the direction of Scammon's Pond. Later in the afternoon I was at Simms Point."

"During this time you were alone?"

"No. Mr. Delancey was with me."

"Oh, was he? Now, in view of what later happened, does anything stand out in your memory?"

"No," she said.

But, after a moment's thought, she amended her answer.

"We went up in my plane, and were nearly wrecked by another aviator. But that had nothing to do with my brother's death."

"By 'we,'" the judge suggested, "I suppose you include Mr. Delancey."

"Yes."

"How long was he with you?"

"We separated at my gate about sunset."

"And your brother did not come. Had you any message from him?"

"Not a word."

"When did you first think something might have happened to him?"

"This morning."

"Then last night——?"

"I went to bed and slept. It was not unusual for him to stay out late. And he was rather careless about explanations."

The judge nodded.

"Some of us are. . . . I don't suppose you recognize this?"

He held up one of the revolvers in evidence.

"Not at this distance."

She leaned forward.

"Do you mind handling it?" he asked.

At that she faintly smiled.

"No. I am quite used to firearms."

The judge extended the revolver to the sheriff, who placed it in her hands. With a swift scrutiny, turning it about, she lifted her head:

"It looks like one of ours."

"'Ours'?" the judge echoed.

"My brother's and mine. We both used them."

"This one, then?"

The second revolver was placed in her hands. She glanced at it with equal care.

"They're alike," she said, a minute later. "And either ours, or duplicates."

The judge again cocked an eye at the pattern of the ceiling.

"Tell me," he said, "where you got them, if you remember; and where you kept them? And what became of them, so far as you know."

As she answered she kept the pistols in her hands, with the easy closeness of familiarity.

"My brother bought the revolvers in New Thetford in the hour or two we spent there before taking the boat for here. We were both used to small arms, and rather better shots than the average. These short Colts were the best the dealer had for target practice, and three were all he had in stock. We took the lot."

"That's plain," said the judge encouragingly. "Now where were they kept?"

"On a shelf in the closet of my brother's bedroom, at Mrs. McCardle's house, where we had rooms."

"Who knew the place?"

"My brother and I, and probably the maid who took care of the rooms. No one else I think of."

"Were the revolvers usually left on the shelf?"

"Except when we took them out for practice in shooting; and sometimes my brother carried one."

"Did you know that he had one with him yesterday?"

"Not until I returned to the house about dark. Then I assumed so."

"Why?"

"Because one was gone then."

"I trust I am not tiring you with questions?" the judge said solicitously.

"No," Greta replied, with her steady look. "I know you are making it as easy as possible."

"Thank you. Now, may I ask you how you made the discovery that one of the revolvers was gone?"

"I went to the closet to get one."

"That was——" the judge began.

"To loan it to Mr. Delancey."

"Mr. Delancey? Why did he want a revolver?"

Delancey half-started from his chair, as if he would speak. The judge did not even glance in his direction.

"He didn't ask for it," Greta explained. "I insisted that he take it."

"Why?"

"I thought he might need it."

"What was the danger?"

"I learned that he had been threatened by men who thought he had something to do with Ericsson's swindle."

"And you felt sure he had not?"

Greta's chin went up a trifle. The judge hastened on:

"Was Mr. Delancey averse to taking the revolver?"

"At first he refused. I think he only took it to please me."

"Was the revolver loaded when you gave it to him?"

"Yes."

"Fully loaded?"

Greta pondered.

"I don't know," she presently said.

"What do you think?"

"But you see, I'm not certain," she pointed out.

"I understand," said the judge. "Maybe we can help you out."

Once more he silently appealed to the ceiling.

"Was it your habit to reload these revolvers after using them?"

"Yes."

"And your brother's habit also?"

"Yes."

"And there were cartridges in the revolver you handed to Mr. Delancey?"

"Yes."

"Then aren't you pretty sure it was fully loaded?"

"I think so. Still, I did not examine the cylinder carefully enough to make sure. I can't say, 'Yes.' Can I?"

"I suppose not," the judge said in friendly fashion. "I only thought I might help you to remember. . . . As you perhaps realize, the question is important. Each of the revolvers here has been discharged once since it was loaded; and we want very much to find out when. Also, by whom. Nobody seems to know."

"Excuse me, Judge," petitioned the sheriff.

"What is it, Mr. Sheriff?" asked the court.

"About these shots. I think Bill Macy can tell you somethin'."

With a discoverer's pride he turned to the individual who had accompanied his return with Greta. A man in jumper and overalls; honest looking, and ill at ease.

"What is it, Bill?" asked the judge informally.

"I heard two shots down there."

"Down where?"

"Towards the Point."

"When was it?"

"Tol'rable late, yesterday afternoon."

"Where were you?"

"Cleanin' stones out of Frank Shannon's pasture."

"Did you investigate?"

"No."

"Didn't attach much importance to the shots at that time?"

"No, Judge. If anybody'd asked, I'd have said 'twas some bird shooter gettin' a drop on the season."

"Now what do you think?"

The witness looked more embarrassed.

"I don't know. Sheriff said I'd better come in and tell you."

"That's right. We're much obliged. If that's all you think of, and need to get back to work, you can go."

Bill slapped on an old felt hat, and immediately pulled it off again. With some muttered apology he hurried out.

"I might have told you about the two shots the man mentioned," Greta said when the little group had readjusted itself.

"You heard them, too?" the judge asked with lively interest.

"Two distinctly, and no more."

The judge turned to Delancey.

"Then you must have heard them."

"I heard some."

"Why didn't you mention them?"

The judge spoke with an accent of sternness. Delancey responded curtly:

"Because I attached no more importance to them than Bill Macy did. Even now, I'm not sure——"

"That doesn't matter," the judge interrupted. "Since it's not your duty to conduct the investigation."

Now he turned to Greta, and his manner was gentleness itself.

"We are greatly indebted to you. I trust it won't be necessary to question you further. I know Dr. Pugh will do all he can to protect you. And anything within my power——"

"Thank you," said Greta.

She rose, and half-turned to go. Then, reconsidering, she walked brisk-ly to where Delancey sat. It was so sudden, so unexpected that she stood before him with outstretched hand before he could rise.

"I believe you are leaving the island to-morrow. If this is 'Good-bye,' I trust we shall meet again."

"You are very kind."

Holding her hand, Delancey flushed with gratitude.

"I do not feel benevolent," she said. "Good-bye, Dr. Caswell. I hope you will remember me."

To the others she nodded, and was gone. Silence hung heavy with her departure. The sheriff looked expectantly at the judge, who examined pa-pers before him with an air of absorption. When his mind was made up he leaned back in his chair, the better to give Delancey and Caswell his atten-tion. As he addressed them he spoke slowly:

"Being sensible men,—men of experience, you must realize certain circumstances connected with Beddle's death have for Mr. Delancey pain-ful import. So far as we know, he was the last person, his sister excepted, who saw Beddle alive. And he finds the body."

"To get things straight," Caswell observed, "I found the body."

The judge brushed aside the interruption.

"At any rate, you were together. . . . And a cigarette case Mr. Delancey identifies as his property was on Beddle's body. Further, a revolver of the calibre used in the killing is found in his possession, with one cartridge fired. He admits he had the weapon when the murder was committed."

"I don't know when Beddle was killed," Delancey protested.

For the first time the judge frowned.

"It must have happened," he said with heavy emphasis, "after noon yesterday. Probably the medical examiner will be able to fix it more closely. Such matters must await a formal hearing. Meantime——"

Of the four grouped about the judge the sheriff most eagerly awaited his suspended utterance. He was moving towards Delancey as Caswell froze him with a sudden look.

"Meantime, I shall treat you gentlemen with courtesy in excess of that required by law. Off on this little island we sometimes act informally. . . . So I do not order you, Mr. Delancey, into custody, as probably I ought in view of circumstances; but you must not leave the island without the court's per-mission. And I shall ask you to report daily to the sheriff, after the sailing of the morning steamer."

Not waiting for Delancey's promise, Judge Fitzmaurice turned his eyes on Caswell.

"I regret," he said with his usual amiability, "this trouble for you. As matters are shaping, we apparently need your evidence. Do you prefer to give bail for appearance when needed? Or can you remain here a few days?"

Caswell's left eyebrow moved upward.

"Since one of the friends who came with me is lost, and the other strangely suspected of crime, I do not think of leaving. My patients must wait."

"I am glad you can stay to help us straighten things out."

The judge bowed with an air of finality, put into words with his "Good-day" as Delancey and Caswell stood up.

They went silently together down the stairs, and stepped back into the doorway as a gust of wind clutched furiously at their hats. Leaves drove by in clouds, but the street seemed deserted.

"I guess you're sorry you brought me, Pop," said Delancey ruefully.

"Nonsense," answered Caswell sturdily. "Queer bunching of circumstances; that's all."

"I suppose," Delancey went on, "they can't send me to the chair without putting you down as a liar and horse thief. But it's bad business."

"One thing at a time is enough. Our first job is to find Ed."

"Maybe he's waiting for us," said Delancey.

Having fought their way to the corner against raving opposition of the gale, they turned towards the hotel with quickened gait.

It was not astonishing to find the piazza deserted, and the big front door tight closed; more than that, apparently locked. For a minute or two they competed with the screen door. Still on, it swung to and fro with spiteful whacks while they went on pressing the bell. At last Stella came. They heard her pull the bolt.

"Excuse us," she said with a smile as they stepped in. "We had to fasten it. Something wrong with the catch. The wind kept a-blowing it open."

"That's all right," said Delancey. "Any news of Mr. Anthony?"

"Is that the gentleman that was lost?"

"Yes," eagerly. "Where is he?"

"I guess," said Stella, "they haven't found him yet."

"Is the searching party still out?" asked Caswell.

"I can't just say. Mr. Flaherty's in there. Maybe he knows."

"You mean—there?"

Delancey followed with his hand the direction of her nod.

"The office, I mean. . . . Somebody's callin' me."

She dimpled, and fled. They found Flaherty standing over the hotel register; apparently turning its leaves with his left hand. A yellow sheet that looked like a telegram was tucked into his right coat pocket as he turned at the sound of their coming.

"Hullo! You didn't get out this morning."

"No. One thing and another kept us in town."

Caswell answered with his choppy briskness of speech.

"No, thanks." Delancey waved away Flaherty's proffer of a cigarette. "What luck with Anthony and Miss Strong?"

"No luck at all. Only this——"

Flaherty took from an inner pocket a woman's handkerchief. A little square of white linen, with the initials "E. S." in a corner.

"I found this to-day," he said. "On that hill near the place where we started last night's search. I think it must be hers. I know no other woman here with those initials; and it isn't the sort of handkerchief one of the island women would carry."

As Delancey held it in his hand a perfume unquenched by the night's dew invaded his senses.

"What's your theory?" he asked, handing the handkerchief back.

"I haven't any," said Flaherty.

"Not even a guess?" queried Caswell.

"Well, I'm still hoping they're only lost; but it begins to look as if there had been an accident. Whatever it is, we'll probably know by night. Every man we could get hold of is beating the moors and shore-line this afternoon. I'm sorry I can't be there the rest of the day. This thing holds me here."

He pulled the telegram from his pocket.

"We're grateful for all you've done," said Delancey. "Considering a friend of ours is one of the lost ones, we've done mighty little."

"Oh, that's all right," said Flaherty easily. "You're strangers here; and you've had the bother of discovering Beddle's murder. If you want to join the search this afternoon, just 'phone Mitchell's garage to send my car around. I won't be using it. . . . I must run along now; see you this evening. Let's hope we'll all have good news then."

"He's really been rather decent," said Delancey as the sound of Flaherty's footsteps died away.

"Circumstances," said Caswell sagely, "have much to do with our view of the character of fellow-men."

Further philosophizing was prevented by evidence of some one advancing with ponderous haste; and then, very flushed of face, Dr. Pugh filled the doorway.

"I was looking for Flaherty," he said unceremoniously.

"Just gone," replied Caswell.

"Thanks."

The medical examiner swept them with a glance they could only interpret as expressing intense emotion of some sort.

"Beddle is gone," he blurted.

"'Gone'?" echoed Delancey.

"How can the dead depart?" asked Caswell.

"How do I know?" The examiner spoke aggressively. "While I was at the judge's office the body disappeared from the undertaker's shop."

"But that's impossible," said Caswell.

"I tell you it's true."

With a final snort, the examiner charged towards the open air.

Delancey and Caswell stared at each other—dumbfounded.

CHAPTER 8

AFTER THE FASHION OF HOUDINI

In a fog, a heavy blanketing cloud, Anthony struggled to rally from nausea and unutterable weariness.

Dully he heard a rushing like the great voice of unwearied wind. Or was it but auditory delusion? A derangement of the senses?

Something cold lightly brushed his cheek. Travelled to his eyelid with ghostly fingers, and was gone. Again that touch, impersonally inquiring as the fingers of the dead.

His flesh congealed. A third time he felt it, with the sensation of one upon whose body water is poured, inexorably, drop by drop. Dread bordering terror swept him back to acute consciousness.

He tried to move to the left, to lift his right hand against the thing. And he could do neither. His feet were bound, and his hands tied together on his breast. Once more that touch at which he shuddered; light as gossamer, yet searching the core of his being. He caught a shriek on his lips.

There must be no panic. Alert now, but faint, he tried to pierce the blackness in which he lay. Strain as he would, his eyes reported nothing.

The place was not cold, but slightly damp. A faint mustiness like that of places underground made Anthony wonder if it was a cellar. Whatever, and wherever it was, it held no sound save that of his quickened breathing.

Without, the wild. He had not imagined the sound that was his awakening impression. Steadily vehement, and sometimes roused to wild proclamation, a wind-storm held his prison in its grasp.

As a cry froze on his lips the cord sank into his wrists, with a convulsive effort to free his hands. That cold touch from nowhere again upon his face. Now it was more inquiring; it paused on his lips.

But a moment, and it was gone. He lay there helpless, trembling. By grim effort he regained sufficient poise to consider what might be done.

The first question was of physical resources. While his head ached with tenderness that brought back crashing sensation of his last conscious moment on the moor, he did not deem himself seriously injured.

There was no keen pain; no feeling of fracture. But he felt weak and sore, with inevitable numbness of impeded circulation in hands and feet.

Considerate enough to put something with burlap covers under his head, his captors had been ruthlessly thorough in binding ankles and wrists. Wriggling to test it, he felt the cord bite to the bone.

These movements were gingerly. For besides the pain they caused he realized loss of such balance as remained would leave him doubly helpless; probably face downward on the floor.

What was that?

A slight stirring above. He listened, with every atom of energy thrown into the effort of hearing. It came again. . . . Footsteps.

Footsteps of more than one. The first heard seemed heavy-footed, with a dragging gait. Another stepped lightly, yet with rhythm and accent that left no doubt of sex.

There were two men above him. He felt sure he heard a bolt shoot home, after the cautious closing of a door. Then a murmurous parley almost directly overhead. . . . Instinctively he held his breath.

Without warning, almost without sound, a square that was dark, and yet in relief against the framing blackness, appeared. And in it the partial silhouette of a man's figure.

It began to descend. Cautiously, with a slight scraping, it came down, step by step, until it was swallowed by the darkness.

No word was spoken. And practically helpless Anthony forbade himself the slightest movement. Flat on his back, his eyes fixed on that faintly luminous opening, he waited for another figure to appear.

It came backward, with more noise than had attended the first man's descent; despite the fact that it moved gingerly. The eye's automatic readjustment, and the intensity of Anthony's concentration, combined for a clearer impression of the second unknown.

Just as the man's head became darkly outlined an arm was raised. Seemingly, something grasped came slowly down; then it was pitch-dark again.

Hearing his own heart beat, it seemed to Anthony that it stopped. Stopped with that recurrent touch of ice on his eyelid. He felt upon his forehead beads of sweat he was powerless to wipe away.

A foot in contact with something broke the silence with a slight clatter. Then he closed his eyes against the dazzling invasion of an electric torch. Closed and opened them again, just as his flesh instinctively recoiled from still another contact with his terror of darkness. It was that he sought, rather than the men at whose mercy he lay there bound.

He sought the mystery, and found it. A tendril of ivy, responsive to surges of the gale, came swaying towards him; touched him for a moment, and retreated towards the wall. With comprehension came relief, despite the desperate peril of his situation.

In this minute that seemed infinitely longer the light had not left his face.

"Well?" said the man behind it. Anthony recognized the voice of Bjerstedt.

"Well?" he answered coolly.

"How are you getting along?"

"I've been more comfortable."

"You should have been more careful."

"It strikes me you're the one that needs to think about that," retorted Anthony, trying to keep his eyes steady under the torch's harsh invading rays.

"Aw, let's bump him off," urged a voice on the right, and near at hand in the darkness.

Through Anthony's mind flashed recollection of a dark forelock overhanging a black scowl. And an opponent announcing: "Say, you—you piece of cheese, I'm going to knock your block off."

"Hello, Lever," he said, "so you're in on this party. Weren't you satisfied with the licking I gave you the other night?"

"It's my turn now. When I get through with you——"

There was no need of seeing Lever's face for Anthony to gather the meaning of his unfinished sentence. . . . Then Bjerstedt cut in.

"Who's boss here?" he rasped.

No answer.

"I mean you, Sam," he said.

"I suppose you are," said Lever sulkily. "But——"

"Never mind 'Buts.' You'll do as I tell you, if you know what's healthy. . . ."

An inarticulate murmur from the darkness where Lever waited. "All right, that's understood. Now you——"

Bjerstedt turned his attention to Anthony. Leaning towards him, he said:

"What's your game on the island?"

"I haven't any," replied Anthony.

"Are you a secret service man, or a prohibition bull?"

"Why should I tell you? Supposing I'm either."

"Because you want to live. I've known secret service fellows forced into this rum hunting job. But a man that picks it——!"

Lever contributed a snarl.

"Then you admit you are rum runners?" said Anthony.

"Admit nothing. I'm asking the questions. What's your game here? And the game of the two with you?"

"Why not ask them?" countered Anthony.

"Oh, they're being taken care of all right," said Bjerstedt with a peculiar inflection.

On both sides Bjerstedt's statement was followed by a moment of thoughtful silence. Anthony spoke first.

"What have you done with Miss Strong?"

"I don't know what you mean."

Bjerstedt's voice held a note of astonishment. His face, with the light between them, Anthony could not read. Doubt sharpened anxiety gnawing at his mind since first the mist of unconsciousness cleared away.

"What's the use of lying?" he said. "She was with me when one of your thugs hit me on the head."

"Do you hear that, Sam?"

Bjerstedt spoke across Anthony to Lever.

"You tapped him a bit too hard. He hasn't come to yet."

"If you ask me," growled Lever, "I didn't give him half enough."

By a pressure of thumb Bjerstedt plunged the place into total darkness.

"I guess it's no use," he said. "We'd better leave him till his mind clears."

"As you like," Anthony answered. "But if you think you can frighten me, guess again. You know what I'm driving at."

"Sometimes," came Bjerstedt's voice from the darkness, "men are sane on every subject but one. We'll leave Miss Strong out, and try again."

Suddenly the full power of the electric torch forced Anthony's eyes to close. And Bjerstedt resumed:

"Once more, what are you?"

"My question first," Anthony retorted. "Where am I?"

No answer. He went on:

"If it's the house on the moor, you know you can't keep me here long. There's going to be a search."

"I'll humor you to that extent," said Bjerstedt deliberately. "You're not in the house on the moor."

"Then where——?"

"Where nobody'll ever find you, cully," chuckled Lever. "You're as good as buried."

"Shut up, Sam," Bjerstedt admonished him. "I can give him all the news he needs."

"We've no time to waste, Anthony," he went on. "Who are you? And what are you here for?"

"I was here for a yachting trip. I'm a teacher of mathematics."

"That sounds innocent enough," said Bjerstedt. "Where did they teach you to put out an ex-middle-weight champion?"

"Oh, he isn't much of a fighter," Anthony observed, wishing he might see Lever's face. He did hear him growl.

"As to the yachting," Bjerstedt said coolly, "how did it happen to send you down to the water-front, and out the Cliff road, the night of your arrival? And away off to the shore, bright and early the next morning? And just to spots where things were going on?"

"What things going on?" asked Anthony.

"Never mind. You know what I mean."

"But I don't know," Anthony protested. "There's been a heap of misunderstanding since you took my friend Delancey for somebody named 'Griffis,' the time we first landed."

The hand in which Bjerstedt held the torch shook with his exasperation.

"I wasn't fooled," he said roughly. "I never supposed a poor fourflusher like Ericsson had anything to do with Griffis. All I wanted was to get hold of his pal. And we nabbed him. He'll make good for his sneaking partner, too. Or we'll take it out of his hide."

"Oh, croak 'em," grunted Lever.

"I suppose you don't know Ericsson has run away with about eighty thousand dollars of our money."

"I certainly don't."

"Well, he has. The sneaking dog. I didn't think he had the nerve to do it."

This turn of events, if Bjerstedt spoke truly, was at once productive of surprise and dismay. Suppose Delancey and Caswell were also imprisoned. Who in the island would take interest enough to institute search for them, or himself? . . . And what of Nell? There was the keener pang. For her sake a speedy way out must be found.

He felt like a squirrel in a cage, as his mind ran on, seeking some avenue of escape.

"Well?" said Bjerstedt.

"So you think Delancey is Ericsson's partner."

"He admitted it, didn't he?"

"That was only a joke."

"I've known men killed for less."

"Anyway, Dr. Caswell has nothing to do with it."

"The old fellow? Perhaps he hasn't. He's got a chance to show us."

"I don't see," argued Anthony, "how we can show you anything, if we're shut up, and tied up, too. . . . Is that what you've done to them?"

"That's telling."

"We don't get anywhere," said Anthony presently. "To satisfy you, I could only tell you lies. . . . What are you going to do?"

Bjerstedt shifted the light to Lever.

"Untie his hands," he ordered.

As Lever bent over him, fumbling at his wrists, Anthony read in his eyes desire to kill.

"That will do," said Bjerstedt when his hands were free. "Keep still."

With the torch in his left hand, and keeping Anthony under observation, he stooped to pick up something. Then in his cramped way he covered the distance between them.

"This is better than you deserve," he said roughly. "But killing by starvation is not in my line."

Anthony put forth a tentative hand, feeling it very weak, and fumbled at a small parcel beside him. A packet of bread and meat. And beside it a small can of water.

"I don't know if I ought to accept it," he said. "But the temptation is great."

Pangs of thirst and appetite denied were sharpened to imperious pain. He ate and drank ravenously. Meantime Bjerstedt sat watching him, with his torch in the left hand, and a revolver in his right.

"That will keep you alive long enough to think," he remarked when the last crumb was devoured. Rather clumsily, with his bad foot, he rose and beckoned to Lever.

"Here, take these," he said, extending the torch and revolver. The fighter silently received them.

Not sure of his intention, Anthony beheld the big man clumsily approach. Then, finding the effort of stooping too much, Bjerstedt got down on his knees beside him. Lever meantime held the torch, and too lovingly fingered the revolver.

"Put your hands together," Bjerstedt commanded.

"I can do that better," Lever suggested.

Bjerstedt did not look up.

"I trusted you once to-day," he said grimly, as he fumbled for the cord with which Anthony's hands had been bound. Then he found it, and proceeded to tie them again.

To Anthony the effort was painfully painstaking. When it was done Bjerstedt rose with a grunt.

"We're ready now," he remarked, as he took back the torch and pistol. "You go first, Sam."

With the light on his back Lever began climbing what Anthony now saw was a ladder leading to the floor next above. Near the top he lifted his right hand to push up a trap-door. Again the luminous square appeared.

Bjerstedt also set foot on the bottom rung.

"How long are you going to leave me here?" asked Anthony.

"That depends," said Bjerstedt, slowly climbing.

"At least, tell me what time it is."

"I can't do that, either."

The trap-door was lowered. Again he lay in complete darkness.

To what was prepared for him he had no clue. For the present that troubled him less than the fact, if Bjerstedt spoke truly, that Caswell and Delancey lay helpless somewhere. . . . Who would think of the disappearance of three strangers? Nell would be sought. But what miracle of luck would offer searchers any clue on that hillside of the moor?

Trapped, he lay there in fruitless cogitation. At times he listened to the wind.

The gale seemingly had passed its zenith. True, sometimes a gust shook the house so passionately he felt it tremble. But it was like the rear-guard attack of an army that slowly, stubbornly retreats. The wind was no longer continuous as a wild symphony.

He wondered what time it was. That night prevailed he assumed from the deep darkness. By day a cellar, any place but an underground dungeon, would admit some ray of light.

When his hands were free he had not thought of investigating his watch pocket. Now, since his coat was buttoned, he could not get at it. He tried to determine if the watch still ticked. It would be proof that more than a day had elapsed if he found it run down. Trying his utmost, he could neither hear nor feel its beat.

What his mind measured off for minutes seemed otherwise like hours. From sheer nervousness he began twisting hands and feet in their bonds. While it hurt abominably, it quickened circulation of the blood a little, and helped to sustain a feeling of life.

What would Houdini do? That was told in a book by the wizard. One of those volumes of half-revelation that never profit a reader much. Thinking hard, Anthony began drawing the left hand, which was tied under, slowly back. And at the same time he sought to thrust the right hand forward, with a turn of the wrist inward. A trifling movement in either case; and the pain was excruciating.

Still he kept on. For after several efforts it seemed to him that he had loosened the bond a bit. But suffering incident forced him to desist.

When he had rested a few minutes he began again. Now the progress was unmistakable. He could turn his left hand.

Raising his hands to his mouth, he found the confining cord with his teeth, and tugged at the knot. Without sight to guide him it was difficult business. Pulling this way and that, he was half-convinced he bound himself more tightly.

Yet he kept on. It seemed the only hope. After what seemed almost endless exertion he was conscious of a providential slip.

Careful to seize only upper strands of the knot, he took a fresh grip with his teeth, and jerked his head sharply to the right. The knot gave perceptibly. Pulling again, he was conscious of further progress.

His wrists felt freer, with the ache of surging blood that rushed to its accustomed channels. Again that initial movement, with the left hand forward and the right drawn back. Then cautiously he pulled the left hand through. It was free.

In a transport of thankfulness he extended his arms. What was ahead he could meet,—up and fighting.

CHAPTER 9

CERTAIN DEVELOPMENTS
IN A SOU'WESTER

The sun shone, and the wind roared. The air was electrical. In the bright wildness gulls rejoiced, as they banked and soared, with screeches the gale rent to wisps of sound.

Caswell and Delancey emerged from the hotel, after belated luncheon in which Stella's fascinated interest made them aware they were now suspect to the villagers. In what fashion it was easy to guess. That Judge Fitzmaurice, Dr. Pugh and Flaherty had said nothing abroad of the Beddle affair was as probable as the sheriff's loquacity.

From the piazza they looked up and down the empty street. The town seemed to be taking a siesta.

"Looks as if everybody was hunting for Ed and the girl," suggested Delancey.

"We'd better get under way, too," said Caswell.

"Do you think they'll let us?"

"I guess so. After all, as the islander said of the escaped prisoner, it's a 'smart swim to America.' And I suppose they've got the *Viva* guarded in case we're rash enough to think of bucking this blow. . . . Will you drive the car?"

"Do you want to accept Flaherty's offer?"

"Why not?" answered Caswell.

"All right. I'd like to find out something about the disappearance of Beddle's body. But that can wait. And every hour is important with Ed and Miss Strong. Come along."

As he finished speaking Delancey stepped from the piazza to the flagged walk. Getting a firmer grip on his cigar, Caswell followed him. Little was said as they picked their way to the garage; for gusts of wind that sought to tear their hats off reduced conversation to fragments.

There was no open objection to giving them Flaherty's car.

"Yes," the man on duty said. "Mr. Flaherty telephoned. Shall you be wanting it?"

"That's why we're here," observed Delancey, a bit irritated by the fellow's manner in asking the question.

"It's a rough day for riding."

"Do you call this much of a wind?"

This question from an off-islander was grievously wounding to a native's pride. The mechanic's face darkened. But he kept a civil tongue.

"There's the telephone," he said, and seemed to listen. "Will you wait a bit while I answer it?"

With that he vanished into a boxey room boarded off from a corner of the garage, carefully closing the door behind him.

Neither Caswell nor Delancey had heard the telephone before. Now they were aware the mechanic was using it. Certain cadences, and breaks of talk in part overheard, were evidence enough as his voice came to them through cracks in the wall.

"Where's the sheriff?" they heard him say. "Well, get him, will you? . . . Yes, I'll hang on to the wire."

Then a brief silence, followed by conversation with an effort at caution on the part of the garage man.

"All right, if you say so," he ended. "I thought you ought to know."

A minute later he appeared. Not hurrying, for that is foreign to Nyatt's creed, but with almost the appearance of alacrity.

"Women is hard on cars," he volunteered and expectorated freely. "I'll be with you in a minute."

From the far end of a line he detached a roadster and backed it out. Caswell and Delancey got in, the latter at the wheel.

"Be out late?" asked the mechanic.

"Not unless we get lost," said Delancey.

"Better not; that's kind of dangerous nowadays."

The garage man's face contracted in a grimace meant for a smile. He gave no further evidence of obtrusive interest until following with his eyes, he saw them turn to the right as they reached the street.

"Hey!" he called. And "Hey!" again.

Delancey shut off power and turned in his seat.

"Goin' out to the moors?" called the mechanic.

"Maybe."

"Better not be leavin' the car out there."

"Why not?"

"Miss Strong had hers, yesterday, and they went together."

"Thanks," said Delancey, and touched the self-starter.

"You'll have to tell me the way," he said to Caswell. "It's as strange to me now as it was last night."

"To the left here," Caswell suggested. "I'll nudge you now and then."

Save a woman who seemed somewhat distracted between efforts to keep a sunbonnet on her head, and her skirts below her knees, they encountered no person within the village limits. On the wind's holiday it had exclusive possession.

On its hill the old mill stood, with an air of offended dignity and locked arms. And a few sheep turned tail to the blast.

Following the rutty way across common and moor Delancey was fully occupied with the car. For it was a light roadster. In sudden assaults of the hurricane he instinctively moved to take the shock quartering, as one jockeys a sailboat in the teeth of the wind.

Caswell seemed absorbed in the rising voice of the sea. Louder and louder it came to their ears, until the sound of surf on both north and south shores was a continuous chorus. Once, when they were perhaps a half-mile from Surfside, they saw spray tossed in a glistening fan above the line of trees.

Soon after members of the party searching for Nell and Anthony were revealed as moving specks on the moor. Once they were picked up, it was easy to see others. Delancey stopped the car for an observation.

"What's the best thing to do now?" he asked.

"Wait till we see some one we know," said Caswell.

For a few moments they watched figures that seemed to move aimlessly in small groups. Except that as they looked it twice happened a few collected with the appearance of haste and definite interest. But it was only momentary. They drifted apart again.

As they kept on slowly Caswell and Delancey came close to squads whose members regarded them apathetically, without salutation or sign of interest.

Then Caswell, suddenly alert, tapped Delancey's arm.

"Wait a minute," he said. "I think the man who led our party last night is over there."

He leaned out to wave a salutation answered by one of a group a few hundred yards away. As Caswell got out the man came towards them.

"What luck?" inquired Caswell when he was within hailing distance.

"Nothing, so far."

"What do you think?"

The man hesitated; he was middle-aged and of serious aspect.

"I don't know what to think," he said at last. "It's strange business. If they'd just lost their way, they'd been back before now. And if either of the two was hurt, you'd think we'd have found them. I don't know——"

He passed a forefinger reflectively over the stubble of his chin.

"'Tisn't as if there was rocks to fall off, and be drowned. I don't know of one more'n ten feet high on the whole island. . . . And the tide don't come fast enough to ketch anybody with a leg to stand on. . . . I snum, I'm stuck for an answer. There's just one thing I can think of."

He paused again.

"What is it?" asked Delancey.

"The bog. There's quicksands by it. I don't know's any man, woman or child has been lost there in my time. But I've heard of cattle that disappeared, and horses. There are many contradictory stories."

"How were they traced?" said Caswell.

"Tracks. And folks have sounded there with pretty long poles. They never come to bottom."

"You mean the place you took us to, last night?" put in Delancey.

"Yes, the same spot."

"I'd like a look at it this afternoon."

"All right, if you want to. . . . We've been over it."

"Will you take us?"

"Sure," said the bog foreman. "Of course, it's pretty well tracked up now. But there wasn't any tracks we could find when we started in."

"I understand."

With one foot over the side of the car Delancey remembered the garage man's warning.

"Is it safe to leave the car here?" he asked.

"I guess so. Nobody'll touch it with so many folks about."

They had proceeded only a short distance when Caswell's attention was directed to a group on the left. One of these looked after them as they passed, and took a few steps in their direction. Then he stopped, and turned back again. It was Bjerstedt.

Whether this man whose mistake about Delancey was the beginning of their trouble in Nyatt was there to help search for the lost pair, or intent on watching himself and Delancey, Caswell wondered as he brought up the rear. With their guide just ahead he said nothing.

The mysterious pond was only a mile or so distant. But fighting the wind, it seemed much farther. As the ground grew soft the bog man cautioned them.

They went in single file through the stretch of long grass. Since the night before its rank growth had been beaten by the wind, until it no longer had strength to rise between attacks. Here and there they saw brackish pools in which a pale purple flower grew.

"All around there's ticklish places."

The bog man employed both arms in his comprehensive gesture.

There was nothing poetic in the aspect of the pond by day. Heavy with the scum upon it, its darkly dirty water was only wrinkled by the wind. But its reeds were agitated. They swayed and rustled with dips so sharp they conveyed a suggestion of conscious energy. More purple flowers peeped from a tuft that rose near the pond's centre.

"What other approaches are safe?"

Caswell put the question.

"The other shore will hold you, if you know where to put your feet," said the bog man. "Want to go round?"

"I suppose it's no use."

"We've been over it."

"Let's go," said Delancey.

He had a disturbing vision of bodies held in slimy depths. With hardly a word they went back to the motor.

"I suppose you wonder why we put you to the trouble of taking us to the pond," Delancey said half-apologetically.

"No," the bog man assured them. "I understand. . . . Is there anything else I can do?"

Delancey turned to Caswell.

"I don't think of anything," the *Viva's* owner answered. "Thanks for your kindness."

"That's all right," said the bog man equably. "I guess I'll see what's going on yonder. Maybe they've turned up something."

But nobody did turn up a clue. And as the day lengthened the searchers grew apathetic, like men working with thoughts on the clock. They had done their best; and they were baffled.

Likewise, Delancey and Caswell went about aimlessly. Until slanting shadows established the first outpost of night. The sun turned deeper red, preparing the abdication of day.

The dispersed parties slowly came together again, and turned towards home. Nyatt's hunt for Nell and Anthony had ended in failure.

Because of their deep personal interest in the search that had failed Delancey and Caswell left last. When they passed the corner of the willow lane, hard by the old house in which Anthony discovered a revolver the day before, only a crimson splash remained on the gray rim of the horizon.

Village lights were lit, and village families at supper before they reached the town. The inquisitive mechanic was smoking in the doorway to the garage.

"I see you got back the same day," he observed as they stepped from the car.

"I believe it is," conceded Delancey.

"Everything all right?"

"All that I know of."

Such taciturnity was too much for the curious one. Turning his attention to the car, he let them go without further questioning.

Stella greeted them at the hotel.

"Sheriff's here to see you," she said hospitably.

"Now?" asked Caswell, screwing up his left eye.

"In the office."

"Thank you. We'll be in to supper in a few minutes."

Caswell ahead, they went on to the office door. The youth whose pleasure was reading, and his work a mystery, was much occupied with a red-covered periodical. And the village Jack Ketch leaned against the cigar case.

"Some one here to see me?" inquired Caswell.

"Sheriff," said the youth, with a jerk of his thumb.

"Ah, yes."

Caswell's expression was devoid of recognition as he waited for the sheriff to speak.

"I just dropped in," that worthy explained, blinking nervously.

"Yes?"

"To see if you was here."

"*Yes?*"

"The judge said I was to——"

"Ah, yes."

While Caswell's voice was not raised, a note of authority entered.

"You see we are here," he said coldly. "And it will not be necessary for you to call again. Good-evening."

Delancey following, they left the zealous limb of the law open-mouthed.

"He won't make trouble?" queried Delancey.

"No," snapped Caswell. "We can't be bothered by him every five minutes."

They were near the end of supper when Stella entered, brimming with self-importance.

"There's a telephone," she announced, "for you, Mr. Delancey."

"For me?" he said, wondering. "Do you know who it is?"

She rallied to the effort.

"The Count—I mean the Countess—Soc——"

"The Countess Sacardi."

She brightened with relief.

"That's the one. Mr. Beddle's sister."

"What is the message?"

"She's holding the line," Stella said.

"Oh!"

Delancey was instantly afoot, and on the way. "Hullo!" he said, picking up the receiver.

"Is that you, Mr. Delancey?"

"Yes."

"Can you come here?"

Unmistakably her voice.

"Surely," he said.

"At once?"

"Where are you?"

"At the house. Mrs. McCardle's, I mean."

"I'll be over directly."

"Thank you—Dick."

Much as it touched him, he smiled at her use of the diminutive. It came with a rush, as one hurdles an obstacle.

"Off for a few minutes," he called to Caswell, still at the table, and was on his way.

She met him at the door, pale, but composed, and wearing the black in which he had seen her last.

"Shall we stay outside?" she suggested. "I mind the wind less than an awful closeness I can't describe. Somehow I feel stifled in the house to-night."

Then, as they found a corner sheltered from the raking blasts, she said abruptly:

"Have you heard?"

"About——?"

"My brother."

"Is it true," said Delancey, "that his body has disappeared?"

"Dr. Pugh says so. What do you think it means?"

"I can't imagine. It seems so strange."

"Will it make any difference to you?"

"I don't see how it can. Anyway, that's not to be thought of now."

A feeling that was new awoke at this evidence of her solicitude.

"But they have been so horrid to you."

For an instant he felt her light touch on his arm.

"I suppose they're only doing their duty, as they understand it," he said.

"All the same, it is abominable. And Guy would be so sorry for being the cause of it."

"Of course he isn't."

Delancey offered his assurance hastily, feeling the little break in her voice.

Now they sat in silence while the wind rose in splenetic wrath. As it died away he said gently:

"If it isn't too painful, will you tell me what you have heard?"

"That is why I asked you to come. I wanted you to know. . . . It isn't very much; and it sounds too simple to be true."

"Yes," he said encouragingly.

"It seems Dr. Pugh left the body at the undertaker's when he went to the office of Judge Fitzmaurice. And when he came back it was gone."

"But how did it go? It must have been taken."

"I suppose so. Dr. Pugh says he finds a small boy was left to mind the place. And a man he is too young, or too stupid to describe came in, asking for his employer. He was told the man was out, and said he would wait. Then he discovered he needed cigarettes, and asked the boy to get some for him. The boy came back——"

"And your brother's body was gone."

"Yes," she said. "And the man who wanted to see the undertaker had vanished, too."

"He couldn't carry the body without assistance."

"That is explained, in a vague way. I'm told a blacksmith on the opposite corner saw a cart backed up to the undertaker's door about that time, and two men putting a long box in it. It didn't occur to him there was anything extraordinary in the happening. All he can say is the men were strangers."

"He must be less curious than most villagers," was Delancey's comment.

Briefly he turned the matter in his mind.

"What are the authorities doing now?"

"Searching, Dr. Pugh says. He thinks they will find Guy, even if the body is hidden outside the village."

"And what do you think of Dr. Pugh?" he asked.

"I don't like him," she said. "But that's no reason to suspect him. Is it?"

"No," he agreed. "Not strictly speaking. I think he's a queer fish. And that's as far as I get. . . . Thanks for all you have told me."

He rose to go.

"I wonder," she said, rising too, "if you would do me a favor?"

"Command me."

"The revolver I loaned you has been taken by the officers."

"Yes."

"Won't you let me lend you another?"

"The only one you have left. I can't take it."

"But I don't need it," she urged.

"How do you know? With things that are happening."

"They won't attack a woman."

"I'm not sure of that."

"I am safe," she persisted. "But I feel you are in danger. Please take it, just for to-night, if you won't keep it longer."

"It's sweet of you to care. But I can't do it."

"You must—to please me. . . . If you will wait a moment——"

Protest was forestalled by her quick turn and disappearance. Chagrined, but touched afresh by her solicitude, Delancey waited on the piazza. She was gone only a few minutes.

"There," she said, as she came to where he stood in the darkness, and put something hard and rather heavy in his coat pocket. "Thank you."

"I feel I should be whipped for accepting this," he said as his fingers closed on the butt of a revolver.

"That's nonsense. . . . Will you call me if anything of interest develops later in the evening?"

"Certainly. Or if it is too late, then early in the morning."

"To-night, please. I can't sleep. And I will keep within reach of the telephone. Is it a promise?"

"Yes," he said.

"Au revoir."

Again she was gone. But for all its coldness the revolver upon which his fingers still closed seemed a link between them. He went carefully down the dusky path to the gate, and with an effort of memory determined the way to the hotel. Some one's advice, some written or spoken word influenced him to keep close to the curb, and away from houses and trees.

As he turned in to the hotel he first saw the glowing tip of Caswell's cigar. It was furiously smoked, so that it burned with steady brightness. Until it was removed for speech as Delancey put foot on the steps.

"Hullo," said Caswell.

"I've been over to see the Countess."

"Yes."

From Caswell's inflection one could gather that, under the circumstances, he thought the call peculiar. Delancey went on to explain.

"She wanted to tell me about the disappearance of her brother's body."

"That's interesting."

Again Caswell puffed vehemently, and took the glowing cigar from his mouth.

"Because," he resumed, "Dr. Pugh has just been here to explain the same thing to me."

"Then we've nothing to tell each other," said Delancey. "The Countess heard about it from him."

"Still, I'd like to check up. What did he tell her?"

"Not much. While he was with us at the judge's office some man came to the undertaker's, and sent a boy in charge out to get cigarettes. When the lad got back the man was gone. Also, as they later ascertained, Beddle's body. . . . No clue, except that a blacksmith on the opposite corner saw a cart backed up to the door, and two men put a long box on it. He can't describe them. That's all."

"Not quite," Caswell said deliberately. "Another person saw the men with the cart and box. One was a tall man with a limp."

"Bjerstedt?"

"We have the same idea. Did you see him on the moor this afternoon?"

"No."

"He was there. And I had a feeling he was spying. He half started after us when we went off with the foreman."

"Why didn't you tell me before?" asked Delancey.

"Our guide was too close then. And he would have misunderstood it; or understood too much."

"There isn't anything we can put a finger on. But I think he's a bad egg."

"He'll bear watching," said Caswell. "To get back to Beddle. It is reported that around noon a cart with two men aboard, and a long box in it, was seen near the water-front, headed east out of town."

"If they know all that, why can't they trace it?"

"Why can't they trace anything?"

In his gesture of irritation Caswell's cigar described a glowing arc.

"If I were in Boston, in New York, in any place with a decently organized police system,—I'd know what to do about the disappearance of Ed and Miss Strong. As it is, we're stumped. . . . All I can think of is engagement of some detective agency. That means days. And every hour is precious."

"At least," said Delancey, "we don't have to sit still. Let's walk down to the wharf."

"A good idea. There may be a guard to keep us from going out to the *Viva*. But they can't prevent us from talking to Andersen, if he's there."

They rose together, and picked their way to the nearest street leading down to the harbor.

"Only one trouble with Andersen," observed Caswell; "he executes orders so faithfully I have to be careful what I say."

Stumbling a little over depressions and hummocks in brick sidewalks, they went past the row of fish-houses, and the Yacht Club aristocratically aloof. And down the long wharf, with the persistent slap of rollers under their feet as they walked out to the end.

The harbor was very dark, and seemed more so in contrast to the white rim of waves toppling here and there. Red lanterns of boats they could not see bobbed fantastically in unruly water.

Straining at details of the scene before them, they were unaware of a rowboat's approach until it tied up to the gangway on the lee side, with a sharp command:

"Now—up!"

Delancey's fingers closed instinctively on the revolver in his pocket as Caswell cried out:

"Hullo, Andersen!"

"Yes, Captain," came the decorous answer from below.

As they leaned over the rail, the last of three figures in glistening oilskins stepped from the tossing dory and started up to them.

"I thought you might be here. Did you send a boat in at noon?"

"Yes, Captain."

"Sorry I forgot about it. I was busy. Any news?"

Andersen hesitated, pulling his mustache.

"Only this, Captain. This afternoon a man came, and say he is the sheriff. That he has a right to come aboard. He wants to find something."

"What did you do, Andersen?"

"Told him to go to hell, Captain."

"Quite right, Andersen. Did he?"

The skipper's blue eyes retained their look of perfect seriousness.

"He went ashore, Captain."

"Anything else?" asked Caswell.

"I discharge Johnson."

"What for?"

"I find him in your cabin, Captain."

"You fired him for that?"

"He was in your desk, Captain."

Caswell whistled.

"I wonder what he could want there."

Andersen pulled his mustache.

"You remember, Captain," he said presently, "the white yawl?"

"Where was it?"

"By the *Viva* it anchored, yesterday morning."

"It must have come in after I went ashore. And I didn't see it last night, or this morning. What about it?"

"When we come back from taking you ashore, I find one of her crew on the *Viva*. I kick him off."

"That's right."

"He is Johnson's brother. One time I have both under me."

Caswell pondered, while Delancey stood by, mystified.

"What does this mean to you, Andersen?" he said presently.

"I don't know, Captain," the skipper answered. "On the yawl, a man watches us, all the time. I see him often."

Caswell turned to Delancey.

"What do you make of it, Slim?"

"If I were to guess, I'd say our friends the rum runners, supplementing Nyatt officials."

"But what do they want of me?"

"Must I remind you, Pop, 'A man is known by the company he keeps;' and it seems everybody is after me."

"Rogues and jackasses," rasped the *Viva's* owner, and turned to Andersen.

"Been hearing any gossip to-day?"

Andersen shifted his balance, and looked uneasy.

"About us, I mean."

"Some little talk there was on the wharf. I knock one man down."

"Thanks for the compliment. Since I have to rely on you, I want to explain. First, Mr. Anthony has disappeared; and we've got to find him."

"Yes, Captain."

"And the Nyatt officers are foolish enough to think Mr. Delancey had something to do with the killing of a man named Beddle. That's why they're snooping around."

"Yes, Captain."

"That's all. Only I depend on you to keep a sharp lookout. I may need your help any time."

Andersen gravely inclined his head.

"You go aboard?" he asked.

"Not now. As matters are, I think we'll spend the night ashore. But I'd like to have you within reach later. No knowing what will turn up. Let's see——"

He looked at his watch by the light of a match, and closed it with a decisive snap.

"It's about nine-thirty. Pull out to the boat, to make sure there's no trouble aboard, and be back here about eleven."

"Yes, Captain."

As he spoke Andersen turned toward the gangway. Caswell and Delancey watched him go down and step into the boat. He took the tiller with a word of curt command, and the men at the oars shoved off vigorously.

"The best skipper I ever had," said Caswell when the boat was swallowed by darkness. "He's a real friend."

They picked their way up the wharf in silence, each pondering the same thing. Until near the gate at which hackmen in summer clamored for the tourist trade something in the inky darkness of a freight shed fell with a clatter. They turned as one. But nothing further was heard; and nothing appeared.

"A box, probably," said Caswell, as they started on. "But it gave me a start. I suppose we ought to be armed."

"I have a revolver," observed Delancey.

"Another one. Where did you get it?"

"The Countess lent it to me."

Caswell puckered his lips, but did not whistle.

"As I remember her testimony, it must be the last of the three her brother bought. I don't want to be nosey. But what's up?"

"Nothing," said Delancey a bit sharply. "I didn't want to take it. She insisted. Somehow she got the notion I was likely to be attacked."

"That's no dream, is it?"

When Delancey did not answer Caswell permitted himself a slight grimace.

"I see," he observed, and the matter was dropped.

As they reached the corner of South Water Street a car driven from somewhere on the Cliff road swung sharply into a lane straight ahead. Its tail-light, the only one displayed, made a diminishing blob of red. That vanished as they traced it up the hill.

"Let's go that way," said Delancey. "It will be less windy."

Mutely assenting, Caswell took the lead. Cautiously, for what was left of a brick walk set snares for heel and toe, they picked their way. There were no street lights; and houses showed only as dim shapes on either side.

Caswell walked on the right. Stooping to avoid an overhanging branch, he brought his head into sharp contact with some obstruction. Delancey halted at his exclamation.

"What's the matter?"

"A car with the lights off," said Caswell resentfully. "I feel as if my skull were split."

Waiting for him to emerge, Delancey took stock of surroundings. A high fence overrun with vines shut off all but chimney and roof line of a house behind it. A little to the left a square that was dark, yet somewhat different in hue, might be a gate. He took a step towards it as a thread of brightness brought out the lustre of its ivy mantle.

Another step, two steps; and a man ran into his arms. Mutual surprise preceded mutual attack.

Closing in, each sought to throw the other. In this the stranger had the better grip. Delancey's first impulse had been to draw his revolver; but the foe had his right arm pinioned. He felt himself give way as they swayed towards the open gate. It seemed this new enemy meant to dispose of him in the yard.

Farther backward, and the dim line of light crossed his foe's face.

"Ed!" panted Delancey.

"Hush!" muttered Anthony.

It was over in a minute. They fell apart as Caswell, free from perplexities of car and foliage, hurried to Delancey's aid. Anthony checked the exclamation on his astonished lips.

"Shut up, Pop! And be quick. We must get out of this."

"But where——?" Caswell persisted.

"Sh! Come on!"

Stooping as he hugged the wall, Anthony ran towards lights not far ahead. As Caswell and Delancey, bringing up the rear, toiled after him they were conscious of a disturbance in the house behind the high fence. A sound of confused voices.

Anthony veered to the right, and vanished. They dived after and landed, one might suppose from fragrant softness, in a flower-bed.

"Don't ask me a thing," Anthony whispered.

They sat there listening to their quickened heartbeats, until a rush of feet up the street stopped almost opposite their refuge.

"What do you think?" asked a voice thick with excitement and exertion.

"He must have gone this way," came the answer.

"Come on, then. He can't be far off."

Running again, Anthony's pursuers passed into the mystery of the night.

CHAPTER 10

AN APPARITION AND INVASION

"Holy Smoke!"

Caswell had his first fair look at Anthony as they came under a street lamp. Walking now, they had gained the comparative security of Centre Street.

"Not so pretty, I suppose," said Anthony, looking at dried blood on his right hand and coat sleeve, and purple marks of rope on both wrists. "I had to break the glass panel of a door in getting out, and my fist was the only thing handy."

Stretching both arms above his head, he rotated his body, testing its flexibility.

"Anybody got a cigarette?" he said. "Thanks."

He took one from the box Delancey silently offered.

They waited while he struck a match and flipped it away with the first deep inhalation.

"What news?" he asked with obvious effort to keep his voice even. "Of Nell—I mean Miss Strong?"

"If you know anything about her, you're the man everybody is looking for," observed Delancey.

"We were blackjacked together. . . . To think they could do a thing like that to her!"

Anthony paused, shocked to silence by the thought.

"Go on," Caswell prodded. "Tell us what you can. There is more than you know of to be cleared up."

Thinking back, Anthony quickened his gait. And he condensed much in eagerness to reach the climax of his story.

"I don't know if you've heard anything about what happened after we separated. I was pulled into a fight with some bruiser set up to put me out."

He pulled hard at his cigarette, and went on.

"So I didn't get back to the boat that night. And Nell asked me to go out to the moor with her next morning. I left word for you at the hotel. Did you get it?"

"Yes," Caswell answered. "But we couldn't find hide or hair of you afterward."

"Good reason," said Anthony grimly. "We motored out towards the South Shore. Pretty day, and all that. Away out near the beach we got out to look at an old black house on a hill."

"What!" exclaimed Delancey. "Were you there?"

"I don't know where I was—for a long time. What day is this?"

"Sunday."

"Two days since we landed. Well, I was out from Saturday morning till two or three hours ago. . . . They got me; and must have got Nell, too, on a ridge just above the shore.

"We wandered over there from the house I spoke of, and left the car. I was ahead going up-hill. I heard her scream, and turned as quick as I could. She wasn't in sight. I thought, though, I saw her dress; just a glimpse. And I pelted down to the place. There was a sort of juniper screen about it.

"As I got there somebody tripped me. Two or three piled on. And a cloth saturated with something was jammed down on my face. I hadn't the ghost of a chance. I just know I was yanked into a hole in the hillside."

They had reached the hotel, and Anthony pushed the gate open.

"We'd better stay outside," said Caswell. "It's easier to tell who's around."

As they drew three chairs tilted against the wall into position for service he continued.

"And the next thing you knew?"

"I was in the cellar of the house I escaped from, just before I ran into you."

"Did you see anybody there?" asked Delancey.

"To-night Bjerstedt appeared."

"That dog! I felt he was at the bottom of our trouble."

"All the same, I think to-night he saved my life. Lever, the handsome pug I beat in the little scrap mentioned, was along, too, and keen to cut my throat. I guess he'd have done it, if Bjerstedt allowed. With hands and feet tied I couldn't offer much resistance."

"How did you get away?" said Caswell.

"Thanks to Bjerstedt's clumsiness with knots. He loosened my hands to take a little food, and bungled tying me up again. After awhile I worked loose."

"Hurt much?"

"Only sore and bruised. Are you game to start right now looking for Nell?"

"Of course. Got anything for a starter?" asked Delancey.

"The men who had me probably know where she is. They practically admitted it in working on me. Tried to make me believe they had you, too."

"What did they seem to be driving at?" asked Caswell.

"I couldn't make out. Some nutty notion we came here looking for the gang; whatever they are."

"My little joke," Delancey observed, "has led to unfortunate results."

"Of course," Caswell interjected, "you don't know that Slim is suspected of murder."

"Who's killed?"

"Beddle was found on the shore this morning, shot to death. We found him. And Nyatt officers make a lot of the fact that Slim had a revolver of the calibre the murderer used."

"But you're not under arrest," said Anthony to Delancey.

"Only informally detained. The Island's my jail."

"It's rotten. I'm sorry."

After a moment filled by the voice of the wind, Anthony added briskly, "But you'll come out all right. Right now we've got to find Nell."

Caswell's question was interrupted by the opening of the hotel door. Turning, they saw the youth enamored of reading framed in the light. He peered about, and called:

"You there, Mr. Delancey?"

"Yes." Delancey leaned forward. "What is it?"

"Somebody wants you on the telephone. Very particular."

"All right."

"In the office," the boy said as he hurried past.

Delancey picked up the receiver, and was instantly saluted:

"Is that you, Dick?"

"Yes," he answered.

"It's Greta speaking. Forgive me for calling you again. I'm so nervous. And I've a feeling that something has happened. I wanted to know about you."

"We've found Anthony. Or rather he has found himself."

"Where was he?"

"Tied in the cellar of a house in the village."

"And Nell?" she asked.

"He thinks the same men had her, too."

"Does he know who they are?"

"No."

"What are you going to do?"

"Hunt."

"Isn't there, please, something I can do?"

"I'm afraid not—now."

"But you'll let me hear from you again to-night, won't you?"

"Yes."

He thought he heard her sigh.

"Well," she said, "I must not keep you. Good hunting!"

He turned away, slowly, ignoring the open-mouthed guardian of the office. Caswell and Anthony suspended conversation as he regained the piazza.

"What's up?" asked Caswell.

"The Countess wanted to know if there was any news."

"Oh!" said the *Viva's* owner with the same inflection by which he had greeted disclosure of the loan of the revolver. After a moment in which Delancey offered no further information he resumed:

"Ed and I have been putting things together."

"What do you make of everything?"

"Nothing definite. But it seems we stumbled into a pretty desperate band of crooks."

"Does Ed think as we do about Nyatt authorities?"

"Nothing doing," Anthony said decisively. "We're better off on our own. First, let's give the house I escaped from a thorough looking-over. Got your revolver?"

"Yes," Delancey answered, feeling a bulge in his pocket.

"If those thugs are still there, perhaps we can wring something from them. I'd like," piously, "a chance at two of them in a fair fight. Come on."

Just as the trio rose a large figure came lurching through the gate. They paused while it advanced. It reached the steps, and they recognized Dr. Pugh.

"Good-evening," he said in his cold, queerly pitched voice.

"Good-evening," Delancey answered for the three.

"Have you anything to report?" the medical examiner pursued, bracing himself against a pillar.

"Our friend Anthony has turned up," Caswell said in a matter-of-fact way.

"Is that so?"

The doctor appeared to ponder this development.

"Where is he?" he asked at length.

"Here."

Caswell waved his cigar in Anthony's direction. Dr. Pugh leaned forward, seeking to pierce the shadows.

"What happened?" he asked.

"I got a blow on the head, and was out for a while," answered Anthony concisely. "Came to this evening."

The doctor digested this meagre explanation, and put his next question deliberately:

"What about Miss Strong?"

"I don't know."

In a forward movement of his great body the doctor leaned towards Anthony like some amorphous monster of the night. His voice remained the same,—small, evenly metallic.

"She was supposed to be with you."

"We were together yesterday morning."

The inquisitor waited. But no further explanation was vouchsafed. Caswell broke heavy silence with a question:

"Is Beddle's body found?"

"No."

"What's your theory about the reason for taking it?"

"The only one I can think of would not appeal to you," said the doctor deliberately. With this observation he swayed again, so that he stood upright and balanced.

"I must be going," he said, and looked down at Anthony. "You know, you ought to communicate with the authorities."

"I realize it."

"Good-night."

"Good-night."

Slowly the doctor stepped down from the piazza, and receded with a squeaky signal of the gate. There was a moment of quiet.

"That was about fifty-fifty," said Delancey. "Nothing told, nothing learned."

"Was I right in holding back with him?" asked Anthony. "I somehow don't fancy the cut of his jib."

"All we know," observed Caswell, tossing away the butt of his cigar, "is that he is a playmate of Flaherty and Bjerstedt. They're the unfathomable three."

Stepping into the streak of light from the hotel office, he looked at his watch.

"We'd better be going. And I think we'd better pick up reinforcements. Andersen's a grand man. And there'll be two huskies with him."

With anchoring hands to their hats they started down the nearest lane. They ploughed through windrows of withered leaves; and what was left of hardy foliage rustled wildly above them.

Still strong, the wind had yet abated, so that only occasionally its shrill crescendo covered the persistent boom of surf ringing the island. The sinking moon played hide-and-seek with masses of solid looking clouds. In a bright moment, like speeding specks they saw against the moon's face a flock of wild duck southward bound.

"Storm's blowing itself out," said Caswell. "But it'll be rough for another twenty-four hours."

"That probably means," Delancey remarked, "we'll find the sheriff arriving aboard the *Viva* with a posse, so we can't run away."

"I don't think," Caswell responded, "he will come again with anything less. Andersen has a chilling eye."

"Look out!" said Anthony sharply, and laid hold on each. With a powerful jerk he pulled them back from the street to the curb. In the nick of time; for promptly as he acted a lightless motor nearly grazed them. It swung wide on the corner a few yards ahead, and sped towards the shore.

"Thanks, Ed," said Caswell dryly.

Anthony did not answer. Oblivious, he darted across the street, and stooped by the fence on the opposite side. They saw him fumble with the leaves, feeling about impatiently. Presently he rose, sifting a handful until he held a scrap of something in his hand. To see it better he impatiently lighted a match.

And he lighted more than one. As sometimes happens with little cards closely packed, he incautiously ignited the lot. The spurt of flame scorched his fingers, and the piece of paper he had found. His fingers relaxed their grip in a stab of pain. The packet fell blazing to the ground.

To extinguish the fire and set his foot on what remained of the paper was the work of a moment. Then, shaking his burned hand, he came towards Caswell and Delancey, who waited under a corner light.

"What is it?" asked Delancey.

"Something thrown from that car," Anthony explained. "I saw a hand at the window, just as it went past. Unless I'm mistaken, this piece of paper was blown across to the fence over there, and held by the wind."

"Maybe," said Caswell. "Let's see."

Three heads together, they bent over what was left of a small square folded in Anthony's hand. It had been burned through at the corner of the fold, and charred a little in the edges. The writing left was plain enough.

Nobody spoke until they had read it twice, confirming their first impression of its contents. Even when intact it had been brief. This was left:

> ". . . to anybody that will help . . . been abducted . . . to-night (Sunday) . . . look also for Edward Anthony . . . fear serious harm . . . death threatened if I refuse. . . . But I do not mean to yield.
>
> "Ellen Strong."

For a moment no one spoke. Anthony stood staring at the ground.

"As near as that," he said at length. "And we missed her."

"That's spilled milk. It's no good to moon. The question is,—What shall we do now?"

Caswell prodded him with friendly sharpness.

"This alters our plan," suggested Delancey. "There's no use in going to that house now. It's probably abduction by water."

"What do you advise?"

Anthony turned to Caswell.

"Ask Andersen," Caswell answered promptly. "It's providential he is here; and the boat, too. . . . Let me see the note again."

He took it from Anthony's hand, and scanned it once more.

"That's good," he remarked as he returned it. "Writing firm and well spaced. She's got her wits about her. Now let's get down to the wharf."

With Anthony setting a pace hard to follow they hurried on to the end of the pier. At first the tossing water seemed tenantless. But as they leaned over the rail on the lee side Andersen called from the dark:

"I am here, Captain."

Half-way up the gangway, he stepped into the light.

"Do you come aboard?"

"Perhaps," said Caswell. "I want to talk with you. How many men have you?"

"Two, Captain."

"Good. Now come up a moment."

In a minute he stood beside Caswell, a figure of composed expectancy in dripping oilskins.

"You see Mr. Anthony is here."

Andersen nodded, and said gravely:

"I am glad."

"But a lady in whom all of us are interested has been abducted. . . . You know this word in English, Andersen?"

"Yes, Captain."

"Then I'll explain further. We think she is being taken aboard a boat to-night. We've got to stop it. We must find her."

"Very well, Captain."

There was no sign that Andersen's pulse had risen a beat. Delancey regarded him with curiosity. Anthony somehow took comfort. In Caswell's air authority and deference were about equally blended, as he said with a characteristic grimace:

"I forgot to tell you her name, Andersen. It's Strong."

On this observation the skipper retired to self-communion.

"Well?" said Caswell presently, with a tinge of impatience.

"I think, Captain, she will be aboard the white yawl."

"Why?"

Caswell pounced on the suggestion. Unhurried, Andersen continued:

"The black power boat you remember?"

"Yes."

"It ran alongside about one hour ago. Some message for the yawl. And soon the yawl it towed to the south'ard."

With a slow sweep of his right hand Andersen pointed over the harbor.

"But why," said Caswell, not waiting for him to marshal afresh his conversational forces, "do you think Miss Strong will be on the white yawl?"

"Both boats, they belong to a gang. . . . Rum runners. . . . For a lady the yawl is a more pleasant boat, and safer."

"In other words," cut in Caswell, "it's a hunch."

Andersen inclined his head.

"But a sensible one."

"Fine. Then let's get at her."

Caswell was already at the top of the gangway when Andersen checked him.

"We cannot do it to-night, Captain."

"Why not?" snapped the *Viva's* owner. "If they get about, we can."

"Shoals there are," explained Andersen unruffled, "where the *Viva* might go aground. I know."

"Then why won't they go aground, too?"

"If they do, we get them easier."

"But suppose they get away to-night," the *Viva's* owner expostulated.

Andersen looked over the leaping waters, just then lashed afresh by a burst of the dying gale.

"To-night, in the dark, they will not dare go past the Point. . . . If you order me, I go. But Pete Farren, her skipper, will not take the yawl out. I know him."

Caswell turned to Anthony and Delancey.

"I guess he's right, boys."

And then to the skipper:

"What's your plan, Andersen?"

"They are, I think, in a cove of the South Shore. Small place, but shelter and enough water. We start at daybreak. If they are gone, we catch them. . . . The *Viva* sails faster."

"What about the crews?"

"The number is about the same. Their men, they are reckless. Mine are good fighters."

With a moment's consideration, Andersen added seriously:

"I can whip three men, Captain."

"If you do, Andersen," said Caswell, "I'll give you a wrist-watch. Let's get aboard."

"Look sharp," called Andersen to his men somewhere below, and started down the gangway. Caswell and Anthony picked their way after him. But Delancey hung back. He hesitated, and hesitated even more to say what was on his mind. The necessity, however, became imperative when the dory was alongside with sailors at the oars.

Andersen stood by as Caswell and Anthony prepared to step in. At that moment the *Viva's* owner noted Delancey's disappearance, and turned inquiringly.

"What's the matter?" he called, seeing Delancey's figure outlined against the rail.

"Can you wait a few minutes?" Delancey responded, making a trumpet of his hands.

"What for?" said Caswell with what power he could command in a rush of wind.

Delancey did not answer at once. He looked down at them for a moment or two, then proceeded to make himself heard:

"I want to speak to the Countess before we go."

"What for?" trumpeted back Caswell, while the others stood by.

"I promised to."

Caswell turned to Andersen.

"Will it make any difference?"

"I think not, Captain."

"All right," shouted Caswell to Delancey. "Make it short."

As he hurried away from the wharf Delancey was half-irritated with himself. "Why am I doing this?" he asked. "I am making myself ridiculous. For nothing."

What if he had promised to telephone Greta again that night? Promises involving other persons were always conditional. He could explain to-morrow. At a corner he paused, momentarily resolved to turn back; but he went on.

He found his feet taking him in the direction of the hotel. After all it was the thing to do. The McCardle's house was doubtless locked for the night, and there would be no way of making his presence known to Greta. Unless he threw pebbles against the window like a larky boy.

The hotel was locked, too, and dark to boot. He applied himself diligently to the bell, which presently threatened to part company from its connection in his hand. At last he heard a stir within, preceding gingerly opening and a suspicious query:

"Who is it?"

It was the stout proprietress of the hotel.

"Richard Delancey," he answered.

"Do you want a room?"

"No," he explained. "I want to telephone."

"Oh!"

Her accent was significant of displeasure. After silence so prolonged he half-expected to see the door shut against him, it was opened wider, and she said:

"Come in."

"Thank you," he responded to her retreating form, briefly defined as she paused to turn on a hall light.

"You know where it is. Be sure you close the front door when you go out."

With the swinging motion of a stout person in slippers she climbed the stairs and disappeared. Delancey breathed easier as he picked up the receiver. A snoozing telephone operator answered sooner than he expected, and gave him the number with only one mistake.

"Not 'R,'" he reminded her. "'W,' please."

From the speed of her response he judged Greta must have been sitting within reach of the instrument at her end.

"Yes, Dick," she said.

"How did you know who it was?"

"It's easy. What is the news?"

"We have heard from Miss Strong."

"What happened?"

"Kidnapped."

"That is fantastic."

With a moment's reflection she went on:

"Who did it?"

"I can't tell. The fact is, we haven't rescued her yet."

"Then how do you know?"

Her voice vibrated with impatience.

"Anthony picked up a note signed by her. Or, rather, part of it."

"What are you going to do?"

"Take a chance in going after the boat of some fellows we suspect."

"I'll go with you."

"But you can't," he expostulated.

"Why not?"

"It's too dangerous."

"Nonsense. I drove an ambulance in Belgium during the war, and was at a first-aid station near Ypres for three months."

"But that was war—and duty."

He mentally braced himself against further attack, and moved to forestall it.

"There are only men on the *Viva*, you know."

"Aren't they gentlemen?" she demanded.

"I trust so," he floundered. "But——"

"Aren't you hoping to rescue Nell?"

"Of course."

"You can't tell what condition she will be in. Anyway, she will need a woman."

"I understand. But what will Caswell think?"

"He is intelligent. . . . Come, and get me."

He heard the click of a receiver returned to its hook. So that was the end of it. Baffled, he felt his way along the dark hall, and left the hotel, carefully closing the door behind him. Greta was waiting when he reached McCardle's.

"My luggage," she explained as she placed a small bag in his hand.

With little said, for he was perturbed by dread of his companions' resentment, and Greta appreciated his mood, they walked rapidly to the head of the wharf. The light at the shore end was out. Pausing a moment, they heard far above migrant wild geese calling.

"Keep close," said Delancey.

Without mishap they reached the far end. There a figure waited at the gangway. It was Caswell.

"Not coming?" he asked as they approached.

"Yes," answered Delancey. "The Countess wants to go with us."

"I'm afraid——" Caswell began.

"I know you are," said Greta. "Danger for a woman—and only men aboard. I know all that. What you haven't thought of is that if you find Nell, she will need a woman with her. . . . You can imagine what she is going through. Do I sound reasonable?"

"I suppose that is so."

Caswell seemed struck with the thought.

"That is it." Greta clinched it briskly. "And I am not in the least afraid. As to sailing, I am better than most men. . . . You agree with me now, don't you?"

"I suppose I must." And he added, "I admire your courage."

"I told you Dr. Caswell would appreciate my reason for coming."

She gave Delancey a half-smile as they went down the gangway. If the rest of the party were astonished at her appearance they gave no sign. Anthony greeted her with a little bow, as imperturbable Andersen helped her into the boat.

Waiting a minute for a long swell to pass, the sailors pushed off, and Andersen headed the boat into the wind. Wet with flying spray, they passed from feeble light to darkness in which waves seemed to reach for the boat with hands that slipped along its side, then vanish in a mocking salute. They headed steadily for a spot of red that rose and fell, often lost to view but fixed in its station.

Seated midway, and facing Andersen, Greta saw the Point light wink and turn, wink and turn,—wink. In a sky that somehow seemed to be bearing down upon the earth stars framed in heavy clouds shone with implacable brightness. The hoarse voice of waves that thundered incessantly upon the shore penetrated to the marrow of being. Greta shivered.

From his station aft the voice of Andersen, steady as the heart that beat in his breast, came occasionally to the party so completely committed to his charge.

"Easy with the port oars. . . . A little starboard. . . ."

The spot of red that so magnetized straining eyes grew larger, and associated itself with the dark shape of a boat. Then the seawise recognized the forward lantern.

A few boat lengths from the *Viva*, Andersen blew a whistle. At that dark forms appeared on deck and ranged themselves along the rail. The dory edged in, caught a rolling crest, and Caswell planted his feet on the ladder at Andersen's word of command. Next came Greta, with a buoyant spring disdaining assistance to the deck.

Presently all were aboard without mishap, and the boat slung in its davits. Caswell turned to Greta with a little bow of the old school,—stiff, but instinct with courtesy.

"Welcome to the *Viva*. Present accommodations are not all I would offer a lady. But you will pardon that, I know. Will you do me the honor to occupy my stateroom?"

"I think," she said, "you are very kind. And you understand so well why I have done this thing I will not attempt to explain it further. . . . As to rest, I confess I am very tired. I think I had better say good-night."

She allowed Caswell to steady her as they went carefully to the companionway. There she paused for a comradely nod before she went below.

While the crew jumped to Andersen's directions, making the boat snug for the night, Delancey and Anthony stood silently at the rail. Both looked questioningly over the waters. But Anthony's was a more sombre thought.

"I wonder——" he began, breaking off abruptly. Such anxieties are not discussed.

It was but a few moments before Caswell joined them.

"Hadn't we better turn in?" he said. "We pull anchor at daybreak."

"I think so," Anthony answered, and they moved away from the rail. Caswell stopped for a last word with the skipper.

"I leave it to you, Andersen. Remember we want to start the minute it is safe."

"Yes, Captain," said the skipper composedly.

Activity on deck continued a little longer. Then, last of all, Andersen went below. The bobbing lantern forward and the red light aft continued their mutual curtsies as the *Viva* swayed and swung.

An hour or so elapsed before a stout working boat with two men at the oars appeared on the crest of a wave hard by. By skillful seamanship it was held nearly stationary as a big man sitting amidships inspected the *Viva*. If there was vigilance aboard the yacht, it gave no sign.

At a word from the man in charge the boat was brought alongside. He noted the fact that the yacht's ladder was not drawn up for the night. Carelessness, or trust in the guardianship of wild weather.

With difficulty, for he had a club-foot and missed connection in his first effort, the leader of these midnight marauders reached the ladder and drew himself up as the boat was swept from beneath him. Carefully, and it seemed painfully, he climbed to the deck. His crew meantime stood by, ready with their oars.

He moved from the murkiness aft to the comparative brightness of the swinging lantern. There he stood a full minute, a picture of concentration. Slowly, putting his ailing foot forward with extreme care, he went down the companionway.

CHAPTER 11

A SACRIFICE AND A SEQUEL

Nell emerged from unconsciousness with the feeling of one flung aside by a tornado. She gropingly recalled a great darkness, a flash of light, and a deafening roar.

It was very difficult to understand. She had stooped on a slope by the shore to look at a heart-shaped purple flower.

That moment a feeling of danger possessed her. She had turned,—but not quickly enough. . . . A large hand came over her shoulder, clapping a handkerchief on her mouth and nostrils.

All this was clear. And the look of her assailant, a thin-faced man of a Latin race. This, with a moment's comprehension of an opening in the hill.

She shook herself free sufficiently to scream. Only once. Then the cloth saturated with something sickish sweet was over her face again. And she felt herself grasped by more pairs of hands than one. With vanished light her mind drifted to sleep.

When she had checked up these impressions the problem of the present emerged. . . . Where was she? What further had happened? . . . And what was the tumult in her ears?

She was somewhere on a bed. A poor bed, apparently, with broken springs. At each movement it contributed to the pangs of nature.

Seemingly night prevailed. A window was outlined between dimness without and the murky dark within. In the absence of knowledge nothing in the room defined itself to her eyes.

Now she understood clamor that enveloped her. The uproar of the wind. A great storm raged, with spurts of wrath Wagner sometimes suggested in superb moments of The Ring.

From exterior circumstances she turned back to herself. She was on a bed, apparently fully dressed. And free to move;—to scream, too, if that would help her. With no sign of life about, and the wind's shrieking outside, it was palpably useless.

She was cold, and hungry, and thirsty, and faint. Her physical and mental energies at low ebb, she lay there—waiting.

After a while, when the strain of self-imposed inactivity had fretted her nerves almost beyond endurance, she heard a movement near by. Apparently just outside the room.

It was one of those noises that, unidentified, somehow suggest human agency. Nell looked in the direction from which it came; in a minute or so a streak of light showed. She judged it entered under a door.

Next the sound of a key inserted, with fumbling, as if it did not fit perfectly. Then it turned raspingly, and the door was opened.

No rush of light flooded the room. Behind a meagre candle, which she held aloft, stood a dark woman of foreign aspect. As she approached to set the candle on a table by the bed Nell saw she was middle-aged, with the look of mixed races in South Pacific islands. Not one, however, of those dark-skinned children of pleasure. Her appearance suggested toil and maternity. Some laborer's wife, probably.

"Who are you?" Nell asked as the woman put the candle down.

The woman shook her head.

"Don't you speak English?"

Another shake of the head. And the woman was in retreat to the door. She walked, despite her clumsy look, with a free stride.

She vanished, but speedily appeared again. Now she carried a basin, a towel, and a pitcher of water, even a cake of soap. These she deposited on the table with a gesture of invitation.

Once more she vanished. This time she closed the door.

While food would have come more graciously, Nell was not without gratitude as she rose for the meagre toilet possible.

As she examined the room in the candle-light she saw it was of generous size, and nearly square. From the fireplace, darkly cold now, a ceiling so low she felt herself almost able to touch it, and the low, deep windows with their heavy casing, she judged the house must be one of those New England survivals of colonial days.

Was she imprisoned in the lone house on the moor? She could not tell with shuttered windows. Wondering if she might free one of the bars, she had taken a step in that direction when she heard a hand at the door.

At once she turned from the window, with an air of nonchalance towards the bed. She was standing beside it when the door, pushed from without, opened wide. At the sill a figure stooped, and straightened up.

A third time the mute woman entered, bearing a tray. Giving Nell, who sat on the bed, a casual glance, she put the tray on the table, and threw back the enfolding napkin.

Coffee, eggs and toast. Nose and eye were practically synchronous in their registration. And the senses rejoiced.

This time there was no attempt at conversation. When the woman turned away Nell concentrated on the table. As she ate and drank life's aspect became more tolerable.

Why she had been abducted defied conjecture. At least it was some comfort to know that her captor did not mean to make her go hungry. In a contemplative way she explored a coat pocket. So her hand came in contact with a little package. With definite purpose she explored the pocket on the other side. From that she drew a card of matches. With anticipatory pleasure the daughter of the age seated herself on the bed, and lighted a cigarette.

She was smoking when a man came in. Whether he exercised greater care, or the door opened more readily through previous use, she did not know. At any rate, he stood on the threshold before she realized any one was near.

He halted in embarrassment she was quick to sense, though he sought to hide it with an air of unconcern. Now he forced a propitiating smile, exposing his teeth.

The expression released a memory Nell had been half-conscious of from the moment of his entrance. The memory of a second of horrified surprise on the moor hillside. This man had been the first assailant in her capture. Then, as now, his lips were drawn back ferociously.

He was short, and slight, and furtive. A jackal that would be a popinjay. There was loathing in her glance as she faced him.

"I remember you," she said.

"Don't be afraid."

He was edging in closer.

"I'm not in the least afraid. Just stay where you are."

He paused, coerced by her firmness.

"Tell me," she commanded, "who sent you. I know you are only some one's servant."

Her contempt stung him. She saw his eyes grow ugly. And he moved a little nearer. Regarding him steadily, she seated herself on the side of the bed, with a foot on the floor. For a minute or so the duel of glances continued. While he did not look away, he shifted his feet uneasily.

"Who sent you?" she said again.

"I can't tell you," he replied sullenly.

"What do you want?"

"I've come to take you away."

"I don't care to go."

With this crisp announcement she turned to press out the embers of her expiring cigarette in a saucer at her elbow. Then she explored her coat pocket for another, seemingly unconscious of his presence.

"You got to go."

He spoke roughly now. But his threat was without visible result. She ignored it until she had lighted the fresh cigarette. She seemed quite at ease. And her voice was even.

"I don't know where I am," she said, "or how I came here. But I won't be taken by surprise again. . . . I'm going to stay here until you let me go, or my friends find me."

"They never will," he asserted.

"Perhaps so. But Nyatt is a small place." As he seemed at loss for words she continued: "I suppose you realize you will go to prison for this."

He bristled at that.

"My friends can take care of me, lady. That's more than your friend can say."

He chuckled in his relish of some mental picture. Nell's glance grew keener; but there was no sharpening of her tone.

"I don't understand," she said, "who it is you mean."

He tilted forward, leering confidentially.

"Then I tell you. Yer gentl'man friend that was with yer on the hill."

"You mean Mr. Anthony, I suppose."

In a reflective moment the match she tossed away fell at his feet.

"What have you done to him?" she asked at length.

"I?" He shrugged his shoulders. "I done nothing."

"Then what have your friends done to him?"

"You saw him fight?" he countered.

"Yes," she answered, "if you mean that affair in the hall, a few nights ago."

"You remember the man he beat?"

"Yes," she said again, and impatiently. "What has that to do with where he is now?"

"He's with him now."

The man made his disclosure about Anthony with undisguised satisfaction.

"Then," said Nell coolly, "perhaps he'll beat him again."

"No." Her informant gloated. "Not with his hands tied. And gagged, too."

"What will they do to him?"

The question slipped from her lips in the shock of surprise. An instant later she would have recalled it.

"I think," she declared, "you are only trying to frighten me."

He reached into a side pocket, and silently extended his closed hand. It opened, and she saw in its palm a lock of brown hair.

"That shows you."

Her recollection was sharpened by a thrill piercing and new. Still she dissembled. The little ferret eyes regarding her dulled with disappointment.

"Will you tell me," she said, "why you brought that to me?"

"They thought you might want to save him."

As she pulled thoughtfully at her cigarette he stood jingling loose change in his pocket. He had rather the air of one on trial.

"I don't see," she said presently, "what he has to do with me. Or what I do has to do with him."

At that his lips writhed again, with a fiercely jocular expression.

"I suppose you know your business, lady," he observed. "But they're goin' to croak him unless you come through."

"'Croak him'?" she questioned.

"Yes. Bean him. You know what I mean."

She considered again.

"And what do you mean by my 'coming through'?"

"Go with me, like I said."

"Where?"

"I dunno."

He shook his head.

"To whom? Who sent you?"

"I can't tell yer."

His face took on an obstinate look.

"You mean you won't tell me. . . . You'd better go. I shall stay here until I am free to go where I please."

"We'll see," he snarled, with a new look of appraisal,—as if he estimated her power of resistance.

A knock at the door checked some supplementary threat on his lips. He broke off to call,—"Come in."

The woman who had thrice visited Nell entered, bearing a note. Silent as before, she went straight to the man and placed the piece of paper in his hand.

"All right," he said, with a gesture towards the door. She departed as softly as a shadow.

Moving a little into the candle-light, at which Nell, inwardly shrinking, nerved herself for battle, he held the note up before his face with the intentness of one to whom reading is a special exertion.

First he stared at the superscription, as if suspecting its source. Then he pored over the note, and laboriously read it again. The distance was too great for Nell to make it out, though she had a view of the few lines scrawled, and a rough drawing in the upper left-hand corner.

Folding the note, the man placed it in his pocket.

"Well," he said, "made up your mind?"

"I've already told you, 'No,'" she answered.

"Then you don't want to save him."

She stood up at that, with a thrill of satisfaction in the fact she was at least his equal in height. If worse came to worse——

"If I believed you," she told him, "I might yield. But I feel what you have told me about Mr. Anthony is a lie."

"You got to take my word."

"But I don't take your word."

A match snapped in his fingers.

"Anyway," he said with a pugnacious thrust of his head, "you leave here to-night."

"I refuse."

"Keep on refusin'. You got to go."

"You can't make me," she asserted, and deliberately reseated herself to emphasize contempt for him.

He made no attempt to touch her, but indulged his eyes in a deliberate inventory. Then he spat on the floor.

"I guess," he said deliberately, "Rosy and me can manage it together."

"She won't help you," Nell asserted with a show of confidence she did not feel.

"Watch, and see. Rosy's goin' with you on yer little trip."

"You'll gag me, I suppose," she said scornfully.

"Oh, no," he leered. "I don't like gals that scratch and bite. There's something easier than that."

As her eyes questioned his meaning he took from a waistcoat pocket two little vials. One yellow, the other green. With a showman's air he held them up to the light. Then together in his hand.

"How long," he asked her, "do you think you been here?"

"Since noon to-day," she answered without hesitation.

At that he laughed, looking at the little vials.

"It's good stuff."

"If it is longer than I thought," she said in sudden doubt, "when did this outrage happen? . . . Tell me."

Still he looked at the vials.

"I've known men," he said, apparently to himself, "kept under by it for a week. . . . The first sleep," holding up the yellow; "and the second." Now he held up the green.

"What good will it do to keep me?" Nell argued, feeling the effort futile. "My friends are sure to find me on this island."

"That's why we're going."

"Where to? I must know."

She looked at him sharply, suspecting a double meaning. Then she went on:

"In a storm. . . . And at this time of night."

"Oh, you don't have to walk," was all he would say. He went on smiling mysteriously.

In a sudden rising she brushed by him. While he moved to place himself between her and the door she walked to a window, and stood there facing its shutters that shook in a blast of wind. From the storm she drew fresh fortitude.

"I won't do it," she said again.

"That's hard on the gent."

Again that new pain disarmed her. She turned, and walked slowly back to the bed.

"Supposing," she said, "I did what you want. How do I know they would let Mr. Anthony go?"

"I'd write a line tellin' them it's O. K."

As she pondered he looked at her encouragingly.

"Anyway, I'll escape, if possible."

"I don't worry about that."

"Write the note, and let me see it."

As though their positions were reversed, she spoke commandingly.

"Sure," he said. "Now you're bein' sensible." He stepped to the door and called: "Rosy, come here."

In a minute or so the woman appeared.

"I want some paper," he said. "And a pencil. You got one?"

She nodded, and vanished. They waited in silence. Once he opened his mouth to speak, but was intimidated by her aloof regard for the ceiling. He was visibly relieved when Rosa came.

Paper and pencil in hand, he approached the table by the bed with a certain diffidence. At his, "Excuse me," she moved away to give him room. Putting the pencil into his mouth, as if to connect it with the organ of speech, he bent in laborious composition. It was finished with a grunt.

"Here," he said, and held the paper out to her.

She read the few words in two sprawling lines:

> "All O. K. with the gent the girl is comin' thru
> "Tim"

"It doesn't say, 'Let him go,'" she observed.

"They'll savey," he said, holding out his hand for the note. "That's the agreement."

"Put in the lock of hair. Then there'll be no mistake."

"If it makes yer feel any better."

The lock was produced and wrapped in the paper.

"How will they get it?" she asked.

"I'm goin' to send it," he snapped. "Give me time."

He walked to the door, which closed after him with creaking emphasis. Then a key grated in the lock.

Nell's eyes ranged slowly over the room, and came to rest on a barred window. She looked back to the door again, and sat a minute or so, listening for some sound without. Within the house it seemed absolutely still.

There might be a chance. Moving swiftly to the window, she raised both hands to the knobs of the bar on its shutter, and pushed upward with all her might. It held fast.

With a little sigh she walked back to the bed. Then suddenly the idea came to her. On the table there her jailor had left an extra sheet of paper and the pencil. She took them, and with a precautionary look at the door wrote a few lines rapidly.

The sheet of paper she folded repeatedly, until it was only a little square. This she concealed in her loosely coiled hair, over the left ear.

Again she reclined and smoked. Still the man signing himself "Tim" did not come. Noting her wrist-watch had run down, she proceeded to wind it. Its faint ticking somehow brought a feeling of comfort.

Her vigilance was a little relaxed when the door opened suddenly and the man stepped into the room.

"I done my part," he said. "You ready?"

She looked about with a shrug.

"It appears my packing is done."

At this bit of satire he blinked stupidly.

"You want Rosy?" he inquired.

"No."

At that he vanished again. Evidently her refusal was of no consequence to him. For the woman Rosa came with a cloak of dark blue stuff, which she extended to Nell. When it was wrapped about her it fell to her heels.

Searching the woman's face, Nell found it neutral. Or was it compassionate?

"Tell me," she hurriedly appealed, "what place he is taking me to."

A hand to her lips, Rosa answered only with a mild smile. With a nod she indicated the open door. As Nell stepped that way she came noiselessly after her.

It was but a short way to go. Along a dusky hall with uneven flooring to a wide door showing discolored white in fluctuant light of a candle the man Tim held. He produced a large brass key, and opened the door to a rush of wind.

Instantly the candle was out. They passed from the house, and Rosa laid a touch of light restraint on Nell's arm. Pausing, she heard the key grate in the lock. In a swift encircling glance she sought to identify her surroundings.

By the faint light filtered through heavy, fast-moving clouds she guessed it was a place somewhere in the region jealously held by old Nyatt families. In the general direction of the moors, and a considerable distance from the shore.

With some inarticulate observation the man took her by the elbow. She flinched at his touch, but made no protest. With Rosa following he guided her a few yards to the right, and along a short walk arched with vines. At its end he opened a gate, and stepped out before her.

Across a street so narrow two cars could hardly pass stood a limousine, with a man at the wheel. He did not turn at their approach. Nell's captor opened the door, and motioned for her to enter.

"I'd rather sit on the left," she said.

"What's the difference?" asked the man suspiciously.

"I always sit on the left."

"Well——" he grumbled, after a minute in which she felt him rein his temper. "Get in."

By a gesture he directed Rosa to follow, pointing to one of the small turned down seats in front. Then he himself stepped in, carefully avoiding Nell's feet, and took a seat on her right.

"Give me a little air," she requested as he swung to the door.

"There's enough. . . . The wind's blowin'."

"I want more," she insisted.

Again a silent debate with himself. At its end he lowered the window on his side a little.

"That won't do," she said, and proceeded to drop the left-hand pane somewhat lower.

Just then the car started, and quickly picked up speed as they swung into a wider street. Seemingly, it was the chauffeur's theory that he had a clear street. For that matter, no one was seen or heard, save once at a corner near the centre of the village.

Two men jumped back to the sidewalk, barely saving their shins as the chauffeur swung right with a quick twist of the wheel. In the swerve Nell lost her balance, so that she was thrown against the door. To protect her face against the lowered window she put up her hand.

Something white whirled from the car, as it sped down a street to the shore.

* * * *

"Ding . . . Dong . . . Dong . . . Ding."

Heedless of night or day, the bell-buoy uttered incessantly its warning. Only its sides emerging from the encompassing waves began to glisten in gilding light.

Of day's approach the man clinging to the bell-support was hardly more conscious than the buoy itself. In stupor his hands sustained the desperate grip by which he had locked them. . . .

With snatches of song a scallop boat came chugging by. It came closer, and closer still, with a change of course that brought it within easy hail.

"What's the matter?" bawled a Down East voice.

The figure on the buoy stirred only with its rise and fall.

"Run alongside," the Yankee voice directed. . . . "Careful."

Canting, the buoy almost buried itself in a wave. In that advantageous moment sinewy hands seized the man who seemed frozen to its surface. With a mighty heave they hauled him over the rail of the *Minnie*.

"I snum!" ejaculated the skipper. "What do you s'pose——?"

The rest of his observation was lost in the accelerated sputter of the engine.

The bell-buoy continued its self-communing:

"Ding . . . Dong . . . Dong . . . Ding."

CHAPTER 12

MORNING

In somewhat abated, but unceasing violence of the sea the *Viva* tugged at her anchor. The wind of dawn struck chill.

From quarters below Andersen appeared, and stood at the rail. As though cast in bronze he kept his post, the while his eyes swept the clarifying scene.

Now the false sky gave way to the real. Clouds streaked through the mist. And in the progressive transfiguration a rising glow where yellow met orange, and the orange melted into flame. Across that glowing band a gray gull flitted in silhouette.

Pressing a button in the rail, Andersen greeted two of the crew who speedily appeared with a curt order. Now he began a thorough inspection of rope and sail. While the wind had veered somewhat, it was still against them.

Satisfied, he gave another order and took the wheel. Free from the anchor, the *Viva* shook herself like a dog from its leash, and drove forward. Andersen brought her about smartly, heading for a cove he knew; a cove on the South Shore. His narrowed eyes constantly swept the horizon.

The *Viva's* course brightened. Presaged by copper flame, the round young sun rose from the sea. Brighter, yet brighter it grew. With sudden radiance above the tossing water day was born.

Easily braced, Andersen drove the *Viva* under full sail. Crests climbing her cutwater were sometimes grayish; again nile green, or the color that is neither blue nor green, but the complexion of deep water. No nuance escaped the skipper's eyes.

Caswell added himself to the scene. A small figure he picked his way, staggering as the wheel turned sharply, to Andersen's side.

"It seems," he said with an accent of slight exasperation, "you don't count much on me."

"Yes, Captain," the skipper answered tranquilly.

"How is everything going?"

"Very well, Captain."

Andersen did not take his eyes from the course. Lingering at his elbow a minute or so, while the seascape told him nothing, Caswell turned to go below.

"I'd better see how Slim and Ed are feeling," he reflected.

Just forward of the companionway his self-communing was interrupted. In sharp impact he collided with a man emerging from the cabin in which he had slept. It did not look like one of the crew.

"What are you doing here?" he said sharply.

No answer.

"Who are you?"

Now the intruder from stooping in the dim light stood up.

"It takes a little explaining," he said.

The impression leaped from Caswell's brain to his lips:

"Bjerstedt! Of all the nerve!"

"For an amateur you are quick on the trigger."

Caswell looked at him in close scrutiny.

"May I take the liberty of asking: Where are the blotches on your face? And where is your pumple foot?"

"I've just left them in your cabin."

"You mean——"

"They're just make-up. Let me explain."

"Another time," Caswell interrupted. "This is a busy morning. And since I didn't ask you aboard, and don't trust you at all,—for the present I'm going to have you tied up."

"Better listen to what I have to say."

"Why should I?" Caswell exploded. "You steal aboard my boat. And there's been nothing but trouble since you fastened on us that first day at the wharf. It wouldn't astonish me to learn you're a thief, and a murderer."

The big man barred the way.

"I am neither of these," he said calmly.

"What, then?"

"I am a secret service man."

"You're a first rate liar."

Caswell's accusation wrought no change in the tall man's face.

"See here——" he began.

Caswell reached for a button summoning men aft.

"Don't do it."

The curtly authoritative voice stayed his hand. As he stood uncertain the big man went on:

"Or rather, do ring, and ask your friends to come here."

Pressing the button, Caswell kept his finger on it to assure prompt response.

"You seem to have thoroughly explored the boat," he observed.

His invader ignored the rebuke.

"Shall we talk in your cabin?" he suggested.

"By all means," Caswell assented ironically. "I didn't know you desired a conference."

A sailor hurrying aft stopped on beholding his employer.

"Ask Mr. Delancey and Mr. Anthony to come to number two cabin," Caswell directed. "As soon as convenient."

The sailor vanished with a rough salute.

"Suppose," the suspect said, "we step in there now." Reading Caswell's hesitation, he continued: "If I wanted to attack you, I wouldn't suggest that you send for your friends."

With a shrug the *Viva's* owner pointed to the open door and followed in. "There's Bjerstedt."

Following a gesture, Caswell saw a large malformed boot in a corner and the wash-bowl half-full of liquid suggesting a failure with dyes.

"The foot was easy," the unknown observed. "But that complexion was a daily job."

Caswell gave him a lengthy look of appraisal.

"I don't believe you yet," he said. "But, supposing Bjerstedt was a disguise, what and who are you really?"

"I'm a secret service man, as I said before. As to my name, it's William Marr. . . . Do you mind if I sit down?"

Sounds of haste without came to their ears.

"In here," Caswell called.

Anthony appeared first in the doorway. At sight of a stranger he looked half-incredulous. Then he stared with fierce curiosity, with a bending of his body as if about to spring. Delancey behind him wondered at the silence, and looked curiously over his shoulder.

"Yes," said the target of all eyes. "You're right."

Anthony advanced one step—deliberately.

"Did you come," he asked with cold repression, "to finish the job?"

A hand the ghost of Bjerstedt withdrew from his pocket held his pipe.

"I came aboard," he said pleasantly, "to help with your job."

"I don't mind saying," Delancey interjected, "that short of seeing you behind bars I've had all I want of you."

The accused one leaned forward, tapping his left palm with his pipe.

"Just listen. Time is precious. And I won't take much of yours. But you, Anthony, aching to put your hands around my throat. And you, Delancey, thinking I've got you into the worst mess of your life,—just listen to me a few minutes. I know I can count on Dr. Caswell for that."

"We'll give you just that," conceded the *Viva's* owner, with an explanatory aside:

"He says he's a detective."

"So I am. . . . Does it happen that one of you had anything to do with the secret service in the war?"

"I was in the military intelligence," said Delancey.

"Then maybe you'll know this credential for emergencies. Right now seems to be one."

He held something before Delancey, who stepped forward. A small shining disk.

"It looks right," Delancey admitted.

"And is. . . . Now let me explain a bit. My name's William Marr. And I've been in the service for ten years. Mostly gunning counterfeiters."

"I thought your friends were rum runners," put in Anthony.

A grim smile curved Marr's lips.

"Still being snorty," he observed. "Well, I don't blame you. . . . The fact is, one job runs into another. And nowadays bootlegging gets into 'most everything.

"My present 'friends,' as you call them, are rum runners. And their moniker is the Red Triangle. I guess you've seen it. It's frightened a considerable number of villagers pink."

"Just what does it mean?" asked Caswell.

"Hands off. Like staking out a quarter-claim. Only what right there is to this stuff is backed with blackjacks and pistols. And they're used good and plenty. . . . Three members of the bunch you brushed into at the hotel have done time for felony. The others——" he fastened his teeth on his pipe stem. . . . "I guess one of them is eligible to the chair."

"On account of Beddle, you mean?"

Caswell leaned forward. And the detective nodded.

"But I wouldn't say which one," he went on. . . . "To get back to my being here,—Anthony's friend, Lever, is pal to a slick-fingered artist that operates a bank-note factory in Brooklyn. I'm pretty sure of it. And the stout, bald-headed feller you remember in the bunch is in cahoots with him. Or I'm a liar. But I can't pin it on them yet. The trail led here, and I found them hug-and-honey with the pirates of rum row. Naturally, I had to join the gang. Savey?"

They nodded.

"It seems counterfeiting," he philosophized, "is only a side-show now. The big money's in bootlegging. . . . Up here in Nyatt these fellers have been able to strongarm competition. And the way they clean up on Scotch, Rye, and Bacardi is a temptation. . . . Easy come, easy go. Seventy-five thousand dropped to that simpleton, Ericsson."

"Another crook," put in Delancey. At which Marr shook his head.

"Not dyed-in-the-wool. Just a jackass with no backbone. With plenty of money he'd run straight. He's putty with women. That blue-eyed Jane he used to fleece the gang here will get it all away from him."

"Anyway, he made you think I was Griffis."

"Not for a minute. I just wanted to find out how you fitted into the gang."

"And how do you fit in?" inquired Caswell, who had listened with somewhat the air of an alert terrier.

"Oh, they think I'm a con man ready to turn bootlegger. I got on the blind side of Lever in New York."

"I suppose that was lucky for me," observed Anthony.

Marr's lips parted in a grin.

"It was a good idea," he allowed, "for me to be along last night. Sometimes Sam acts hasty."

"What was the idea in kidnapping Miss Strong and me?"

The detective looked at him blankly.

"I didn't know they took her. They swore to me they didn't."

"She was with me when I was knocked out," said Anthony.

Marr scratched his head reflectively.

"It's no mystery about you. The gang have a notion you fellers are either prohibition agents, or belong to another rum-running bunch that wants to horn in. They'd bump you off either way. And not worry about it."

"That doesn't explain about Miss Strong," said Anthony.

"I've an idea," the detective went on slowly. "But not being sure, perhaps I shouldn't spring it. Give the devil his due."

"If it isn't too indelicate," said Caswell, "do you mean Mr. Flaherty?"

"What's he got against you?"

The detective looked at Anthony.

"He just doesn't like me. And certainly I don't like him."

"Hates you like poison. Better keep an eye on him. He's the kind that hires somebody to kill in the dark."

"You haven't answered my question," Caswell reminded him.

"I can't."

The detective chewed his pipe stem reflectively. As the four in the cabin revolved an unspoken thought the *Viva* heeled over in abrupt alteration of her course, and they were busy a moment with recovery of balance. Then slowly, as if the effort were detestable, Anthony freed the idea preying upon his mind.

"Suppose Flaherty is responsible for the abduction: Do you think he'll hurt Miss Strong?"

Marr looked at him sharply.

"Not in the sense you mean. He hasn't the nerve. . . . What would be his game with the girl, anyway? Has she got money?"

Delancey and Anthony looked blank. But Caswell answered:

"She's supposed to be quite rich."

"Well, Mr. Flaherty would do a lot for a million."

"Has he a record?" asked Delancey.

"Jail, you mean? Not yet. But he's going there when a little account he has with Uncle Sam is adjusted."

"My claim first."

Anthony's grim observation seemed more to himself than to the others.

"You'll have to catch the goose before you cook him," observed Caswell with a shrug, and cocked his head to listen. "I wonder what's happening on deck."

Sounds of voices came to their ears. And the boat seemed to be losing momentum. The nickel clock on the cabin shelf grew suddenly clamorous with its "Tick—tick——"

"I wonder——"

With Anthony and Delancey at his heels Caswell headed for the door.

"Do you mind," called the detective, "if I come along?"

"No," Caswell answered without turning.

They hurried up the companionway. Summoned for some emergency, even to the cook the crew had preceded them.

It was broad daylight now, with a glint in the water, and a free wind. To starboard shore was near. And the comparatively shallow depths were creamy with short seas. A boat that looked like a fisherman was working its way alongside.

"What's the matter, Andersen?" Caswell demanded.

"A sick man they say, Captain."

Though he spoke with his usual slow evenness, Andersen was manifestly perturbed.

"What of it?" barked the *Viva's* owner. "This isn't a hospital ship."

"Say, there, throw me a line," called a man in the bow of the boat edging in.

"Can't stop," replied Caswell, taking Andersen's megaphone.

"Picked up a man we want you to take aboard," explained the persistent stranger.

"Don't want him."

"Can't you be decent?"

"We may not go back to-day."

"I won't be back for a week. Say, throw me a line."

"May as well get rid of him," snapped Caswell to Andersen. "We can't wait here all day."

As if still mutely protesting he withdrew to the far side of the boat while the line was secured, and the ladder let down. With Anthony and Delancey beside him, and Marr standing near, he watched for the charge thrust upon them.

As one of the *Viva's* crew pulled, and men of the fishing boat pushed below, the head of a man appeared at the rail. Bjerstedt was a second or two ahead of the others in his grasp of identity.

"There goes your murder case," he said, turning to Caswell.

The man landed on deck like a bale of goods was Beddle. Unshaven, in oilskins, and a fisherman's shirt pulled almost up to his chin, he was still as unquestionably himself as the Mona Lisa.

His first act on sitting up was to salute his rescuer, who lost no time in getting under way with a great sputtering of his engine and hearty sea oaths. Now he turned back to the *Viva* with a slow survey of surroundings.

Caswell, Delancey, Anthony, and Bjerstedt,—his gaze swept them all in turn.

"So it's you," he said at length, still sitting calmly on the deck.

Caswell stepped towards him, half-incredulous.

"How do you happen to be alive?"

"Luck," said the one seemingly risen from the dead. "Luck twice."

"But I found your body," Caswell expostulated.

"You found *a* body, you mean."

Carefully, and with manifest difficulty, Beddle pulled himself up, and stood leaning against the rail.

"May I ask," he said, "what port you are bound for?"

The *Viva* was again tearing along with bellying sail.

"I don't know," said Caswell, with a tug at his beard. "Why aren't you dead?"

"Some gentleman," Beddle reflectively stroked his unshaven chin, "made a mistake of identity."

"Oh!" blankly.

"I had a brother that was a bootlegger. And he looked very much like me." . . . He paused with a slight grimace. . . . "Of course, it's a little family secret; but circumstances entitle you to know. I hadn't seen him for years until I came to Nyatt. I traced him there. The family wanted him back. But he had a notion of pride, and wasn't keen to come."

Beddle looked at his fingers, flexing them. He seemed to have forgotten his listeners. But presently he went on.

"He'd promised me his decision the afternoon he was killed. Fate sent his murderer to the spot, and just ahead of me. . . . I don't know why he was killed. Some rum-runners' row, I think. He represented a syndicate trying to get part of the business here. . . . Anyhow, some one shot him down.

"I was near enough to see him fall. My first feeling was it might be an accident. I stooped over him,—and that's all I know. Evidently some one behind me struck a terrific blow."

Beddle touched the back of his head gingerly.

"Hours afterward I came to. It was dark; and by a rolling motion I knew I was at sea. The next thing I realized was a row over me just the other side of the wall. From the voices there must have been four or five rowing over whether to murder me forthwith, or contrive a way to let me go. Against the good old doctrine that 'Dead men tell no tales' was the notion that the British government would be inquisitive about my disappearance. The chicken-hearted had their way.

"Just before daybreak they put me into a rowboat with the traditional can of water and loaf of bread. To be picked up, or drown. Being fair at the oars, I might have kept on indefinitely. But I misjudged a buoy that capsized me coming up. I managed somehow to grip the bell-support, and held on until a fisherman picked me up. . . . That's all."

Beddle seemed wrapped in thought, as he touched with inquiring fingers his unshaven chin. While the *Viva* drove onward the circle about him was held in suspense.

"Have you no clue at all?" said Caswell with a trace of impatience.

"I know the boat that dropped me. It's a black launch. And there was a name mentioned that I know."

"Flaherty!"

The word burst from Anthony's lips. Beddle looked at him with interest.

"Exactly," he said. "Mr. Flaherty."

As they closed the mental circuit of an idea Greta came on deck. Delancey saw her first, and went to meet her.

"You see——?"

By his explanatory gesture he embraced her brother, still leaning against the rail and unaware of her presence. As she stepped towards him he turned.

"Hullo, Greta," he said calmly.

"It's really you?"

An accent of wonder was in her voice. She put a hand lightly on his shoulder. He moved slightly.

"Are you hurt much?"

For all its coolness, her voice betrayed the strain she was under.

"No," he answered with a rueful half-smile. "But shipwreck on a buoy is hard on the arms and knees. And one's appearance."

"Tell me——"

"Not now. I've just been over the story, and nobody wants to hear it again. You shall have it all later. . . . Do you think,"—he turned to Delancey, "I could borrow a razor?"

"You can. And I will outfit you, too." Delancey looked him over. "We're about the same size."

"Thank you," Beddle said with more effusiveness than he had shown in his rescue from the sea. "That's a leg up I appreciate."

They moved towards the companionway.

"You'll be all right for a few minutes?" Delancey queried Greta.

She answered with a nod, and a faint smile.

As they made their way below Delancey revolved a question he hesitated to put. Beddle, for his part, was not thus deterred.

"Do you mind my asking," he inquired coolly, "if you and Greta are going to hit it off?"

"I don't know," Delancey answered with confusion. "I hope so."

"Then it's settled," said Beddle equably. "Greta knows her mind. And I see signs."

"I hope you're right. But," Delancey felt it incumbent upon himself to explain, "I haven't proposed yet."

"That's no matter," serenely. "Congratulations. . . . I'll join you presently."

Delancey went on deck a little dazed.

From the general stir about he surmised contact with their quarry was expected soon. Two or three of the crew were equipped with revolvers, probably Andersen's provision in view of the new piracy of the North Atlantic Main; and all were at their stations.

Greta sat calmly where he had left her, a patrician figure.

"Don't you think you'd better go below now?" he suggested. "There'll be trouble soon."

"I'm not in the least afraid," she assured him.

"I understand. But to oblige me,—please?"

"If you wish." She rose slowly. "But you must let me know when I can be of service."

"I promise," he said.

He looked after her with more wonder in his eyes than when he turned to survey the shore towards which the *Viva* drove before the wind. Tumbling over flats, the sea sucked at the base of a gravelled bluff split for a narrow passage with clear green water.

"Is everything all right?" asked Caswell, standing at Andersen's elbow.

"Yes, Captain."

Straight as an arrow he sent the *Viva* through, a bare boat's length to spare on either side. They drove into a small harbor, where water was never rough. Evidently a popular resting place for birds. Great numbers floated in the water, or preened themselves on the sand.

That was all. No boat. Beyond the *Viva* no sign of human presence.

Shortening sail, Andersen made the circuit of the basin, his eyes searching its irregular and somewhat wooded shore. With a little headway the *Viva* was now again near her point of entry to the harbor. Caswell standing beside Andersen, with Bjerstedt at his heels.

"What do you think?" he asked.

"That way."

With his free hand Andersen pointed north. As his eyes followed Caswell could see no break in the shore.

"Is there a way out there?"

Now Bjerstedt came in.

"Yes, if you're careful. Launches of the rum fleet use it. . . . Only," he added, "if you head that way you may run slap into a nest of them."

"I don't care," snapped Caswell. "Hornets or bootleggers, it's all the same. We've got to find Nell Strong. Now drive her, Andersen. We've only lost a few minutes here."

The skipper nodded, and agitated the expectant crew with a gesture. They jumped to the ropes, with a will hoisting canvas. In a puff from the hills that was followed by sustained pressure the sails filled. Heeling somewhat, the *Viva* quickly picked up speed. Andersen brought her over for the short tack past the point that challenged entrance to the northern passage.

He was nursing her prettily when Bjerstedt bellowed:

"Look!"

As he cried out he pointed. And looking backward they saw what excited him. A white yawl had just entered the basin by the channel the *Viva* used.

"It's the *Sarah*," he said excitedly.

"How do you know?"

Anthony clutched his elbow.

"I've been aboard her a dozen times."

Caswell turned to Andersen, who answered his unspoken question:

"It looks like her, Captain. I know her rig."

"Gorry! They've run into our arms."

It seemed so. Though those on the *Sarah* must have seen the *Viva*, she came tearing on while Andersen jockeyed to come about at the precise moment that would enable him, with headway he had, to block the passage.

Whether the *Sarah* would sheer off was never tested. It was Bjerstedt again who made a discovery.

"See there!"

He grasped Caswell's elbow to emphasize his observation. Through the southern passage streaked another boat.

"A revenue cutter," said Bjerstedt, his mouth to Caswell's ear.

The newcomer closed in behind the *Sarah*, with brownish plumes from forced engines streaking the horizon. As those on the *Viva* watched her creep up a sharp bark preceded a light puff of smoke on her forward deck.

Was the *Sarah* hit? She gave no sign. The revenue boat came still closer to its quarry. Now the silence was rent with a curious rattling sound.

Anthony straightened as if struck.

"A machine gun!" he ejaculated. And then, as if communing with himself, a single word:

"Nell."

With the *Viva* ahead, and a pursuer in action at her heels, the *Sarah* suddenly headed for the inner shore. And the cutter, following, gave her another shot. At that the considerable number on deck dodged to shelter, leaving only the man at the wheel exposed. Heading straight for the beach, he had almost reached it when the *Sarah* went aground.

Driven on a bar, she stood like a creature chained, her rent mainsail swinging dangerously. At once figures reappeared on deck and vanished over the side, with two boats hastily lowered. After them went a boatload of the cutter's crew, with unheeded shouts of command.

It was a race to the beach with the rum runners leading. Both pursued and pursuers vanished in the orange fringe of autumn foliage. Another shot sounded, and fainter shouts marking the receding chase.

Aboard the *Viva* Andersen took matters into his own hands. As after a short tack they again approached the helpless *Sarah* he half-turned to command the waiting crew:

"Lower sail."

Down came the canvas, with the *Viva* still gliding. In a minute or two she was nearly opposite the stranded boat, and a few yards in the margin of safety.

"Let go the anchor."

With a splash it dropped and held. The boat rocked easily in a light swell. Now Andersen turned to Caswell, whose eyes had been glued to the *Sarah* while his own boat came to anchor.

"Shall I lower, sir?"

"Give us a dinghy."

As it went over the side Caswell turned upon his associates a spray of staccato observation:

"You come with me, Anthony. . . . And you, Bjerstedt. . . . You'd better stay aboard, Delancey. Responsibilities here. . . . No, not you, Andersen. Feel safer with you on the *Viva*. Give me two men. . . . Got a gun? Thanks."

As the sailors shoved off a petty officer on the cutter, which also had dropped anchor on the far side of the *Sarah*, sang out:

"You'd better keep away."

"Go on," said Caswell in a low voice to the men at the oars.

As they touched the *Sarah* Anthony led the scramble up the ladder. The yawl seemed deserted. At the foot of steps leading down to it the cabin showed dark beyond its opened door.

Anthony led again. His first observation in the dim light showed shutters sealing the cabin windows. With a strong shove he pushed one aside. And the morning sunlight poured in.

The cabin was tenanted before them. In a chair Flaherty sprawled. His head rested on the table, with his arms about it. His attitude was suggestive of drunken stupor.

Caswell's professional instinct outran Anthony's craving for vengeance. He stooped over Flaherty, touching his shoulder. Then he saw a pool between the cradling arms.

"Blood," he said. "He's hurt."

Anthony shook him, calling into his ears:

"Wake up!"

Flaherty stirred, and with the appearance of enormous effort turned his head to one side. His eyes half-opened mirrored no thought. Then he recognized the three about him. First Anthony, then the other two.

"You here?"

He spoke thickly, with the accent of exhaustion.

"What do you want?"

"You," said Bjerstedt, stepping nearer. Anthony caught him by the shoulder, and silently pushed him to the rear.

As Flaherty slightly moved his head a trickle of red under his left ear ran faster. A convulsion of shoulders preceded his effort to speak:

"So you're a spy. . . . I told them so. . . . Anyway . . . Can't bother me."

"We'll see," asserted the detective.

Caswell lifted a hand to silence him, then laid it persuasively on Flaherty's shoulder.

"What happened?" he asked in a calm professional voice.

Flaherty seemed to ponder, finding the effort almost too much. At last he spoke, never lifting his head from the table, on which the red rain slowly fell:

"Cabin window open. . . . Bullet hit me in the neck."

Another silence, and he finished with a heavy sigh:

"Bleeding to death inside."

Now Anthony brushed aside Caswell's hand to take the failing man by the elbow.

"Where is Miss Strong?"

He bent low for the answer. But Flaherty did not stir.

"What have you done with her? . . . Tell me before you go to hell."

Anthony poured his demand into Flaherty's ear, as if by vocal concentration he would force a way to the dulling brain. And Flaherty opened his eyes—very slowly. At first dazed, his expression somewhat clarified. He met Anthony's threatening eyes with a look neither defiant nor malicious. Still he did not speak.

"What have you done with Miss Strong?" Anthony reiterated.

"Can see . . . I haven't got her."

Flaherty spoke with more difficulty now, very slow and faintly.

"Where is she?"

"Don't . . . know."

With whispered denial Flaherty closed his eyes in the peace of the dying.

"It's no use."

Caswell checked Anthony's purpose.

"You can't get anything out of him now."

"Then what shall we do?"

"You and Bjerstedt go on deck. They may have some tip on the *Viva* by this time."

"And you——?" Anthony queried.

"I stay here. There's no hope. But as a physician I can't leave him."

"Then take this."

Anthony offered his revolver. Caswell shook his head.

"You forget I have one," he said. "Go on with the job. And good luck to you."

They went up the stairs, leaving him there with what was left of a gentleman that became a rogue.

As they looked from the bow of the *Sarah* there was no obvious change in the surrounding scene. On one side the cutter, with steam up and rather the air of a hound straining at its leash. On the other the *Viva*. They saw Andersen at the wheel, and Delancey talking with Beddle. Noting their re-appearance, he came towards them as if to speak. Whether question or assurance, it remained unuttered.

At that moment Anthony and Bjerstedt turned towards the shore.

"Did you hear that?"

Anthony spoke softly, as if fearing to dissipate a sound.

"It was what was left of a scream. . . . Right over there."

Bjerstedt pointed to a clump of oaks on the neighboring shore.

"Do you think——?" said Anthony.

"Let's see."

They dropped into the waiting dinghy, and the pair at the oars pulled lustily. It was a matter of brief minutes before, timing the last stroke with an advancing wave, they leaped to the glistening sand.

Anthony was ahead as they scrambled up the gravelly bluff, with the tier of trees still in their mahogany dress a little inshore. Nothing further was revealed until, just as they reached the grassy level, they caught sight of a black patch that was part of a shanty's roof, and a stovepipe chimney.

Without looking for a path they forced their way through. And suddenly they burst into a little clearing. At the farther end, its rear to the encircling trees, a black hut stood, with a litter of fisherman's gear beside its tightly closed door.

Anthony rapped sharply—three times.

"Hullo!" he called, and rapped again. Still there was no reply.

He put his shoulder against the door, which gave way with the rasping sound of a forced hasp. And daylight poured in after them.

In a little room which was destitute in its furnishing their eyes leaped to the figure hunched in a chair partially obstructing a door leading somewhere. A big man whose sagging head almost rested on his knees. Bjerstedt pushed it roughly, with impatient salutation:

"Hey, there! Wake up!"

The man straightened himself slowly, until they saw his face. It was Dr. Pugh. But somehow changed, with a bloated look, and a strange expression in his little eyes. His skin was red and white in patches.

"What are you doing here?" Bjerstedt demanded.

The answering expression was at once laugh and sneer.

"Hasn't a citizen of Nyatt a right to travel in the island? . . . Ah!"

With a snarling cry he clutched at something Bjerstedt grasped, in a swooping movement to the floor. With satisfaction the detective held it up to the light.

"I thought so," he observed. "A Majendie needle. Did we interrupt you taking a shot?"

"You're a fool," said the doctor in his small, cold voice.

But Anthony saw his face grow more mottled. And twitching fingers dug into his palms. Bjerstedt's eyes never left his face.

"You're a morphine addict," he said with his overbearing manner. "See."

Grasping the doctor's right arm, he pushed the sleeve to the elbow. From the wrist up it was peppered with small red sores.

"I know your kind."

The detective stepped back to hurl his next question:

"Who else is here?"

Dr. Pugh sat mute. Only his protruding tongue moved, and his restless eyes that never left the needle in Bjerstedt's hand. Now the detective again stooped suddenly, and came up with a bottle half-full of white powder.

Rolling helplessly in his chair, the doctor cried like an animal in pain. While it still echoed in the brains of the two before him they heard a muffled cry from the rear.

In a flash Anthony cleared the doctor's sprawling figure, and lifted the latch of the lean-to door. It was so dark there he stood on the threshold, readjusting his eyes to the dimness. They had hardly glimpsed something dark in a far corner when his whole being responded to a sound. A sound that was not intelligible speech; yet his blood answered.

"Nell!" he ejaculated in a ferment of wonder.

In a moment he was touching her with half-incredulous fingers.

"Are you hurt?"

By her effort to answer he realized her plight, and began feverishly tugging at knots of a cruelly tight bandage over her mouth.

"My hands, too," she said faintly.

With impetuous care he cut through a cord fastening her arms to the back of the chair. She was free.

Heedless of half-articulate cries in the outer room, he drew her to him, holding her steadily in a strong embrace. Her desperate fingers clutched his shoulder; and she shook with sobbing breath.

"Tell me," he said presently, "that it is all right."

His voice broke with the strain.

"What?" she answered, steadying herself, and all at once understood.

"Yes. It was dreadful. But not that."

"Thank God!"

In the darkness she held her head a little apart, listening as if she still feared her recent captor. Then hurriedly went on:

"He wanted me to go away with him. When I laughed he seemed to go mad. He threatened me—all through the night. But he never touched me until just before you came. He said he was going to give me something to make me unconscious. Then I screamed. . . . Oh, it was so horrible!"

"Never mind," he said soothingly. "I've got you."

"Take me away," she pleaded. "I can't breathe."

"Come," he said, and went before her, still holding her hand.

He led her quickly to the outer door. A brief passage made terrible by Bjerstedt's baiting of his frenzied quarry.

"Do you need me?" asked Anthony.

"No, I can handle him," answered the detective, again dangling the magic bottle before Dr. Pugh's protruding eyes. "Better get the girl away. It ain't pretty. But," with grim satisfaction, "it works. He's admitted the abduction. And the killing of Beddle, too. That was for money to get away with the girl. He's nuts about her. . . . No, you don't."

As he dexterously withdrew the bottle from snatching fingers a choking cry more terrible than any before came from the doctor's lips. Nell fled before it. And Anthony followed, closing behind him the shanty door.

Purging themselves of noxious contacts, they breathed deeply the clear autumn air. Blue sky above, and all about the friendly oaks in harvest dress. In that moment torment just past dropped from them as a garment.

As Nell turned to Anthony he saw again the brightness of her eyes.

"I knew you would come," she said.

In Nature's music their kiss and the ecstatic song of a lark somewhere in the blue were one.

* * * *

"Ding . . . Dong . . . Dong . . . Ding."

Sometimes clear, again half-smothered by shrieking wind, with mournful reiteration the bell-buoy uttered its warning. The sea climbed it as it swung and rang. Half-over, then poised an instant, it slid down the hissing slope. Now it plunged its iron side into the oncoming wave, and climbed again.

"Ding . . . Dong . . . Dong . . . Ding."

Over and over the brazen notes of that desolate cry. None heard it. Consciousness had so departed from the figure outstretched on its iron side that it seemed like something in bas relief. The hands of a man who had gripped a bell support with desperate energy were automatically locked now.

It was near daybreak. That hour when the wind strikes chill, and insistent emptiness crawls up into the bottom of one's throat.